Martha Rogers is a new writer who has stepped into the art of storytelling with flair and expertise. A splendid first novel.

—DiAnn Mills
Author of *A Woman Called Sage*

Becoming Lucy offers readers a powerful message of love, hope, and transformation. Set in the historic ranch lands of Oklahoma, this story is packed full of action, adventure, and romantic tension. Highly recommended to all readers who are on a journey to "becoming" all they are meant to be in Christ.

—Janice Hanna Thompson
Author of *Love Finds You in Poetry, Texas*

This book is a wonderful debut novel. A real winner. It has a variety of multidimensional characters, a realistic and well-defined setting, and a story that pulls the reader into the nineteenth century and doesn't let go until the last page. I can hardly wait for the next book in the series.

—Lena Nelson Dooley
Multipublished, Award-winning Author of *Minnesota Brothers* and *Love Finds You in Golden, New Mexico*

A new voice in historical fiction, Martha Rogers pens a compelling tale of faith, hope, and letting go of past regrets. Set in the Oklahoma Territory, bits of historical truths are woven into this story about a young woman from an affluent background and a young man carrying a burden too large to bear, who finally find their God-chosen place of belonging. I delighted in the growth and change of the characters. Treat yourself to a step back in time—you won't be disappointed.

—Kim Vogel Sawyer
Best-selling author of *My Heart Remembers*

Becoming Lucy is a retreat from twenty-first-century chaos. Martha Rogers's voice and historical detail transport her reader to life lived at a different pace. Despite burying both her parents on the same day, Lucinda Bishop meets the challenges of the rugged plains of Oklahoma with faith and grace. I turned the last page fulfilled, inspired, yet somehow rested. A satisfying read.

—MARCIA GRUVER
AUTHOR OF THE TEXAS FORTUNES TRILOGY

Martha Rogers's sweet debut novel radiates redemption and love: God's love for man and a man's love for a woman. Combining the romantic element with a realistic old west setting and strong characters makes for a truly enjoyable story.

—MIRALEE FERRELL
AUTHOR OF *LOVE FINDS YOU IN LAST CHANCE, CA*

Becoming Lucy

MARTHA ROGERS

REALMS

Most CHARISMA HOUSE BOOK GROUP products are available at special quantity discounts for bulk purchase for sales promotions, premiums, fund-raising, and educational needs. For details, write Charisma House Book Group, 600 Rinehart Road, Lake Mary, Florida 32746, or telephone (407) 333-0600.

BECOMING LUCY by Martha Rogers
Published by Realms
Charisma Media/Charisma House Book Group
600 Rinehart Road
Lake Mary, Florida 32746
www.charismahouse.com

Unless otherwise noted, all Scripture quotations are from the King James Version of the Bible.

The characters portrayed in this book are fictitious unless they are historical figures explicitly named. Otherwise, any remblance to actual people. whether living or dead, is coincidental.

Cover design by Amanda Potter and Nathan Morgan
Design Director: Bill Johnson

Library of Congress Cataloging-in-Publication Data:

Rogers, Martha, 1936-
  Becoming Lucy / by Martha Rogers.
      p. cm.
  ISBN 978-1-59979-912-4
  1. Young women--Fiction. 2. Ranch life--Oklahoma--Fiction. I. Title.
  PS3618.O4655B43 2010
  813'.6--dc22
                                          2009036100
E-Book ISBN: 978-1-59979-992-6

14 15 16 17 18 — 11 10 9 8 7 6
Printed in the United States of America

And ye shall seek me, and find me, when ye
shall search for me with all your heart.

—JEREMIAH 29:13

Prologue

Boston 1896

*L*ucinda Bishop accepted the condolences offered by well-meaning friends. In one brief moment, her life had changed forever. The two people she loved most in the world lay ready to be covered by mounds of fresh dirt. She squeezed back tears and tried to listen to the words of those who spoke to her, but her mind grasped none of them.

Despite the warmth of late summer, a chill coursed its way through her weary bones. The thought of leaving Mama and Papa here among the weathered headstones of the church cemetery brought tears yet again. She blinked her eyes, vowing to remember their wonderful love and not to dwell on their passing.

Aunt Amelia's hand fell like lead on Lucinda's arm. "Come, my dear. We must return home. Guests will be waiting."

It couldn't be time to leave yet, but Aunt Amelia, Uncle Ben, and she were the only mourners remaining in the cemetery. Their driver waited by the carriage, but Lucinda didn't want to leave. If she left Mama and Papa here, then their death became a reality.

Aunt Amelia wrapped her arm around Lucinda's waist. "We must go. Ben and I can bring you back later if you wish."

Lucinda winced at the thought of more people who really had no idea of the depth of her grief. However, good manners required her to greet those friends and neighbors who would come to pay their respects. Church friends provided a bounty of food to share with the guests, and she would not shirk her duties.

A slight breeze stirred up dust from the clumps of dirt near her feet. The scent wafting from the floral wreaths in memory of her parents filled the air. Would she ever smell a rose again without thinking of this day? The trees dancing in the wind mocked her sadness with their vibrant green leaves. With a sigh she laid a pink rose on her mother's casket and a red one on her father's, then she turned toward the road.

Uncle Ben assisted her up into the carriage. Lucinda settled and adjusted the folds of her skirt. She bit her lip and offered up a silent prayer for patience and endurance to face the afternoon. The carriage rolled down the dirt path through the cemetery. A wheel struck something and swayed. Was this what her parents had felt before their carriage overturned? A shudder coursed its way through her body.

Aunt Amelia held a lace-trimmed handkerchief to her mouth with one hand and grasped Uncle Ben's hand with the other. Aunt Amelia mourned the loss of her sister and had traveled to Boston all the way from Oklahoma Territory to attend the services. For that Lucinda thanked them with all her heart. Without her aunt, all the details would have been more than Lucinda could have handled.

Uncle Ben cleared his throat. "Lucinda, your aunt and I have discussed your future. We know you have no one here to take care of you, so we are offering you a place at our ranch. We want you to come out west and live with us."

Lucinda gasped and shrank back against the leather cushion. Leave Boston and her home? How could she? Everything she loved and held dear was right here. The idea of leaving it numbed her as much as when she first learned about the carriage accident that killed her parents. Her entire life had been spent in Boston, and if she left, she'd be leaving everything she knew and loved behind.

"Thank you, Uncle Ben. I don't know what I'll do just yet. I hope to stay here. However, Mr. Sutton will help me decide what must be done." He had already told her to wait until he read the terms of her parents' will this evening.

The carriage stopped at the entrance to the Bishop home. An iron fence and gate surrounded the green space in the front where Mama's roses blazed forth in a last burst of color before summer's end approached. Clouds rolled in to hide the sun as Lucinda alighted from the carriage and opened the gate. The black draping and wreath hanging on the door signifying a death in the household only served to add to her grief.

Lucinda squared her shoulders and prepared to meet her guests. Mrs. Wilson, the housekeeper, opened the door as Lucinda stepped to the porch with Aunt Amelia and Uncle Ben behind her.

"I'm sorry we're late," Lucinda apologized to the housekeeper. "Have many arrived?" Lucinda removed her gloves and blinked her eyes. She would not cry in front of her guests.

The older woman nodded, grief furrowing her brow. "Yes, they are in the front parlor, Miss Lucinda. The table is ready when you wish to eat."

Her stomach rebelled at the thought of food, but guests had to be fed. "Thank you, Mrs. Wilson."

Lucinda removed her bonnet and handed it and her gloves to Mr. Wilson, the butler.

The man's face reflected Lucinda's sorrow. "It was a lovely service. You can be proud, Miss Lucinda. Your parents were fine people."

"Yes, the service was perfect. Thank you for being there."

Lucinda smiled at the gray-haired man she'd known all of her life.

With a deep breath to bolster her courage, she entered the parlor to meet her guests. Aunt Amelia stayed close by as church friends hugged Lucinda and others whispered their words of sympathy. Most of them attended the graveside services, but she retained only a vague recollection of speaking with them there. They meant well, and their words were sincere, but nothing they said could fill the void in her heart.

Aunt Amelia brought her a plate of food, but the colorful array had no appeal. She picked at the vegetables but couldn't put her fork to her mouth.

"Child, you must eat to keep up your strength. We have much to do in the days ahead."

Lucinda nodded. Better to take a few bites than have her aunt hovering about like a mother over a sick child. She ate a bit of meat and a morsel of homemade bread. It landed like lead in her stomach.

Her family's minister and his wife stood before her. Mrs. Gleason bent down and hugged Lucinda. "My dear, these days will be difficult, but trust in the Lord with all your heart. He will see you through. Remember, I am available anytime you need someone to talk to."

Lucinda swallowed the lump forming in her throat. "Thank you, Mrs. Gleason." The dear woman had been a close friend of Mama's. Papa and Mama had instilled their strong faith in Lucinda, and if she didn't have faith now, she'd be dishonoring not only her parents but also God. She must trust God to make provisions, even if it meant moving to Oklahoma. Papa's words were seared in her heart: "If we don't give back to the Lord the tithe of what He gives us, we dishonor His holy name and all He has done for us."

The Reverend Gleason and his wife departed, followed by a train of other guests. In the now silent room, Lucinda drank in the beauty of the parlor. The deep purple of the velvet sofa and two side chairs reflected her mother's decorating skills, as did the cream china vases, lamps, and each piece of furniture in the room. Mama had used her favorite color in all shades and tints in the parlor.

As beautiful as it had always been to Lucinda, today the thick fabrics and heavy drapes adorning the windows only added to the depth of her grief. She walked toward them now to the one overlooking the front yard and street beyond and drew back the lace curtains behind the velvet panels. A light drizzle fell to wash away the grime of the streets. Even heaven itself mourned her loss with drops of rain that trickled down the panes as the tears did on her cheeks.

Mr. Sutton approached, his thick white hair slightly disheveled. He dabbed at the perspiration on his forehead. "My dear, everyone has departed. It's time for us to discuss your future."

She nodded and followed Mr. Sutton into her father's study. Just as the parlor bore Mama's tastes, this room in brown tones with leather-upholstered chairs and a great walnut desk spoke of Papa. The aroma of his cherry-scented pipe tobacco lingered in the room. If she closed her eyes, Lucinda could imagine Papa still sitting in his chair with his fingertips together and his eyebrows raised in question at some request she'd made.

Aunt Amelia and Uncle Ben sat on her left, and Papa's brother Rudolph Bishop sat on her right. She barely knew her uncle, who'd always been the black sheep of the family. In fact, when her grandfather died five years ago, it became known that he'd cut Rudolph out of his will and bequeathed everything to her father. No wonder Uncle Rudolph had barely spoken to her since his arrival yesterday. Indeed, the scowl on his face proved he would rather be anywhere but here.

Mr. Sutton settled himself in Papa's chair and adjusted his glasses. Lucinda blinked to hold back tears because someone other than Papa sat behind the desk. Several stacks of papers lay in front of the lawyer. He cleared his throat before speaking, then peered straight at Lucinda. "Your parents left a substantial estate, Miss Bishop. The bulk of it will be held in trust for you until you are eighteen."

Uncle Rudolph leaned forward. "What did my brother leave me?"

Mr. Sutton frowned, his gray, bushy eyebrows forming one line across his forehead. "I'm coming to that, Mr. Bishop." He held up another piece of paper. "Charles Bishop bequeathed ten thousand dollars to his church, three thousand each to Mr. and Mrs. Wilson, and ten thousand to his brother, Rudolph Bishop."

Rudolph slapped his palm across his thigh. "That is ridiculous. My brother's estate is worth much more than that. He couldn't have left it all to Lucinda."

Mr. Sutton peered over the rims of his glasses. "That's exactly what he did."

Rudolph bolted from his chair. "You can have the funds transferred to my account." He turned to leave the room but stopped and stared back at the lawyer, then Lucinda.

His dark eyes, so like Papa's earlier, now held only malice in their depths.

After he left the room, Aunt Amelia sniffed loudly. "I never did trust Rudolph. He spends money like there's no tomorrow. Will there be a problem, Mr. Sutton?"

"I don't believe so. Your brother-in-law's instructions are quite clear and specific. The money will be held in trust for Lucinda until she reaches the age of eighteen."

Mr. Sutton cleared his throat. "Mrs. Bishop's will bequeaths a sum of five thousand dollars to you, Mrs. Haynes."

Aunt Amelia gasped. "Oh, my. I never expected anything like that. What a generous thing to do."

The lawyer patted the stack of papers before him. "I'll begin probate proceedings tomorrow morning and set everything in motion."

Uncle Ben shook his head. "We won't be able to stay in Boston until that's completed. We must return to the ranch."

"I understand. Leave instructions as to where you want the money to be sent, and I'll take care of it. As for Lucinda, we must find someone to care for her."

Aunt Amelia grasped Lucinda's hand. "We want her to come live with us in Oklahoma. We have plenty of room, and she has two cousins there."

"That is a splendid idea and would be best for everyone." The lawyer smiled at Lucinda. "We can make arrangements for you to leave with them with enough allowance to manage until you inherit your trust. At that time, we can make arrangements for the transfer of funds and create a new will."

"I really don't want to leave Boston just yet. Can't I stay here with Mr. and Mrs. Wilson and other staff for a while?" Lucinda bit her lip and fought the tears.

Aunt Amelia nodded. "Yes, she does need to stay and settle all her affairs. Then she can come west by train and coach."

Mr. Sutton pursed his lips. "*Hmm.* But what about traveling alone? It isn't proper for a single young lady to be without escort on such a long journey."

Lucinda sat up straighter. She had decided herself she would have to leave Boston eventually, but they were being rude in discussing her as though she were not present. "I'll be all right.

It will be an adventure. A month or so here will give me time to prepare for the trip and grieve my parents."

"I suppose Mrs. Sutton and I can look after you and help you close the house. We can arrange an escort for you to make the long journey west." The lawyer slid the papers into his satchel, then he stood and stretched his hand toward Uncle Ben. "Thank you for offering your home to Lucinda. I'll see to the probate immediately and have matters settled so she can leave with no worries."

Lucinda swallowed hard yet again. Would the lumps never cease to form when she thought of her parents? She remembered the Bible verse Mama always quoted from Jeremiah about God having thoughts for her and her future. Trusting Him would give her the peace and comfort she needed for the days ahead. Her life had changed in an instant, and nothing would ever be the same again. Leaving everything she'd ever known would be the most difficult thing she'd do, next to burying her parents.

Chapter 1

Oklahoma Territory 1896

*J*ake Starnes hunkered down in his jacket. He smelled frost in the air, but the cold in his bones came from fear, not the temperature. A gust of wind threatened to take his hat. He shoved it down tighter to secure it.

He peered ahead at the barren landscape and the outline of the town of Barton Creek. Naked trees stretched forth to the skies against a backdrop of prairie grass that spread as far as the eye could see toward distant mountains. It bore no resemblance to the beautiful hills of Texas where he grew up. He missed them, but he'd probably never get the chance to see them again. He sighed in resignation to the life that lay ahead. A life he hadn't chosen. It had chosen him the day he chose to wear a gun.

Mrs. Haynes sat beside him and nudged his arm. "How much longer will we be? Dear little Lucinda. I pray she doesn't have to wait too long for us. I thought Ben would be done with the stock, but since he wasn't, I'm thankful you were available."

"Happy to oblige, ma'am. Won't be long now." Mrs. Haynes had talked about her sister's "poor orphan child" for the past two months. He could sympathize with the child because he lost both his parents just after he turned fifteen. She must be grieving terribly.

The pressure of Mrs. Haynes's hand on his arm brought him to the present. "Jake Starnes, you're not paying one bit of attention to me. If your mind is on the work you left at the ranch, don't worry about it. Ben and the others can take care of your chores."

"I know they will." Gray clouds covered the late October sky. "It's getting darker. Hope we get back home 'fore night sets in. That wind's coming straight down across the prairie with nothing to stop it."

"Dear me, I do pray Lucinda is dressed warmly." Mrs. Haynes pulled her shawl more tightly about her shoulders.

"You said she's coming from Boston, so she knows about cold weather." He peered at the horizon. The few buildings of Barton Creek drew closer. Another ten minutes and they'd be in town.

Jake's stomach began churning like those blue-black clouds rolling across the sky. Were it not for the little girl waiting for them, he'd have turned back home now. If the sheriff in Barton Creek recognized him or had questions about him being a stranger in these parts, he'd be in a heap of trouble.

He'd avoided going into the settlement ever since he came to Oklahoma six months ago. His wanderings ended at the Haynes's spread, where he'd stopped to ask for work. His first intention to stay only a month or so then move on changed when the Haynes showed him a kindness and love he sorely missed. They had become the family he had lost years ago.

Now the thought of entering the town caused fear to rise like bile. What would happen if the lawman in town recognized him and Ben Haynes learned about Jake's past, a past he wanted to forget?

⤚⤙

Lucinda stared down at the dusty ground beneath the worn wooden bench of the Wells Fargo depot and twisted her black-gloved hands in her lap. She searched the area for a familiar face. Where were Aunt Amelia and Uncle Ben? Her escort had fallen ill in the last town, but Lucinda had been determined to come on alone despite protests, and now she sat here with no one to meet her. Doubt clouded her mind over the decisions of the past month.

With no one else to call family, she'd had no choice but to come west. Aunt Mellie and Uncle Ben could never replace Mama and Papa, but being a part of the Haynes family would help take away the loneliness haunting her days.

She swiped at something as it brushed her cheek. An insect of some kind flew away, and she shuddered. What other strange things would she see this day? Her gaze swept across the scene before her. Several buildings across from the depot included a general store. She stood and made her way across the uneven ruts crisscrossing the street, if the hard-packed ground could be considered a street. A sign advertising Anderson's General Store squeaked on its chains. Welcome warmth greeted her when she pushed her way through the double doors.

A woman behind the counter peered at her. "May I help you, dear?"

The aroma of lamp oil and peppermint mingled in the air. "I stepped in to get out of the wind. I'm waiting for my Uncle Ben and Aunt Amelia to pick me up."

The gray-haired woman wiped her hands on her white apron. "Are you talking about Amelia Haynes?"

"Yes, ma'am. I've come to live with them."

The lady beamed. "Welcome to Barton Creek. I'm Bea

Anderson, and that's my husband Carl over there." A slightly bald man helping a customer grinned and nodded in her direction.

Mrs. Anderson pulled up a stool beside the wood stove. "Sit a spell and get warm. Ben and Amelia should be here soon."

A young man by the shelf of canned goods turned and smiled. Lucinda offered a small one in return. Heat rose in her cheeks as he continued to stare.

She broke her gaze and pointed to glass jars filled with a rainbow of colors. "Thank you, but I must go back over to the depot. I'll take a few of those peppermints if you don't mind."

Mrs. Anderson filled a small bag with the candy. "It's a mite colder out now. Sure you don't want to stay here until they arrive?"

Lucinda handed the woman a few coins and grasped the bag. "Thank you for your concern, but I don't want them to have to hunt for me. Maybe I'll see you again."

"If you come to church on Sunday, you surely will." The bell over the door jingled, and another customer entered. Mrs. Anderson turned her attention to the new patron. The young man smiled and nodded as Lucinda turned from the counter. She didn't smile in return. Mrs. Anderson should have introduced him. Were proper manners of no importance here on the frontier?

Lucinda crossed back to the depot that was down from the town's answer for a hotel. The only fully brick building in sight, it had grand windows, and cut glass adorned the wooden doors, but it couldn't compare to the ones in Boston. Of course, nothing in these buildings resembled the beauty of the masonry of her hometown.

She returned to the bench and popped a peppermint into her mouth. The sharp sweetness teased her taste buds as she savored her favorite candy. It brought back memories of Papa bringing a bag of treats home to her every week.

She'd be eighteen in less than six months and old enough to take care of her own affairs. Until then, however, she had to comply with the lawyer's recommendations. At least her aunt and uncle were family, and she longed to be a part of a family once again. She missed having someone concerned about her welfare. Mr. and Mrs. Wilson had been kind, but they had their own affairs to tend to. Her only fear now lay in losing her own identity so far away from everything she knew and loved.

With no idea what lay ahead, one thing was sure: she would have to learn to do without the amenities enjoyed as the only child of a wealthy family. But if Aunt Amelia could come out here and live and be entirely happy, Lucinda had to at least give it a try.

A gust of wind whipped open her dark blue cloak and stirred a small whirlwind of dirt. She coughed from the dust and wrapped the thick wool tighter around her body to ward off the cold. If Aunt Amelia and Uncle Ben didn't arrive soon, she'd have to go back inside to escape the weather.

⤜⤛

Mellie Haynes shivered in the frigid air. In a few minutes she'd be with her young niece. Dear Lucinda. How would she fare in this country? Amelia missed her sister and the wonderful letters they exchanged, but that couldn't begin to compare to the grief Lucinda must bear.

The Haynes ranch house may not be as elegant as Lucinda's home in Boston, but it was warm, comfortable, and large enough to accommodate her own son and daughter as well as Lucinda.

She pictured her young niece and Becky together. Surely Lucinda's upbringing would have a positive effect on her daughter's hoydenish behavior. Of course, Becky was only twelve, but the time had come for her to learn more ladylike ways.

Mellie considered the young man beside her. Jake couldn't be much more than a few years older than Lucinda. Such a handsome face, but so full of sadness, it had drawn her to him like a moth to light when he arrived at the ranch all those months ago. He'd become more like a second son. She wanted to erase that haunted look in his eye and believed she'd succeeded until today.

When they reached the main street, her heart beat a little faster. Her precious niece huddled on the bench, staring at the ground. She would offer Lucinda plenty of comfort and love to help her adjust to all the changes in the days ahead.

≈

Lucinda sat with head bowed against the wind as it blasted around the corner. She yanked on her bonnet to keep it from flying off into the street. She hadn't felt this lonely since the day after the funeral.

Wagon wheels creaked and broke the silence. Her name echoed across the street, and she glanced up. Aunt Amelia waved and called to her again. Relief flooded Lucinda's soul. She bolted from the bench and ran into her aunt's welcoming arms.

Aunt Amelia hugged her tightly. "Oh, my dear, I'm so sorry we're late. Your uncle Ben couldn't leave the ranch, so I had Jake bring me."

A young man in dusty boots and a brown hat stood waiting by the wagon. Hair the color of the wheat fields she'd passed in Kansas escaped from under his hat and brushed his shoulders. He tipped the brim back with a forefinger, and his eyebrows arched as though surprised to see her.

Aunt Amelia hugged her again before stepping back. "Oh, let me look at you. You've grown even more beautiful since we saw

14

you at the funeral." She turned to the cowboy. "Jake, come and meet Lucinda."

The young man sauntered across the unpaved street and removed his hat. Steel blue eyes met Lucinda's gaze and sliced through her with razor sharpness. She gulped. No one had ever looked at her like that.

Aunt Amelia introduced him as Jake Starnes. A muscle twitched in his well-tanned jaw, and a gust of wind blew a few strands of hair across his face. Still, he stared. Curiosity swelled from within, but she averted her eyes. The handsome young man in dirty boots and a blue jacket was like no other young man Lucinda had ever met.

She lifted her chin into the air and turned her gaze toward the station. "My bags are over there."

He stepped behind Lucinda to survey two trunks and a mound of other pieces. He emitted a low whistle. "All that stuff yours?"

At Lucinda's nod, he shook his head, then hefted the smaller trunk onto his shoulder. With his free hand he grasped the handle of her largest bag. "I reckon it'll fit, but we'll all three have to ride on the bench." He strode across the way to a wagon hitched to a pair of horses.

Lucinda scurried to keep up. Dismay swelled in her chest as she surveyed the wooden contraption. No carriage? How far would she have to ride up on that narrow seat? "How far is it?" she asked.

"It's about an hour's drive out to the ranch. Mrs. Haynes, maybe we should have brought the bigger buckboard."

Aunt Amelia covered her mouth with her hand. "I'm sorry. I should have thought of that, but this will have to do for today."

Jake pushed his load into the back of the wagon. He turned to Aunt Amelia and offered his assistance to lift her onto the wooden plank bench. After she settled herself, he nodded toward a step on the side and reached for Lucinda's elbow.

Lucinda tensed at his touch but accepted his help. She perched next to her aunt. Not even a cushion on the boards to soften the impact, but the thickness of her petticoats and coat would ease the bumps a bit.

As soon as she was situated, Jake turned back to the station. "I'll get the rest of your things."

Jake's dark jacket strained across his broad shoulders as he lifted the final two boxes and almost staggered under their weight.

Aunt Amelia leaned against her arm. "Jake's a strong young man and a big help on the ranch."

Lucinda's cheeks again filled with heat. Ashamed to think her aunt caught her observing the cowboy, she let her gaze wander back to the street and the buildings. How different from what she expected, but then she had no way of knowing what awaited her in Barton Creek.

Before she could take time for further inspection, Jake returned to heave the last small trunk onto the wagon.

Jake frowned up at her. "'Tain't Boston, but it's growing."

His words echoed her thoughts and unnerved her even more. She clasped her hands to keep them from shaking.

He unhitched the horses and climbed up beside her aunt, then reached behind him for a heavy wool coat. Jake pushed his long arms into the sleeves and buttoned it around his chest. A flick of the reins and the team moved forward.

Wide-open range and grasslands spread across the scene with distant hills giving character to an otherwise dull landscape with its brown and pale greens. Leafless trees sent crooked fingers into the overcast sky. The land looked as though God had created it and then forgotten it. Lucinda shivered as the wind sent chilling gusts through her cloak.

Aunt Amelia grasped Lucinda's hand. "Our house isn't a big

one by any means, but we have plenty of room for you, and Becky is excited to have another girl around the ranch. You'll share a room with her."

Share a room? Lucinda hadn't counted on that either. What other surprises lay waiting for her? The view of bleak land sowed more seeds of doubt in her mind. She should have insisted on staying in Boston. How would she ever fit into life on a ranch in such a lonely place?

If only Mama and Papa hadn't been so protective, she might not be as ill at ease as she was now. The sound of her name broke into her reverie. "What was that, Aunt Amelia?"

"I said Lucinda is rather a formal name for the west. How about Lucy? It's short and easy to say."

Change her name? What next? She rolled the name on her tongue but didn't care for the feel of it. If she changed her name, then she'd be giving up one more part of herself. Manners restrained her tongue from a sharp answer. "I'll have to think about the name for a while if you don't mind, Aunt Amelia."

Her aunt pursed her lips. "Of course, dear, but you can call me Aunt Mellie. Everyone at the ranch and in town does except for this young'un here." She nudged Jake in the arm. "Don't you think she looks like a Lucy?"

Jake shot her a quick look. "Sounds fine to me, ma'am," he said politely.

"Yes, Lucy is a good name." Mrs. Haynes grinned at Jake but spoke to Lucinda. "His name is Jacob, but we all call him Jake. Even your cousins have shortened names."

Love emanated from her aunt, but Lucinda would wait awhile before agreeing to change her name. She leaned forward a bit to observe Jake just as he cut his gaze to hers. A strange feeling of excitement engulfed her, but the unknown sent an icicle of fear through her heart.

❧

Jake matched Lucinda's stare until she turned her head. Was that fear he saw in her eyes? What had he said or done to frighten her?

He observed Lucinda's ramrod straight back, her hands clutching a dark blue cloak around her. Raven black hair peeked from beneath a bonnet. He didn't know her age, but she had to still be in her teen years. What had led him to think Lucinda was a child? Of course Mrs. Haynes always referred to her as a little girl. Nothing prepared him for the young lady seated on the other end of the wagon bench.

Mrs. Haynes eyed Lucinda's traveling clothes. "We'll have to get you some more comfortable things for life on the ranch."

Jake swallowed a chuckle as Lucinda protested. "No need for that. Mr. Sutton thought I needed a proper traveling gown, but most of the things his wife helped me with are much more practical." More practical? Jake doubted it. A refined lady from Boston like her wouldn't know the first thing about what to wear at a ranch. A twinge of sympathy ran through him. She looked as out of place as a pig at a cattle auction.

"Here we are," said Mrs. Haynes. "Welcome to your new home, dear."

Before them the Rocking H ranch spread out across the horizon. The roof outlines of the house, bunkhouse, and barns drew near. Jake urged the horses forward, eager to deliver his unusual charge and return to his work. Lucinda's troubles were none of his business. Besides, he had enough troubles of his own to carry.

Chapter 2

*A*t sight of the ranch, anxiety wrapped its tentacles around Lucinda's heart, but she refused to let them take hold. Instead, she filled her mind with good things and an eagerness to meet her cousins. She truly wanted to fit in with their way of living.

A sprawling one-story house made of logs and stone stood before her. Two young people ran out to meet the wagon. Uncle Ben stepped down from the porch.

The young girl hopped about in the cold, but her eyes sparkled with excitement. The boy looked older than she first thought and much taller. How they had grown since the last time they visited Boston nearly ten years ago. Jake pulled the horses to a halt and jumped down to come around to assist the ladies. His hands circled Lucinda's waist and lifted her easily from the wagon.

She felt the strength of his hands even through the layers of garments she wore. Her eyes were almost even with his, but she could read nothing in their blue depths. She averted her glance. "Thank you, Jake."

He released his hold and stepped back. "You're welcome, Miss Bishop."

A pair of arms encircled her waist. "Is it really you, Lucinda?"

Lucinda peered into the face of the young girl with her hair tied back with a bow and a spattering of freckles across her nose. "It is, and you must be Becky."

Her cousin nodded and grabbed Lucinda's hand. "I'm glad you're here. It'll be so good to have someone to talk to besides Matt."

Uncle Ben grasped her shoulders, and a warm voice greeted her. "Welcome to Oklahoma Territory and the Rocking H ranch." He hugged her and then slid his arm around his wife's waist.

Her cousin Matt stepped forward, smiling warmly. "I'll help Jake get your things into the house."

When they entered the front parlor, she gasped at the furnishings. She hadn't known exactly what to expect, but the sofa and chairs closely resembled those from her own home in Boston. But of course, Mother had shipped a number of items out west for her sister. To the right she spotted another room, and from the looks of the furnishings, it was the kitchen. The large stone fireplace, now banked with a cheery fire, lent a homey feel of welcome that eased Lucinda's misgivings.

Becky pulled her down a hallway. "You're going to share a room with me. I hope you don't mind. Pa put two beds in it for us 'cause he says I'd probably kick you out of the bed if we slept together."

Lucinda listened to her cousin's explanations and hid a smile. With this little magpie, she'd never have any quiet, but sharing might be fun. This way she wouldn't be as lonely. "That sounds fine, Becky. You'll have to help me go through my things and decide what is best to be worn here."

When she entered the room, Lucinda stepped back in time. The familiar print of floral wallpaper matched that of her room in Boston, and a chest at the end of her bed was almost exactly like hers at home.

A tear formed in her eye. She walked over to the bed nearest the windows and ran her hand over the quilt that covered it. It was her own quilt from her bed in Boston.

Her aunt beamed. "We had it sent out as a surprise for you. Mrs. Sutton helped get it here."

"Oh, thank you, Aunt Amelia. What a nice thing to do." She fingered the delicate lace curtains adorning the windows and realized how much they wanted her to feel at home.

Becky plopped on the bed nearest the door. "Ma and Pa let me help with fixing up our room. It was fun, and I'm glad you like it. I have the bed by the door 'cause I have to get up early to help Ma with the chores."

She leaned back on her hands with her legs akimbo, causing her skirt to rise above her knees. "I hope you like it here. Do you ride a horse? 'Cause if you do, we can go riding together."

Lucinda reached out to straighten Becky's skirts, but stopped short. She mustn't appear too bossy. Besides, Becky would keep things too busy to think about why this trip to Oklahoma had been necessary. Lucinda turned her gaze to the window where a few horses tossed their heads and pawed the ground in a fenced-in area beside the barn. "I've ridden horses back home." But could she ride like they did here?

Jake and Matt appeared in the doorway with the first load of boxes and the trunk. They set them down next to her bed.

Matt shook his head. "Looks like you're really planning on staying with us awhile. I never saw so many boxes and trunks."

Lucinda smiled. "I know it looks like a lot, but it isn't all mine. I have some things for your parents and for both of you too."

Becky clapped her hands in enthusiasm. "Oh, I can't wait to see what you brought."

Jake said nothing but simply stared at her again for a moment before he strode from the room for more boxes. Once more her heart fluttered under his gaze. She removed her coat and bonnet and then fluffed out her skirt.

Becky grinned at her. "He's a handsome one, that Jake Starnes. He seems to be taking a liking to you."

The heat rose in Lucinda's face and warmed her cheeks. "Oh, no, I think he's just curious as to what a girl from Boston is doing out here with so much baggage." She tapped her chin with a slender finger. "I think I have just the thing for you in my valise."

Becky sprang from the bed. "Oh, what is it? Can I see it now?"

With her tactic to change the subject successful, Lucinda grinned. "We'll find it as I unpack."

Her cousin grabbed Lucinda about the waist and peered up at her, her head even with Lucinda's chin. "You're taller than I expected. Ma said you're almost eighteen. I'll be thirteen before Christmas."

Such a chatterbox, but she did have a winsome smile and lovely brown hair. Lucinda held her at arm's length. "Tall women abound in our family. I bet you'll have a growth spurt and add an inch or two to your own height." Then again Becky may be more like their grandmother who had been just over five feet tall.

Becky furrowed her brow. "I pray so. Matt grew a whole bunch over the summer. It's not fun to be the short one when everyone towers above you."

"Oh, I don't know about that. Sometimes I envy my petite friends. Besides, you're a perfect height for your age. Now come and help me decide what I should wear this evening for dinner." The aroma of an apple pie wafted in from the kitchen and reminded her of her meager lunch at the relay station.

She swallowed hard to quiet the rumble in her stomach and reached into her reticule for the trunk keys. If the dinner lived up to the smells in the air, it would be a most pleasant ending to a trying day.

⁓

Jake drove the now empty wagon into the barn after Ben and Matt carried the last load into the house. Then he led the bays to their stalls to settle them in for the evening.

Only three years separated Lucinda and him in age, but miles and miles made the difference in their background. All his life he'd known only farm and ranch work. Miss Bishop most likely knew nothing about either.

The horses jerked their heads, happy to be home and out of the wind. He loved being with the animals. Here he could think and feel safe. The smell of the fresh hay forked in earlier mingled with the odor of the stock quartered there. The swishing tails of the two milking cows and the soft nickering of the horses gave him a peace he didn't often feel these days.

He brushed down the team as his thoughts drifted to Miss Bishop. He'd never met a girl who could face him almost eye to eye. Being six feet one inch in height, most women came only to his shoulder or below. The top of Lucinda's head reached about chin high on him, and she was slender too. The memory of her small waist beneath his hands burned in his mind.

Then the dark cloud of despair descended. He shouldn't be thinking about her or any woman for that matter. He was a man running from the law and had nothing to offer any girl, much less one like Miss Bishop.

He finished with the horses and headed for the bunkhouse he shared with two other hands. The chill of the wind blowing across the plains down from the north cut through his jacket. Late October usually brought the first cold front to the land. At least he'd be safe enough here during the winter months of snow and ice. And if he could trust the signs of nature, that wouldn't be too far away.

Inside, Hank and Monk greeted him. They had cleaned up from their chores of the day and sat playing cards at the only table in the room. Monk's older, sun-weathered face bore a wide grin under its mustache, but Hank, who was a few years older than Jake, smirked and narrowed his eyes.

"How was your trip to town? Miss Bishop looks to be a fine figure of a woman." Monk slapped a card on the table and picked up another one to add to his hand.

Jake shrugged. "She's only seventeen. Not quite a woman yet."

Hank guffawed. "Maybe so, but she's old enough to take a husband and start a family. Wonder if she'd be interested in me?"

Jake bristled. "She's too much of a lady to be having anything to do with the likes of us." He doused his face with cold water from the basin near the door to cool his rising anger.

Of course Hank's thoughts only echoed his own. Maybe that's what riled him. He groped for the towel to wipe his face. He had to think about something else, anything other than Lucinda Bishop.

But that would be difficult seeing as how he'd have to sit at the table with her for dinner shortly. Maybe he'd skip the meal tonight, although Mrs. Haynes's fried steak and apple pie made his mouth water. His stomach rumbled. No, he'd just have to bear being near her again.

Her lovely floral scent lingered in his nostrils, reminding him of the flowers his ma grew back on their homestead when he was a child. She had taught him the names of all the blooms in her garden, but none smelled as sweet as the waxy white flowers of the gardenia and honeysuckle.

He squeezed his eyes shut to keep away the threatening sadness brought on by those memories. The last thing he needed was to have Monk or Hank catch him like this. He'd never hear the end of their teasing. Proving his worth on the cattle drive had won their respect, and he didn't want to jeopardize that now. He splashed more water on his face and raked his hands through his hair.

Lucinda tucked away another garment in the chest her aunt had provided in her new room. Several skirts and shirtwaists already hung in the wardrobe.

Becky sat cross-legged on the bed. "You have such nice things. I'm not fond of wearing all that stuff, but it does look pretty."

Suddenly she jumped up. "Oh, goodness, I'm supposed to help Ma with supper, and I forgot all about it, but I wanted to see what you brought me."

"I'm sure it will be all right if I explain you were helping me. We can wait until after dinner, and then everyone will get their gifts at the same time."

Becky started to protest, but Lucinda placed her hands on her cousin's shoulders and guided her out of the room and toward the kitchen. Wonderful aromas of fried meat and fresh bread tempted the taste buds.

Lucinda stopped short at the door. Two strange men stood near the table with Jake and Uncle Ben and Matt. She hadn't realized others would be sharing the meal.

Becky hurried across the room and headed for her pa. "Looks like everyone is here to eat. I'm sorry I'm late, Ma."

Aunt Mellie set a bowl of potatoes on the table. "It's all right, dear. I knew you were with Lucinda. You may help with cleaning up after."

Becky spoke to the man with the droopy mustache. "Monk, have you had time to fix Daisy's bridle yet?"

The man grinned. "Sure have, Miss Becky. You'll be able to ride her tomorrow."

The young girl clapped her hands with delight. "Oh, I do hope it's not too cold to ride. Ma said we could stay home from school tomorrow in honor of Lucinda's arrival."

Uncle Ben gestured for Lucinda to come to his side. "Boys, this is Lucinda Bishop. She's here from Boston and will be living with us awhile. Lucinda, this is Monk and Hank, our other two wranglers. You've already met Jake."

Jake's gaze locked with hers. His vivid blue eyes sent a chill through her veins. What was the matter with her?

The other two men smiled. The older of the two, Monk, bore whiskers and a drooping mustache on his face with streaks of gray in both hair and beard. Hank, though not quite as handsome as Jake, had the rugged look she expected of a cowboy. His dark eyes sparkled as he nodded to her. "It's a pleasure to have another young lady here. I'm sure you'll be a great help for Mellie."

Lucinda swallowed a gasp. Hired help didn't speak in such familiar tones with a family member in Boston.

When all were seated, Lucinda sat directly across from Jake. She hadn't expected to see him at all this evening, and his presence only added to the uneasiness that fell upon her every time he came near. She kept her eyes on her hands in her lap. Eating with strangers had never been pleasant for her.

After Uncle Ben's blessing, she surveyed the food spread before her. Plates piled with beef and bowls brimming with potatoes and green beans as well as a platter of corn bread squares and fresh bread filled the center of the table. During the meal she noticed how much the men ate. Such appetites must come from living in the country. Of course she had only her father as a guide, and he had not been a heavy eater. She had so much to learn about the ways of the ranch.

Jake's hand grazed hers as she passed the corn bread, and she almost jumped at the spark that lit inside her. "Thank you, Miss Bishop. Did you help Mrs. Haynes with the meal?"

"Um, no, I didn't." No need for him to know she didn't understand the first thing about cooking.

Aunt Mellie passed her the butter. "Fresh churned this morning."

Fresh churned? Butter had graced the table in Boston, but Lucinda had never thought about how it got there.

She glanced up to find Hank grinning at her. "You city girls sure don't eat much."

Jake helped himself to more potatoes but glared at Hank. "After a long day on the stage, I would think maybe Miss Bishop is tired."

Heat rose in her cheeks. How rude for them to discuss her, but at least Jake seemed to know his place as a hired hand. Not like Hank or Monk, who called Aunt Mellie by her first name. She lowered her head and buttered a piece of corn bread.

She listened with great interest as the family and the ranch hands talked about the ranch and its workings. Lucinda didn't attempt to add anything to the conversation, but Becky jumped right in with her comments and ideas. Lucinda had been taught that women and especially young girls were to sit quietly unless spoken to first.

Jake ate steadily, only occasionally lifting his eyes from his plate. Why did he send her heart all aflutter whenever he cast his blue eyes in her direction? Lucinda pushed her strange feelings aside and tried to concentrate on learning all she could about her new home.

Chapter 3

*A*fter dinner, Ben stood by the mantel while his family gathered around the fireplace. Jake and the boys had retired to the bunkhouse for the night. He remembered the exchange between Hank and Jake at the supper table. They both had eyes only for Lucinda. Of course the two would be attracted to his pretty niece. Hank probably wanted to see if he could get a rise out of Jake, and if Ben was a good judge, he had succeeded. Still, she was now his responsibility, and he must be careful about her relationships.

Not that the boys weren't good men, but he didn't know enough of their backgrounds to determine if they were suitable for his niece. He'd keep a close eye on her for the next few weeks until she became more acclimated to the ranch.

He headed for his favorite chair. Becky sat with Lucinda. His young niece reminded him of a hothouse flower, carefully tended until it was in full bloom. He prayed that nothing would take away her innocence and blossom.

Matt set Lucinda's smaller trunk before her. She motioned for everyone to gather around as she unlocked it and lifted the lid. A layer of cloth protected the contents.

Lucinda reached for the first piece. "I wasn't sure about what to bring. Mrs. Sutton and I spent a good amount of time considering what you may need or could use out here." She grasped a bundle wrapped in paper and handed it to Mellie. "These are a few of the linens that Mother embroidered. I saved a few for myself, but I thought you might like to have these."

Aunt Mellie carefully removed the wrapping. "Oh, Lucinda, they're beautiful." She moved her fingers across the fine stitches. "Amanda did have a way with a needle. Thank you." Her cheeks glistened with tears.

The joy on his wife's face warmed his heart. Her love for her sister shone in the way she caressed the pieces. Lucinda couldn't have chosen a nicer gift for Mellie.

Lucinda's voice caught in her throat. "Uncle Ben, I thought you might like to have Papa's pipes and rack. I remember how you and he enjoyed your after-dinner coffee and good tobacco when you visited us in Boston." She retrieved the package and held them toward her uncle.

Ben gasped. "Charles had some of the finest pipes to be found. I've always admired them." He gripped the box that contained three pipes, a stand, and a small can of tobacco. "I'm honored to have these. Thank you, Lucinda." Never had he expected such a generous gift.

Lucinda smiled again and reached into the trunk for the next parcel. "I think this will be just the thing for you." Lucinda placed a wrapped bundle on Becky's lap.

She tore off the paper and squealed her pleasure at the dark green dress trimmed in cream lace. "Oh, look, Ma. Isn't it beautiful?"

"Yes, it is, and it'll be perfect to wear for your birthday party at Christmas." She turned to her niece. "You couldn't have picked a better color or style."

Indeed, Ben could already picture his rambunctious daughter in such a dress, and the image amused him. Becky liked pretty things, but putting on fancy clothes for more than Sunday church or a special party was not one of her favorite things to do. He'd take great delight in seeing her wear Lucinda's gift.

"I just thought of what I wore at Becky's age, and Mrs. Sutton helped me with the size. I'm glad you like it."

Lucinda handed the next package to Matt. Ben grinned when his son held up three books. Just what his boy needed. The few books here had been read until they fell apart. Lucinda had chosen her gifts well.

Matt ran his fingers over the covers. "Mark Twain. I've heard of him but never dreamed I'd have books by him. Where did you get them?"

"Mr. Sutton found them in a bookstore in Boston and thought you might enjoy reading the stories. He bought copies for his own son. The others are from our own library."

Ben chuckled. At sixteen, Matt wouldn't jump up and hug his cousin, but he did give her a warm smile in thanks.

Lucinda handed a vase to Aunt Mellie.

Mellie clasped the gift to her chest. Tears glistened on her cheeks. "This is precious, dear. I know Amanda treasured my gift, and I will treasure her memory with it."

"I knew it was special to you." Lucinda stifled a yawn. "Oh my, excuse me. It's been a long day."

Mellie reached over and hugged Lucinda. "Of course you're tired. I should have realized. And it's time you went to bed too, Becky. Despite the cold weather coming in and my letting you stay home from school, you still have chores in the morning."

The young girl sighed and hugged her new dress. "I think I might really enjoy wearing this dress for my birthday party. Thank you."

"I look forward to seeing it on you." Lucinda wrapped her arm around Becky's shoulders. "Come, let's go to our room."

The girls left the room with Matt, and Ben moved to the fireplace. Studying Mellie out of the corner of his eye, he stretched his hands toward the flames, and warmth bathed his palms. She set her rocker into gentle motion as she picked up her knitting. A softly hummed tune met his ears. He cherished these moments alone with his wife.

He tamped his new pipe, then lit it. After taking a few draws on the stem, he settled into the chair beside her. "Bringing me this pipe was a fine gesture on Lucinda's part. How do you think she's going to take to living on the ranch?"

Mellie laid down her knitting and unwound more yarn from a skein. "I'm sure she'll do right well. Becky already adores her, and that's a good thing. I'm counting on Lucinda's ways to have an effect on our daughter."

"Now, Mellie, I like Becky just the way she is. She brings life to everything around here. She rides almost as well as Matt and loves being around the stock."

"That's well and good, but she'll be thirteen shortly and needs to learn to be a young lady."

Ben shook his head. "My dear, please don't make her grow up too fast. I enjoy having my little Becky around." All too soon she would grow into a young lady ready for a home of her own.

Mellie grinned and grasped her knitting needles. "I know, and if you had your way, she'd never leave the ranch, no matter how many boys might come a-callin'."

Ben leaned back and puffed on his pipe. "You could be right about that." His young daughter already showed signs of the beauty she would be like her mother and cousin. He still had time before young men began taking a fancy to his little one.

"Speaking of young men, I think I saw a spark of interest in Jake for our Lucinda." The emotion in Jake's eyes when he had looked at Lucinda troubled Ben.

Knitting needles clicked in the quiet of late evening, and

Mellie nodded her head. "I noticed too. What worries me about Jake is that I don't think he knows the Lord."

"Don't think he does either, but I gave him a Bible and told him if he had any questions after reading it, to come to me and ask. So far, no questions or interest of any kind." He placed his new pipe in its rack above the fireplace.

"That's a shame." Mellie stuck her needles into a ball of dark blue yarn. "We'll have to just keep praying and setting the example for him. I'm still hoping he'll make it to church with us one of these Sundays." She sighed. "For being a cowboy, he seems like a decent sort. If only he came to know the Lord, they could make a fine young couple."

Ben nodded. "I remember your ma's reaction when she learned her daughter wanted to marry a rancher from out west. She called me a young, mule-headed, cow-loving dust buster."

"Yes, she did. But we made a fine pair and still do. I haven't regretted for one minute leaving the social life of Boston behind me." She held up her project to examine the stitches.

He moved to her side and knelt beside the rocker. "You really mean that? I often think of all the things you gave up eighteen years ago. It's been a good life, hasn't it?"

Mellie lay down her needles and yarn. She cupped her hands on either side of Ben's face. "It's been a wonderful life. You have given me more than I ever dreamed of having when we first arrived."

Ben covered her hands with his. Her love shone through her dark eyes and in her smile. "I love you, Amelia Haynes. You've never disappointed me, criticized me, or argued with me."

Her laughter warmed his heart. "That doesn't mean I didn't think of it a time or two. You can be a stubborn man, Mr. Haynes."

"Oh, really now. I've seen a little streak of mule in you too."

He grinned when the red rose in her cheeks burned like the flames in the fire behind them.

She eased her hands from under his and picked up her needles. "I suppose I must admit that."

Ben stood and strode back to the fireside. "I wish Lucinda hadn't been forced to come just as winter is setting in. Much better here in the spring and summer."

"If you discount the heat of July and August, it is. Anyway, she's accustomed to harsh winters in the east, and from what I've seen of her on our visits back home, she has quite a bit of spunk."

Mellie rose and rubbed her hand across her mid-back. "I just pray we're not making a mistake bringing Lucinda out here where she knows nothing about our way of life."

Ben put another log on the fire, then turned to embrace his wife. "I think she'll be fine. After all, she does come from good stock."

Mellie giggled like a schoolgirl. "You do know the right things to say, Benjamin Haynes." She stowed her knitting project in the basket beside her chair. "We'll be up early tomorrow. I'm going to bed. Will you be long?"

He kissed her cheek, the velvet smoothness of her flawless complexion soft beneath his lips. Years on the ranch and still she had the softest skin he could ever imagine. "No. I'll take care of the fire and then be in. You might check on the girls. It'll be a cold night."

He stoked the logs in the fireplace and stirred the ashes. After making sure the glowing embers were safe to leave, he snuffed out the lamp on the table and picked up the other one to light his way to the back of the house and the room he shared with his wife.

Mellie stopped in the hallway and opened the girls' door. Her oil lamp shed light on Becky with her covers all askew. Mellie set the lamp on a table and stooped to kiss her daughter's forehead. She picked up the quilt trailing on the floor and tucked it back snugly under the mattress. Becky would probably have them all on the floor again with all her tossing and kicking, but she'd be warm for a while.

Lucinda stirred in her bed. What a beautiful young woman she had grown to be, but her face still held the innocence of a child. She had her mother's tact and her father's spirit, two things that would serve her well in the future.

She knelt beside the bed and placed her hand on her niece's shoulder. "Lucinda, I'm very glad you're here. I know this seems like a foreign land to you, but give us a chance and let us love you and take care of you."

A snuffle emitted from the covers. Lucinda turned over to face her aunt. The dim light revealed the wetness of her cheeks. Mellie wrapped her arms around her niece. "I'm so sorry about your mother and father. I wish I could bring them back. If things don't work out here, we'll make sure you have a place back in Boston should you want to return. Just remember, we love you, and God loves you. Let Him help you through your sorrow."

Lucinda sniffed again. "I will, Aunt Mellie. I truly will."

Mellie tucked the quilt around Lucinda and stood to leave.

"Aunt Mellie, please don't go yet."

"Of course, my dear child. Is something troubling you?"

Lucinda swiped at her cheeks. Her eyes appeared dark and luminous in the light of the lamp.

"I'm afraid to go back to Boston."

Mellie gasped, and her heart skipped a beat. Lucinda afraid? "Why, my dear? What happened?"

"Nothing really. It's just the way Uncle Rudolph treated me when he came back to Boston a few weeks ago. He was very angry and said harsh and ugly words to me and to Mr. Sutton."

That man! What Mellie wouldn't give to get her hands on him. She'd known he'd been angry after the reading of the will. She composed her thoughts. "He's just upset; that's all. He won't do anything to hurt you." But she didn't believe her own words.

"I didn't think so either, but two days before I left to come out here, there was another incident with the carriage. This time, though, the driver managed to keep the horses under control."

Mellie's heart jumped with fear at the thought of danger for her niece. "Oh, my dear, were you hurt?"

"No, and I thought it to be just an accident until the next day." Lucinda hesitated. "I hope I'm imagining things, but I went shopping with Mrs. Sutton, and a carriage almost ran us down. I could swear that Uncle Rudolph was inside it."

Mellie's thoughts swirled with images and ideas of the evil that man could produce, and she squeezed Lucinda's hand. "I'm sure it was a mistake." But what if Lucinda was right? Would she be safe here on the ranch? Ben needed to be told.

"Don't worry about it anymore. You'll be safe here. We'll take good care of you." She bent to kiss Lucinda's forehead. "Good night, dear. I'll call you Lucinda until you decide you want us to change it."

"Thank you, Aunt Mellie. I'd like that."

"Of course; I understand." Mellie picked up the lamp and left the room. She and Ben would do everything they could to help their niece adjust to the ways of the West and keep her safe too, but what if her sister's death had not been an accident? She closed the door behind her and went down the hall to join her husband in their room.

Ben turned around when she entered. "What happened? You look troubled."

Mellie closed her eyes and leaned on his chest. "I *am* troubled. I have so much to tell you."

⚜

In the bunkhouse Jake turned over in his bed yet again. No matter which way he turned to get comfortable, he couldn't sleep. The face of a certain young lady from Boston filled his mind, and he couldn't shake it loose. He had a better chance to study her at supper earlier. Brown eyes had locked with his on more than one occasion. He couldn't keep his gaze off her, and when his hand brushed against hers, the shock traveled quickly up his arm and into his heart.

If things were different and he was still a rancher's son, he'd have no qualms about asking Ben Haynes for permission to court Miss Lucinda. But now he was just a cowhand with no business even thinking about a young lady like her.

He sat up and fumbled to light the candle by his bunk. He waited to make sure the light didn't wake his bunkmates, then reached beneath his bed and drew out a Bible. Ben had given him the book months ago, but he'd never felt driven to open it till now.

The book fell open to a page marked by Ben. Jake started the third chapter of John. The words about being born again confused him, but the sixteenth verse caused him to stop. Why would God love a man like Jake so much?

He snuffed out the candle and closed his eyes. The Bible spoke of God's love, but how could God love Jake after what he'd done? He didn't understand any of this business about God. It had been too many years since he'd attended church as a child. He tried to remember those days and what the preacher had said. Nothing came to mind but the fire-filled words telling of hell and the punishment that waited for sinners at Judgment Day.

Just then he heard a pinging against the windows. Sleet. That meant icy ground tomorrow. Must be in for a hard winter if the temperatures dropped low enough for freezing this early. His arms grew cold as the embers turned dark in the old pot-bellied stove.

Tomorrow morning he would be the first up to get the fire going again. He pulled the blanket up to cover his shoulders. If he'd been a praying man, he'd be thanking the Lord for a warm, dry bed on a night like this.

He tried to shut out the sounds coming from the next bunk, but Hank's snores almost drowned out the plunk of frozen rain against the windows.

He turned over yet again. No matter how hard he tried, Jake could not dislodge the image of Lucinda Bishop. He punched his pillow and buried his face in its feathered softness.

Chapter 4

*L*ucinda awakened early the next morning and clutched her quilt about her. At first, she couldn't quite get her bearings, but then she remembered. This wasn't her room in Boston; she now lived out west. She looked over at her cousin's bed. Becky was already up and about her chores. Lucinda cringed. Her aunt and uncle must think she was a slugabed.

Her feet hit the icy cold floor, and she scrambled to slide the rag rug closer. She fished heavy black stockings from her valise and pulled them over her chilled feet. A few minutes later she completed her morning routine and pulled a heavy wool skirt down over her petticoats. Thank the Lord that women here didn't wear corsets or bustles. Ranch work would be most difficult bound and laced into those contraptions.

The sound of pots and pans drew her to the kitchen. A white apron covered Aunt Mellie's brown woolen dress. She opened the oven door and slid in a large pan of biscuits. "Good morning, my dear. Did you sleep well?"

"Yes, I did." The aroma of frying bacon and coffee reminded Lucinda of her hunger. "Aunt Mellie, I'm so sorry I slept late. I meant to be up to help you with breakfast."

"It's your first day here. Time enough for you to help with chores later." She set a large crockery bowl on a counter. "Becky's out gathering eggs for breakfast. She'll be back shortly."

"What can I do?"

"Why not set the table. The dishes and mugs are on the shelves right there." Her aunt pointed out the dishes.

That she could do. Lucinda had learned the fine art of table setting in her class on etiquette. However, the heavy crockery bore little resemblance to the fine china to which she was accustomed.

The large table had been waxed until it shone in the light from the oil lamps sitting about. Lucinda moved around the table laying plates, and when she came to the place where Jake sat, she paused, her cheeks burning. What would people back home think of her being attracted to a man like Jake? Papa would have been furious that such a boy had even spoken to her. She smiled now at how protective Papa had been. She hadn't minded because she knew how much he loved her. Still, she did wish for a bit more experience with the male gender.

Aunt Mellie laid slices of bacon in the black iron skillet. "When the places are ready, you can pour milk for Becky and yourself, unless you prefer coffee."

Lucinda circled the table with mugs. "No, milk is fine. I haven't developed a taste for coffee yet. I do like tea, but that's too much trouble for breakfast."

"Not really, but I usually reserve a little time in the afternoons for a spot of tea. It'll be nice to share that time with you today."

"Thank you. I'd like that." She swallowed a chuckle threatening to erupt at the thought of Becky sitting down for tea and cakes or cookies or whatever else Aunt Mellie served. Would she be able to tame Becky, or would the younger girl have the greater influence?

The door burst open, and her cousin bounded through it in a blast of cold air. "Here, Ma. Plenty of eggs for breakfast and some to spare."

Her aunt grasped the handle of the basket and set it on the counter. "Thank you, dear. You can crack them up for me while

I finish the bacon. The men will be in and hungry as bears after hibernation."

Becky broke eggs into the crockery bowl and glanced over at Lucinda. "I wish it wasn't so cold out today. I have so much to show you around the ranch."

Aunt Mellie laughed. "I'm sure that can wait for warmer weather. We have plenty to do in the house today."

A flurry of activity at the door again caught her attention. Ben stamped his feet and hung his coat and hat on the rack nearby. He took a big sniff. "*Hmm.* I sure love the smell of bacon frying."

Jake and the other two men stood back, but Matt ambled over to the table. "I see Ma put you to work early."

"Yes, and I don't mind helping any way I can." She poured milk into two glasses and set them on the table. Her hands trembled as she held the pitcher.

Uncle Ben pulled out his chair. "Well, I'm hungry enough to eat a whole steer."

Aunt Mellie's laugh rang across the room. "You'll have to be satisfied with what I've got, but you'll have plenty of biscuits and gravy to go with it."

Lucinda heard snatches of conversation about the herd and going out to check them today as the men gathered around the table. She acknowledged the smiles and greetings as the men took their places, but Jake remained silent and avoided her eyes. He seemed bent on ignoring her today.

Lucinda took her seat and bowed her head as Uncle Ben returned thanks for the meal and the hands that prepared it. Again, she felt the love emanating from her family. They promised to take care of her. God had provided for her just as He always had and always would. Nothing else may be certain in her life, but the love of God and family would never change. She repeated Uncle Ben's "amen" and lifted her head.

Matt grasped the platter of eggs and served himself. Then the business of filling plates and passing food took over. The amount each man heaped on his plate amazed her yet again. They must have put in half a day's work before breakfast.

Conversation flowed around her as the men spoke of riding out to fill the feeding bins for the cattle on winter range. Lucinda reached for her milk and sipped. She wrinkled her nose. What a funny taste, not like that at home.

Uncle Ben spread a biscuit with homemade blackberry jam and grinned at Lucinda. "That's milk straight from the cow. Might take a little getting used to."

Lucinda felt the heat rise again in her cheeks. She forced herself to take another swallow. "It isn't so bad." But it was. She set the glass back in place. Seemed like everything she did brought some embarrassment.

Becky mentioned the horses and peered at Lucinda. "You said yesterday you know a little about riding."

"Yes, I took riding lessons in Boston. I enjoyed frequent rides in the park with my father, but I've never ridden on anything but an English saddle."

Uncle Ben stroked his chin and nodded. "Umm, I believe we can take care of that. I'm glad Becky will have someone to ride with." He arched an eyebrow at his daughter. "She takes to riding off alone too frequently to suit me, so you'll be a good companion."

Becky grinned. "Oh, Lucinda, having you along will be more fun than ever. I wish the cold weather would hurry up and leave so we can ride every day."

Ben shook his head. "It'll be soon enough. And Jake, you can select a horse from the corral for Lucinda to have her own mount. I believe we have an extra saddle about her size too."

Jake nodded and stared evenly at Lucinda. She twisted her hands in her lap. "Thank you. I'd appreciate having my own mount." Both hope and fear rose in her throat at the possibility of Jake working with her and the horse.

A grin spread across Hank's face. "If old Jake here gets too busy to help you, I'd be happy to lend my assistance."

Lucinda smiled at Hank. "Thank you. With the two of you teaching me, I should learn to ride on a new saddle quickly." Perhaps he wasn't as rude as she first thought. And again, it may be the way cowboys on a ranch behave.

Jake frowned and pressed his lips together. What was the matter with Jake? That made the third time she'd seen a look of displeasure on his face.

Talk continued on about the ranch until Uncle Ben wiped his hands with his napkin and thrust it on the table. "We need to check on the cattle and make sure we have enough hay for all of them. Chester Fowler's herd most likely will be wandering around the open range too. We'll take care of them, but I don't want any of our herd wandering over to Fowler's place and eating the feed left for his cattle."

Jake furrowed his brow. "Don't you think he'd do the same for our cattle?"

"Maybe, but probably not. We'll take care of his because that's what the good Lord wants us to do, but we have no control over what Fowler will do for us. Sam Morris, on the other hand, will watch out for any strays over his way."

The young cowboy nodded. "Hank, Monk, and I loaded the wagons with the feed you wanted to take out this morning, so we're all set to leave when you are. We should have plenty."

"Good, now let's get on with our day." Uncle Ben stood, then leaned over and kissed Aunt Mellie's cheek. "I'll be back in a few minutes to pick up our grub for noon. Those leftover biscuits will be mighty welcome come noontime."

Jake and the other two men rose to follow Ben and Matt. The

wind howled into the room when her uncle opened the back door. He stood back to let Jake and the others precede him. He tossed one last smile back at his wife before pulling the door securely closed behind him.

Love flowed like honey between them. Someday a man would look at her with that much love in his eyes. Would that someone be Jake? Lucinda didn't understand her attraction to him. But his courtesy toward her and Aunt Mellie proved he had learned manners and social graces somewhere in his background.

The memory of blue eyes and golden hair sent a chill down her arms. The only other males in her life besides her father and two household staff members had been the boys at her church. They had been gawky and clumsy like she had been, but Jake wore the look of a man who had known rough times. How had a man like him come to be a cowboy on a ranch in Oklahoma?

⚜

Mellie couldn't help but notice the looks passing between Lucinda and Jake. *Oh, Amanda, how I wish you were here to advise me how to handle this situation. I don't think either of them is truly aware yet of exactly what's happening.*

"Aunt Mellie, where do I put these?"

Lucinda stood with an armful of plates. "Over by the sink. When you two have finished the dishes, we'll get started on our other chores." She held up Ben's saddlebags. "Right now, I need to finish this pack for the men to take with them."

She busied herself with stuffing the bags with biscuits, beans, and coffee. When Mellie completed her task, she set them by the back door for Ben to pick up.

"Do you prepare a meal for them every day?" Lucinda dried her hands on a towel.

Mellie laughed. "Only in the winter when our trail cook isn't

43

around. Webster is away seeing to his sister. She's really sick, and he went to help out his brother-in-law. When he gets back in the spring, he'll take a chuck wagon out with the boys on the trail. Sometimes they're gone overnight."

Becky retied her wayward apron strings. "That's why Jake and the others took supper with us last night. When Old Webster gets back, they won't be around as much. He likes to cook as much as Ma."

Mellie placed her arm around her niece's shoulder. "I just realized we didn't give you much time to unpack last evening, so why don't you go take care of that now. I'll finish up around here."

"But what about the baking? I'd really like to learn to cook."

Becky giggled. "Want to make a good impression on Jake, huh?"

"Rebecca Haynes, I think you have a few chores to do, and now is as good a time as any to get started."

"Yes, Ma." Becky turned to leave the room but with a grin and a twinkle in her eye.

Mellie sighed. Her young daughter did like to tease. "I'm sorry about that, Lucinda. Becky doesn't mean anything by it." She paused. "He did have an eye for you this morning."

Lucinda averted her eyes. "I've never been around a man like him before. And he is handsome."

"That he is. He's been working here on the ranch about six months. From the little we know about him, he's an orphan too."

"Oh." Lucinda untied her apron.

She appeared as if she wanted to ask something. Mellie waited, but her niece only hung her apron on the hook and said, "I'm going to unpack now."

Mellie shook her head. When Lucinda was ready, she'd open up more and maybe reveal what seemed to be troubling her. In the meantime, she and Ben must be careful to protect her and not let a relationship develop that might hurt her.

The back door opened, and Ben reached for the saddlebags. "Where are the girls?"

"Becky's cleaning, and Lucy's unpacking." She leaned over and kissed his cheek. "You men be careful out there. We want to see you back here for supper. I think we need to talk about Lucinda and Jake tonight."

Ben laughed and returned her kiss. "Nothing will keep me from getting home to one of your meals, and you know that." His expression sobered. "I noticed the sparks between those two again this morning. Lucinda is too inexperienced to understand, and we must watch out for her. I'll speak with Jake if the opportunity arises."

He hefted the load onto his shoulder, winked at her, and headed back into the cold. Her heart filled with love for her husband, Mellie set about checking the supplies for baking later on in the day.

Chapter 5

The chill winds blew, but Jake's last encounter with Lucinda at breakfast warmed him from inside. He mounted his horse to ride with the others out to the herds.

Ben had given him the responsibility of choosing a horse for Lucinda, and he knew just which one it would be. The ebony filly he had ridden last week to see how she took to wearing a saddle would be a good choice. Her gentle nature and ease of handling should give Lucinda a great ride.

The men spread out, and Jake headed to the south side to round up cattle not taken on the last drive. Jake's horse knew his business and needed little coaching from his rider to nudge the cattle into a group. The morning passed quickly with Jake completing his assigned task. The herd would be easier to feed when the snows came if they were on the range closer to the ranch house.

When they arrived at the first of the feeders, Matt sat atop the wagon loaded with hay. He bore the height of his parents and stood eye to eye with Jake.

"Glad to see you made it." Jake swung a leg over his saddle and hit the ground.

"Sure I did. What's been keeping you? I've been waiting hours."

Ben rode up and dismounted. "Let's have our grub first, then we'll get the hay set out for the cattle."

Jake secured his reins to a nearby bush. "You won't get any argument out of me over that."

Matt jumped down from the hay load. "I'm hungry enough to eat a bear. What did Ma send?"

Jake chuckled and bent to get a fire started. That boy could eat more than any sixteen-year-old he'd ever known, except maybe himself at that age.

Ben removed the saddlebags from his mount. "You'll see soon enough." He headed toward the open space sheltered by an outcropping of rock. The other men dismounted and joined him. Ben unbuckled the straps and withdrew a cloth-covered bundle, then spread it out on the smooth surface of the largest rock.

Biscuits lavish with butter and filled with Mellie's homemade preserves tempted the eyes. Jake kindled the fire and stoked it to a nice flame. He poured the beans into a black iron pot while Ben set the coffeepot over the fire.

Soon Jake's tin plate held the biscuits and hot beans, and his cup sloshed with fresh-brewed coffee. After he filled his belly, he moved next to Ben while Matt and the others laughed and talked across the way.

"May I have a few words with you, sir?" he asked, settling in next to Ben.

Ben tilted his head. "Of course, son. Not thinking of leaving, are you?"

Jake shook his head. "Oh no, nothing like that. It's not about leaving. I...I was reading that book you gave me, and I have some questions."

Ben's eyes lit up. "You mean the Bible? Of course; ask away."

"Well, I don't quite understand how Jesus could love me and all my sins. I thought God hated sin."

Ben stroked his chin. "That's the miracle of God's love. He hates sin, but He loves the sinner. The Book of Romans tells us that everyone has sinned and has fallen short of God's glory, but John three sixteen tells us God loved the world so much He sent His Son to die for us."

"Now, that's the part I read and don't understand for sure. Why would Jesus die for anyone, especially me?"

Ben's hand rested on Jake's shoulder. "Because of His great love for you, me, and everyone on this earth. When you give your heart and life to Him, all past sins are washed away."

"It's that easy?"

"Yes. Confess your sins, and ask Him to forgive them. Then He can begin a new work in you."

Jake rubbed his chin. "I gotta think some more on this. Do you mind?"

"No. You keep reading the Bible, and if you have any more questions, come to me and we'll talk about them. You're also welcome to join us at church any Sunday."

They sat in silence a few more minutes. Jake let his boss's words settle a little more in his head. If only he could truly believe God would forgive his sins.

Ben stood and pulled on his gloves. "Time to get back to work."

Jake shook hands with his boss. "Thank you, and I appreciate your being patient with me." He waved at Matt, who climbed up on the wagon again to toss down hay for the feeders.

For the next hour Jake helped fill winter feeders. He wanted to believe what Ben had said, but the words only confused him further. He needed help in understanding what it was that God expected from a man.

⚜

Lucinda entered the kitchen. "I've finished unpacking. Shall I go help Becky with the chores? Two of us can make light work. That is unless you prefer I stay here and help you."

Mellie waved her hands. "I have everything set out for baking, and we'll do that soon as the house is set right." She peered at Lucinda a moment. "Have you ever done any cooking at all?"

Lucinda gulped. "No, I haven't."

"Then it's time you learned. We'll set aside some time after lunch for a cooking lesson."

"I'd like that; thank you." Lucinda hugged her aunt and left to find her cousin.

Becky sat cross-legged on her bed. "I see you have all your things put away. I'll show you where we store the trunks and such."

"I came to help you with whatever needs to be done, so putting away my bags will be a good place to start, but some things will have to wait for Matt because they're too heavy for us."

Becky leaned forward with her elbows resting on her knees. "I'm sorry if I embarrassed you earlier. I just think Jake is the most handsome cowboy I've ever seen." She sighed. "Wish I was four years older."

Lucinda laughed. She had to agree with Becky's assessment of Jake. "Oh, Becky, you'll have plenty of time to meet young men before you're ready to settle down."

"That's what Ma says." She hopped off the bed and led Lucinda to a door that opened to reveal a large storage area. "This is where we store things. We used to put stuff in the barn, but Ma decided the house would be a better place, so Pa added this room. He says it can be an extra bedroom if we ever need it one day."

They worked quickly, hauling the trunks and boxes into the

storage area. "And I'm glad you're home from school today to help me," Lucinda said.

Becky giggled. "We had so much ice last night, we probably wouldn't have gone anyway, but Ma had decided Matt and I could stay home today to help you feel welcome. Besides, Matt loves helping Pa with the cattle. He's going to be a rancher too someday, or so he says now."

"That's a fine ambition. What about you? Any dreams of what you want to do with your life?"

"Oh, I suppose I'll get married and have a family like Ma, but what I'd really like to do is ride the range with Pa. I'm as good on a horse as Matt is."

Lucinda pushed the last trunk into place. "I imagine you are. But the range isn't really the place for a girl."

Becky turned and headed back to the bedroom. "And why not? I think we should be able to do just about anything we want, including roping calves and branding them."

"That sounds dangerous to me." Becky certainly lived a different lifestyle than Lucinda had ever known.

She followed Becky into their room. "What else is there to do now?"

Becky grinned and scampered through the door. "You'll see."

Becky retrieved some cloth from the rag bag, and they began the task of dusting furniture.

"Seems there's a good amount of dust even in winter," Lucinda commented.

Becky laughed. "Just wait until spring and summer. The winds bring in more dirt than you can ever imagine. Gets into everything. Sometimes even the food."

"In the food? Surely not. The list of things to know about Oklahoma never ends. At this rate, I may never adapt to this way of life."

Becky only laughed again. "Oh, I think you will, but it will be fun to watch."

The aroma of vegetables and onions wafted from the kitchen. Becky tossed aside her dusting rag and beckoned Lucinda to follow her.

Aunt Mellie placed steaming bowls of vegetable soup on the table. "We'll eat and then start preparations for supper."

Lucinda eyed the large kettle. Where had the soup come from? Cook said soup took hours to make, but Aunt Mellie had been doing other things. "How did you find time to do this?"

"Ma makes soup in large batches and puts it up in glass jars so we'll have plenty when winter comes."

"Oh, doesn't it usually take a long time?"

Aunt Mellie sat with the girls. "Yes, when we're making it. We use all fresh vegetables then, but like this it only needs to have a few cooked potatoes tossed in and then heated up." She bowed her head and blessed the food.

After Lucinda swallowed the first bite, she knew this was one thing she wanted to learn to make, even if canning soup did sound like a lot of work.

While they ate their lunch, Aunt Mellie gave her an idea of what to expect later. "This is the last of the corn bread, so we'll make a fresh batch for supper. Becky can take care of the vegetables today." She smiled at Becky. "Remember, tomorrow is back to school for you."

Her cousin grimaced. "I hope a blizzard comes."

Lucinda sighed. "You know what? I really miss going to school. When I finished in June, we had hopes of my going on to college, but then with the accident and all, Mr. Sutton thought it better to wait." Even now she questioned the wisdom of that decision but trusted her lawyer. If their suspicions about

Uncle Rudolph were true, then Oklahoma offered safety not found in Boston.

Becky stared at her as though Lucinda had taken leave of her senses. Obviously she didn't like school as much as Lucinda did.

Aunt Mellie wrapped her arm around Lucinda's shoulder. "That's OK, dear. If you want to go later, you'll have the time and money to do so. Right now, let's get busy showing you how to make pound cake."

Half an hour later, Lucinda found herself covered with flour. Two broken eggs lay on the floor. She stooped to mop them up but found it almost impossible to clean up the slippery mess. "I'm so sorry. I don't know what happened. First I had them in my hand, and then they were gone."

Aunt Mellie bent down to wipe up the remains of the yolk on the floor. "It's all right. We brought in plenty this morning, so we won't run out. Let's try again."

Lucinda sighed. "I'm sorry to be so clumsy."

"You'll do fine. My first efforts were something we laugh about now." Aunt Mellie handed her a fresh bowl.

Under Aunt Mellie's supervision, Lucinda measured and stirred the appropriate ingredients for the pound cake.

As she stirred, her aunt cleared her throat. Lucinda looked up, surprised to see the seriousness on her aunt's face. "What is it?" she asked. "Am I doing something wrong?"

Her aunt lay aside her mixing spoon. Her cheeks turned red. "No, this isn't about the bread. I have something else to say." She paused, frowned, then plunged ahead. "Lucinda, as your aunt and guardian until you are of age, I have only your best interests in mind. I've noticed the attraction between you and Jake, and I know Becky teased you about it. But we know so little about him. And from the little we do know, he is not a believer. He hasn't attended church since he arrived."

Lucinda's heart dropped, and her fingers trembled. Not a Christian? She swallowed hard. "Oh, Aunt Mellie, then I ought not be thinking about him."

"That's right." Aunt Mellie seemed relieved at Lucinda's words, and her tone softened. "Ben is speaking to him about spiritual matters and gave Jake a Bible recently. We're praying the young man will read and ask questions and be led to the Lord."

"I will pray for him too." If only she could get her heart to behave.

Aunt Mellie hugged her. "We all must set the example for him and show Jake how God cares about him. We don't know much about his life before coming here, but like I told you, his parents died before he was of age, so he does understand your loss. What Jake must see is your joy in the Lord and how the Lord has seen you through these days of grieving."

Lucinda nodded, but her heart raced with the idea of being a witness to Jake. Until he became a believer, she could only pray for his soul and for her uncle in his talks with Jake. How she wished she could sit down with him and discuss their circumstances and how much God loved her and had provided her aunt and uncle to care for her.

Aunt Mellie finished mixing the cake and placed it in the oven. "We're going to need at least two pans of corn bread." She reached into a cupboard and removed two darkened iron skillets.

"Now these are the best for corn bread. They've been seasoned and will give us a nice crisp, brown crust. But they need to be heated first." She placed them in the oven with a bit of lard in each one. They sat on the level just below the cake.

Lucinda stirred the dry ingredients together. Her mind wandered again to all the work that went into preparing a meal. She glanced down at the cornmeal in the bowl. What else was she supposed to put in? Baking soda and salt. Had she added the salt? Better put some in just in case. She added another pinch, then poured the fresh buttermilk from the pitcher on the counter. Finally it was ready for the oven.

Soon the kitchen filled with the aroma of the baking cake and corn bread and simmering vegetables on the stove. Just before the men arrived, Lucinda removed the corn bread from the oven and frowned. Her pan didn't look quite as golden as Aunt Mellie's, but she placed it on the counter to cool.

The back door opened, and the men stamped in, bringing the cold air with them. Lucinda hastened to finish setting supper on the table, making sure not to look toward Jake. Still, she could feel his presence. She prayed for guidance and wiped her hands across her apron.

After Uncle Ben offered thanks, the food made its rounds. Lucinda bit her lip and waited for them to taste the corn bread.

Shocked expressions appeared on both Matt and Uncle Ben's faces. Matt sputtered and reached for his glass of milk. "What in the world happened to the corn bread, Ma?"

Lucinda tasted a bite herself and suddenly wanted to spit it out. It tasted like salt. Tears welled in her eyes. She'd ruined it. Uncle Ben and Matt wore pained expressions and swallowed gulps of coffee.

She shook her head. "I'm so sorry. I don't know what happened."

Aunt Mellie grasped her arm. "It's all right, dear. It was your first attempt."

Uncle Ben chuckled. "Reminds me of those first meals you cooked, Mellie. Took you a while to get the hang of the kitchen."

Uncle Ben's words did little to take away the sting of failure, especially when everyone reached for Aunt Mellie's corn bread instead. Heat infused Lucinda's cheeks. What must they think of her? She hung her head, not daring to meet anyone's gaze. She couldn't do the simplest things. Not even make corn bread. She'd never learn to live on a ranch.

Chapter 6

*T*he next morning, a Friday, Lucinda's eyes popped open at the sound of the bedroom door closing. The other bed in the room lay empty. She wanted only to snuggle back under the covers, but she had to rise and help her aunt and cousin with the morning chores. Lucinda quickly dressed and headed for the kitchen.

Aunt Mellie stood at the stove, stoking the fire. "Good morning, my dear."

"I'm sorry I'm late again. Becky is so quiet I don't awaken when she gets up." Lucinda glanced around the kitchen. "Where is she? Has she already gone to the barn?"

"Yes. Grab your shawl, and you can help her gather the eggs for breakfast."

Lucinda wrapped the heavy wool shawl around her shoulders. Although the temperature was warmer, a cold wind still cut across the prairie and sent chills skittering through her body. She hurried across the hard-packed ground to the henhouse. So different from the grass-filled yards in Boston, but then they had no livestock back home.

A gust of air almost dragged the door from her hands, but she held on and closed it behind her. "I'm freezing. We didn't have wind blowing this hard in Boston."

Becky retrieved an egg. "It is chilly this morning." She handed Lucinda a basket. "Here, I'll show you how to gather the eggs."

She approached a brown hen's nest. "Slide your hand gently under the hen and wrap your fingers around the egg. She won't protest."

Fifteen nests sat on roosts, and most had hens sitting on them. She slipped her hand into the nearest one and felt the firm oval. As she pulled it out, the hen moved and squawked. Lucinda jumped, and the egg splattered on the floor. "Oh dear, she startled me. I'm sorry." She bent down to try to pick up the pieces of shell.

Becky laughed. "I'll clean that up. And don't worry about it. I dropped plenty when I first started."

Lucinda wrinkled her nose as the slimy mass dripped to the floor from her hand. Two eggs yesterday while mixing cake and one today. Would she ever get over being so clumsy?

Becky handed her a rag. "Here, wipe your hands, and then you can go on back to the house where it's warm. Take these to Ma, and I'll clean this up. I reckon she could use help with the breakfast."

Lucinda nodded and wiped her hands. Her first outside chore and she'd made another mess. She grabbed the basket and stepped outside. The cold penetrated her bones, and her teeth chattered as she scurried back to the house. Would she ever think of this place as home? How she missed being able to stay inside on mornings like this. She burst through the back door into the warmth of the kitchen.

Aunt Mellie shoved a pan of biscuits into the oven and wiped her brow. She smiled at Lucy. "Come over here by the stove. I see you shaking from here."

"Oh, I wasn't prepared for such cold. The wind doesn't bite like this in Boston." She set the basket on the countertop, then stretched her hands toward the warmth of the wood stove. "Can I help you, Aunt Mellie?"

"I'll get the bacon started, and you set the table again. You do a fine job of that." She hefted a large black iron skillet onto the top of the stove and began arranging strips of bacon.

Lucinda sighed and reached for the dishes. At least she could do one thing right. In a few minutes the scent of frying bacon blended in with the rich aroma of coffee. Lucinda's stomach responded with a rumbling. Something about being out here caused her appetite to soar, and Aunt Mellie's good cooking made it grow even more.

Becky backed through the door with her apron cradling some eggs. "Here's a few more, Ma. We'll have enough to bake another cake this afternoon."

Aunt Mellie grinned. "That's a good batch this morning. Come mix up some for me while I finish the bacon."

Lucinda watched as her cousin cracked the eggs and then dropped the contents into a bowl. She wondered if she'd ever be able to do that without dropping one or getting shells in the mixture.

The men arrived before she finished setting the table. They warmed their hands by the stove. Monk spoke to her and took his seat at the table as did Ben and Matt. Hank and Jake appeared to be in a discussion across the room. Hank glanced her way and grinned.

She jerked her head around. Why was she looking their way at all? Then she sneaked a glance at Jake. He moved toward her, and her hands trembled, but he walked around her without a word and sat at the opposite end of the table. Hank pulled out a chair, his gaze moving from Lucinda to Jake and back again. He shook his head and sat.

Lucinda swallowed the knot in her throat. Jake didn't want to be near her this morning. Had her cooking been that bad?

Mellie again pondered the way Jake and Lucinda tried to avoid each other. Their attraction may be obvious to her, but she prayed none of the others took notice, but then she remembered the teasing Becky had given Lucinda. Even Hank seemed to have backed away this morning, as if aware of their attraction to each other.

Her brother-in-law would be turning over in his grave if he thought a young cowboy was interested in his precious girl, especially a non-Christian boy. How she wished Amanda were here to advise Lucinda on how to handle the situation.

"Aunt Mellie, is there anything else I can do?" Lucinda asked.

Mellie shook her head to clear her thoughts. "Check on Becky for me. She should be ready to leave with Matt for school. Tell her he has the horses ready."

Lucinda hurried to find Becky, and Mellie busied herself packing food for the men's noonday meal. She finished with that task and set the bags where Ben could get them.

Ben opened the door. "Where's Becky? Matt's waiting."

"Lucinda's gone for her. They'll be here in a minute." She hugged him. "You men be careful out there. We want to see you back here for supper." She may repeat the same words every morning when he left, but she knew that Ben understood how much she meant them.

He wrapped his arm around her, then peered over her shoulder as Becky and Lucinda came in. "Better get a move on it, young lady. Your brother is waiting for you."

"I'm sorry. I didn't mean to be slow." Becky stretched up to kiss his cheek. "Good-bye, Pa. I love you." She grinned and raced out the door to meet her brother.

Ben hefted the saddlebags over his shoulder and kissed

Mellie's cheek. "This ought to take care of us." He glanced at Lucinda. "And don't give up on your cooking skills, young lady. You'll learn to be a good cook like your aunt."

Mellie shooed him out the door, then beckoned to Lucinda. "Let's sit a spell and talk. We can do the baking and other chores later."

After they settled by the fireplace, Mellie picked up her knitting. "It's always so quiet after the men leave and the children are in school. Having you here will be a joy for me. Your hands will make lighter work for us too."

Lucinda laughed. "Oh my, I don't know how much help I'll be. I've already dropped three eggs and ruined a pan of corn bread."

"You didn't learn to play the piano in one or two days, so give yourself time to practice cooking. You'll be good at it before you know it." Her needles clicked in the quiet room. "I'm sorry we weren't able to have your piano shipped before you came, but Mr. Sutton promised he'd get it here in the spring. It'll be nice to hear you play once again."

"Thank you. I do miss my music." Lucinda clasped her hands.

Mellie had so much she wanted to say to her niece but couldn't decide where to begin.

Lucinda leaned forward. "How did you meet Uncle Ben?"

Mellie smiled at the rush of memories that filled her mind. "His family and ours were good friends. We knew each other as children, but he didn't want to go into his father's business after he finished school, so he up and headed west. His father said Ben was on his own and didn't give him much money. When he came back, we'd both grown. He was so handsome in his boots and western clothes. I was smitten right away."

"What was it like when you first came west with Uncle Ben?"

The knitting needles slowed. "Hard at first, but I loved Ben so much, I didn't really care. When we stopped in Kansas, we lived in a two-room soddy built out of mud and straw and whatever else. We arrived in early summer, so by the time winter came, we had a warm place to live."

How different life had been in those days. They had only a few steer and some land for grazing and farming. "After a few years, Ben decided he liked raising cattle rather than crops, so he used some of the money my parents gave us to stock a herd. That's how we got into ranching."

"Why did you leave Kansas and come to Oklahoma?"

Mellie laughed. "That was the love of adventure in your uncle. When the land down here opened up to settlers a few years back, he came on down to stake our claim. After he had a shelter in place for me and the children, we came too."

Mellie remembered those hard first days. "You never know what those prairie winds from Kansas will bring down this way. I expect we'll see a tornado come next spring, but my prayers are always that we have enough rain so the fires don't start."

"I don't like the sound of either one of those." Lucinda shivered and crossed her arms.

"We've always made it through with God's help." Mellie stuck her needles into the ball of yarn. Time had passed, and the morning was almost gone. "It's time to start our chores. We'll have to hurry to get everything finished by suppertime, but I've enjoyed this time with you."

Yes, the time had been pleasant, but Mellie still hadn't approached the subject most worrisome to her. Lucinda set out to tidy up the room she and Becky shared, and Mellie set about her duties in the kitchen. More discussion concerning Jake would have to wait for another time.

Lucinda performed her tasks with many questions floating in her mind. A powerful love flowed from her aunt and uncle. They had endured many hardships together. Would she ever find such love? She'd seen it in her parents too. Mama and Papa were so different from Aunt Mellie and Uncle Ben, but the love was there for all to see.

With her last task finished, Lucinda dreaded the next job awaiting her because Aunt Mellie would have her making corn bread again. She exhaled a long breath. Having food on the table meant cooking, so she'd just have to learn. She didn't intend to sit around and let Aunt Mellie do it all.

In the kitchen, Aunt Mellie set two bowls on the table. "We'll have a little lunch and then set about baking for the day."

Lucinda savored the warm soup and chunks of sourdough bread. She peered at her aunt. Something seemed to bother Aunt Mellie. "Is there a problem? Do I need to do some other chores?"

"No, no, my dear. You've done a fine job." Aunt Mellie furrowed her brow and leaned forward. "I'm concerned about something." She pressed her hands together. "How I wish your mother were here with us."

Lucinda stared back at her aunt. Did her aunt think her not suited for this life? Was she to be sent back to Boston so soon?

"As your guardians, we a have a great responsibility for your care, and we don't want to see you making wrong choices before you have the experience to understand what is right or wrong in a relationship."

Lucinda gulped. "I'm sorry, Aunt Mellie." She'd tried so hard to conceal her feelings this morning when Jake ignored her, but apparently she had failed.

"As long as you remember our discussion from the other day, things will be just fine."

Aunt Mellie's words hit deep. Inexperience brought on more problems than Lucinda ever thought possible. For a moment, going back home seemed a good idea, until she remembered the loneliness and the threat of Uncle Rudolph.

⋙

Ben sat astride his horse and checked feeding troughs. He'd built a number of wooden bins last fall, and they had worked to keep the cattle well fed during the winter months. Of course, last year hadn't been as severe, and he prayed the same for this one.

With more people coming into the territory to settle, the grazing lands became less. He didn't mind as long as he kept his original spread. He gazed across the land. Fences lined up in the distance where settlers had come in and marked off their plots. Water didn't present a problem, as he'd been sure to include an ample source in his deed.

Jake rode up beside to him. "Looks like they'll have enough for a while. The herd doesn't seem as large as last year."

"It isn't. Didn't breed as many this spring. I figure that as we lose grazing land, we need to trim the herd to fit what we have. I can only pray that our neighbors do the same."

Jake shoved his hat back on his head. "I see some of the new settlers are putting up fences."

"Yes, they are. I imagine we'll need to do the same. The days of open-range grazing are numbered. But that's progress, and if the territory is ever to become a state, she'll need plenty of people, ranches, farms, and stores." Many of the ranchers resented the farmers and their fences, but he believed people had to learn to live together. At least no range wars had happened here.

"I hoped to have a spread of my own someday, but that's just a dream now. Take too long to save up the money for it."

Ben tilted his head. "Son, don't ever give up on your dreams. With the Lord's help, they can come true. Look what He's done for us." If only he could persuade Jake to trust God with his future.

Jake shook his head. "I'm not sure the Lord wants a sinner like me. Things I've done will take a powerful heap of forgiveness."

Ben leaned forward. Still the same doubts and fears. He had no idea what could be so terrible that the young man couldn't accept forgiveness. "Jake, the Lord has more love and forgiveness in His heart than any man deserves, but He gives it freely."

Just then Monk and Hank rode up. Ben wanted to continue the conversation, but such talk would serve only to embarrass the young cowboy. He'd save his words for another time.

Monk tipped the brim of his hat. "This section is done. My stomach tells me it's time for eatin'."

Ben laughed. "Thinking about those biscuits, are you?" He swung down off his mount. "This is as good a place as any to see what else Mellie packed for us." One thing he could count on each day was that Mellie made sure they had a good meal at noontime.

He found the matches Mellie always included for the fire and arranged the kindling he'd collected. In a few minutes the flames shot skyward. Ben set the pots for the beans and coffee over the heat.

Ben wanted to talk with Jake, but the boy sat off to the side and gazed out at the cattle moving about. Jake probably was dreaming of owning land. Maybe someday Ben could help that dream along. He'd leave him alone for now.

After eating, Ben repacked the saddlebags and stamped out the fire. Only a few hours of daylight left to check other parts of the land. He much preferred the summer days when sunlight lasted longer and more could be done both here and back at the barn. He mounted his stallion and beckoned the boys to follow him. He worked alongside his men until the sun fell low in the sky and they headed home.

When they arrived back at the ranch house at dusk, Ben spotted the smoke from the chimney. Mellie had a good fire going and supper on the stove. Jake headed to the stables with Monk and Hank. Ben watched him go, thoughts churning in his mind. *There's good in that boy. I feel it. I pray he will listen to what I've told him. I don't know what he's done, but he sure needs the Lord.*

That young man reminded him of himself in the early days of courting Mellie. The prodigal son, a poor cowboy from the West, he had no idea Mellie's father would even consider allowing him to court his daughter, but Mr. Carlyle had let his daughter have her way. He'd thought that Ben would take his father's advice and stay on in Boston. The memory caused him to chuckle. He and Mellie had surprised them all.

Ben shook his head. Until Jake committed his life to the Lord, he couldn't afford to be as accommodating as Mr. Carlyle. He meant to keep a sharp eye on the two of them and prevent anything serious from developing.

Chapter 7

*F*inally a Saturday warm enough for riding arrived, and Lucinda prepared for her first western-style riding lesson. Aunt Mellie had loaned her a riding skirt. The skirt was actually sewn so that it was split in the middle and formed two sides, much like men's trousers. The same style had been used at home for ladies to ride bicycles. She tucked in her shirtwaist, thankful for a garment that would make riding astride the horse much more comfortable.

Lucinda entered the corral area. Becky adjusted the bridle on her horse. She wore the same trousers and plaid shirt as her brother and father. Lucinda gasped. "My gracious, Becky, you look like one of the men."

She laughed and hooked her thumbs through the belt loops. "Most comfortable way to ride a horse. These belonged to Matt before he grew so much."

"Here, you might want to tie this around your neck and feel more like a cowgirl." Matt handed her a bright red neckerchief like the one he and Becky both wore.

Becky tugged at hers. "I wear mine for fun, but you'll be glad you have it if a dust storm stirs up. The men cover their noses with it when the cattle raise too much dust on a trail ride too."

Lucinda examined the kerchief. She'd noticed the same type of scarf worn by Uncle Ben and his men—now she knew why.

She tied the ends behind her neck. "Well, I guess I'm ready when you all are."

At that moment Jake strolled from the barn leading a dark filly with white markings on her legs. "Oh my, what a beautiful horse." She walked over to slide her hand down its neck. "Is she for me?"

Jake grinned. "Yep. Her name is Misty, and she's well broke."

Uncle Ben checked the cinch strap. "She'll make a fine ride for you, Lucinda. Misty will be your horse as long as you're with us."

"Oh, thank you. I love her already." She hugged her uncle.

"I'm sending Jake with you because he broke Misty and knows her well. He'll help you get accustomed to her ways. Matt and Becky will be along, so you'll be fine."

Lucinda adjusted her jacket. "All right. Now show me how to mount her."

"Just like this." Becky grabbed the saddle horn, slid one foot into the stirrup, and hoisted her leg over Daisy, her black mare. "See? Nothing to it."

Her cousin made it look easy, but when Lucinda tried to mount, she had difficulty getting all the way up. "I had a step to help me back home."

"Here, let me help then." Uncle Ben gave her a little boost, and she found herself sitting astride the horse.

"This is quite different, but I do think it is more secure than the English style." Lucinda loved the feel of the horse beneath her and could detect the strength of the horse as she sat astride. The Western way of riding would be far superior to the one she'd learned at Austin's Riding Academy.

Jake mounted his horse along with Matt. When all were ready, Lucinda followed Jake and her cousins out of the corral and across the yard.

Uncle Ben called after them, "Be careful. Remember it's Lucinda's first day on the range."

Becky and Matt laughed and waved back at their pa. The duo trotted on ahead. Jake stayed back and rode alongside Lucinda. She studied the scenery around her and breathed in the crisp fall air. The sun warmed her shoulders and filled her with a contentment she hadn't felt for many months.

Glancing over, she caught Jake's eye. "You ride well," he complimented her. "None of the bouncing usually seen with riders unfamiliar with this type of saddle."

A flush of heat filled her cheeks. "Thank you. We were taught to follow the rhythm of the horse's movements. The first time I ever rode as a young girl, I was sore as could be for the first few weeks. One thing that is different, I feel the strength of the horse in both of my legs, whereas sidesaddle was..." Her voice trailed off, and her cheeks burned hotter. This was not a conversation to have with a man.

Jake merely nodded. "I think you'll be a fine rider, and that's just what Becky needs to keep up with her."

Lucinda didn't respond. Yes, it would be fun riding with Becky around the ranch and maybe even into town.

Jake rode with such relaxed posture as he sat in his saddle. How could she approach him with questions without seeming to be nosy? At the moment her tongue felt thick as a slab of Aunt Mellie's bacon.

⚜

Jake rode at a slower pace than he normally would, but he didn't want to get ahead of Lucinda or let her ride at more than a walking pace until she had more experience in the saddle.

At least she wasn't a chatterbox like Becky. Even from this distance he could see the young girl's mouth working. He grinned at the bland expression on Matt's face, noticing how tolerant he was of his younger sister.

The sight of them took Jake back to the painful memory of his own sister. She'd been the core of his existence after his parents' death. He'd done everything he could to protect her and keep her safe, but he'd failed at even that.

The hairs on the back of his neck prickled. He sensed eyes other than those of his riding companions watching. He'd developed the knack for listening and knowing when someone followed. He looked about and found nothing amiss. No rider, no stranger rose on the horizon, and no one appeared behind. He hoped it wasn't a mountain cat. Sometimes they strayed down from the hills to prey on cattle. They sure didn't need one today.

"Jake, tell me about your family." Lucinda's voice broke into his worry.

He hadn't shared much of that with the Haynes family. "We had a ranch much like your uncle's when I was growing up. Ma died when I was fifteen of something the doctor called a cancer."

"Oh, how terrible. I'm so sorry."

Lucinda's sincerity and concern opened a floodgate of emotion, and the story spilled from his lips. "Pa couldn't handle life without her, and he took to drinking. That left me to look after my little sister, Caroline. Pa started home drunk one night and got thrown off his horse and was killed."

Lucinda shook her head and closed her eyes. Jake tilted his head to one side. "You know, we're alike in that we were orphaned at a young age and went to live with an aunt and uncle."

"Aunt Mellie mentioned something about that. Is your sister with them now?"

Another innocent question, but this one brought back a picture he'd long put away in the recesses of his mind. It all came back in a rush of color, pain, and sadness. "No, she isn't. Carrie is dead."

"Oh no! How did it happen?" She lowered her head. "I'm sorry, I don't mean to be nosy. You don't have to tell me if you don't want to talk about it."

Talking about it may be just what he needed at the moment. He'd never told another soul, but an overwhelming desire to tell her filled him.

"We were coming back from a visit to town on one of my trips home. We were in West Texas, where it's more like a desert. A rattlesnake spooked the horses pulling the wagon with my aunt, uncle, and Carrie. They took off before I could even think. By the time I galloped after them, the wagon careened out of control. Carrie flew out and landed on a rock. I stopped to check on her, thinking my uncle would control the horses."

The image of Carrie lying so still with blood flowing from the back of her head sickened him even now. She'd been not much older than Becky, too young to have her life taken. He'd known she was dead even before he felt for a pulse and tried to revive her.

"She died right in my arms, and I couldn't do a thing to stop it. Then I heard screams and a crash and looked up to see the wagon overturn with my aunt and uncle. My uncle died instantly, but Aunt Josey lived until the next day. She had too much inside bleeding before I could get her to the doctor. But I don't think she really wanted to live without her husband."

"That's a tragic story. I don't see how you've made it these past few years."

He didn't dare tell her the rest. Ben Haynes would never allow him to stay on at the ranch if he knew. "It's been hard, but your aunt and uncle have taken me in like one of their own."

"I was curious as to how you came to be here. And Monk and Hank too."

Jake said nothing. He knew little about the two men with whom he shared a bunkhouse. He furrowed his brow as the feeling of being watched fell over him again. He scanned the horizon but saw nothing. Whatever or whoever it was kept well out of sight.

"Your uncle took me in as a wrangler. He needed help with the drive, and I hired on and decided to stay on when the others left. They have been good to me." But he was repaying them with secrets from his past.

"What was it like in Boston?" If he kept her talking, then she wouldn't notice his attention to their surroundings.

She laughed, and it filled the air with delight. He'd have to think of other ways to get her to laugh.

"Well, it's certainly nothing like Barton Creek. I went to school, played the piano, did some sewing, and that's about it. Everything is much faster paced, and we have so many of the more modern conveniences."

He'd heard about some of those new inventions. Some could really make a man's life easier.

Again he sensed danger. He didn't want to alarm the others but decided it might be best if they turned back. The moment he started to speak to Lucinda, he caught a gleam of mischief in her eyes.

"Catch me if you can, Jake Starnes." She bolted away with her horse at full gallop. Despite the way she leaned into her horse and rode well, she may have trouble. He had to stop her.

Jake hollered to Matt and Becky, but they were galloping with Lucinda. He raced to catch up to them. He had almost reached her when a loud crack resounded and something whizzed past his head. Misty reared up, and he could see Lucinda's hands slipping from the reins. Before he could catch her, she slid backward and landed with a thump on the ground.

His heart lurched in his chest, and his lungs squeezed so that he could barely breathe. Not again. Not to Lucinda. Jake scrambled from his horse and knelt beside her still form. At least she was breathing. He pulled off his glove and checked for a pulse. It was strong. Becky fell to her knees beside him, her eyes filled with alarm.

After checking for broken bones, Jake grabbed Becky's shoulders. "Ride back to the ranch and tell your ma and pa what happened." He glanced up at Matt. "Help me get her up on my horse."

Matt jumped to the ground, and Becky took off like the wind. The two men managed to get Lucy propped up against Jake's horse. He swung up into the saddle, then Matt helped lift her up to be cradled in his arms. They probably shouldn't have moved her, but Jake wanted her back home as soon as possible.

"Run on ahead and get the doc from town. I'll bring Misty back with us."

Matt nodded and mounted his horse, then took off in a race against time. Lucinda's filly, which had galloped away, now had circled back and nuzzled against Jake as though she were trying to tell him something.

"What happened, girl? Did you hear the shot? Is that what made you rear back like that?" He grabbed her reins and headed back to the ranch, keeping his horse at a slower pace to keep from jarring Lucinda any further. He worried about Lucinda because she hadn't opened her eyes yet, but he could find no visible wounds other than a lump on the back of her head.

Her thick, dark hair had come loose from its tie and spread across her shoulders. Dark lashes lay against pale cheeks. He remembered the painted ladies from the saloons, but none of them could compare to the natural beauty of the girl in his arms. If only he could hold her...no, his thoughts couldn't go there.

He peered toward the horizon and spotted Ben, followed closely by a wagon. Ben pulled up beside Jake.

"What happened?"

Jake shook his head. "I don't know, sir. One minute she was riding beside me and then the next she was flying across the field. Something spooked Misty and caused her to rear back. That's when Lucinda fell. I've sent Matt to get the doctor."

"Good thinking," Ben said.

Hank drove up with the wagon. "Mellie filled the back with quilts and a few pillows. She thought the girl might be more comfortable there."

Reluctantly, Jake let Lucinda slide down into Ben's arms. Ben carried her to the wagon and carefully placed her on the bed. Once she was settled, Jake rode beside Ben back to the ranch.

Mrs. Haynes waited by the front porch when they arrived. She hurried out to the wagon. "How is she?"

"Looks like she got a hard knock on the head," Ben replied. "Matt's gone for the doctor just in case."

Jake helped Ben lift her from the wagon, and Ben carried her into the house.

Mrs. Haynes followed close behind. "I have her bed all turned down and ready. Take her in there, and I'll see to her needs."

Jake grabbed Misty's reins, his heart thumping in his chest. She had to be all right. "I'll take care of the horses." He led them to the stables and brushed down Baron before taking care of Misty. He buried the image of Lucinda and the fall to concentrate on his horse.

As he brushed her coat, he patted her neck and said, "I'd still like to know why you spooked like you did." He ran his hand under her mane along the shoulder and felt something sticky.

When he drew back his hand, his fingers were smeared with a mixture of dried and fresh blood.

"Hank, come here and look at this." He moved Misty's hair out of the way and stared at the wound he'd found.

Hank leaned over Jake's shoulder. "That looks like a bullet grazed her."

Jake remembered the sound he heard just before something passed his head. "That's what I thought. I sensed someone followed us, but who would want to hurt any one of the Haynes family?"

"Don't know about that, but this is something for the sheriff in town to see about. Better tell Ben and let him come take a look."

Jake's hand trembled as he cleaned the area of blood and swabbed it with salve. "It's all right, Misty. This will make it stop hurting. I'll tell Ben soon as he comes out."

Hank shook his head and blew out his breath. "Sure hope it was just an accident." He turned on his heel and left the stables.

Jake shivered. What if a bounty hunter had come looking for him? The shot had whizzed past his head, so it could have been meant for him. That would be even worse than the law being on his tail. It could also mean danger for the Haynes family. He couldn't stay here and let anything happen to them. But where would he go? Ben and Mellie had become like family to him.

He shivered at the trouble he might be bringing to the serenity of the Haynes's ranch. But worse, his heart ached at the thought of leaving Lucinda behind.

Chapter 8

*A*fter Uncle Ben lowered her to the bed, Lucinda relaxed. The memory of Jake's arms holding her close still gave warmth to her whole being. Never had she felt such emotion as she had in his arms. Too embarrassed to let him see her feelings, she had pretended to be unconscious.

She heard the door close and opened her eyes to find Aunt Mellie hovering over her. "Oh, my dear child, you gave us such a fright." She removed Lucinda's boots, then patted her head with a damp towel.

"I'm sorry. It was such a stupid thing." Lucinda attempted to move, but winced at the pain in her head.

"Just lie still. Let me check you over. Matt should be back with the doctor any minute."

Lucinda shook her head. "I don't need a doctor. I'm fine, just a little sore."

"*Hmph.* We'll let Doc Carter decide about that."

Lucinda sat up and tried to stand, but dizziness forced her back.

Aunt Mellie moved Lucinda's legs back onto the bed and began loosening her belt and shirt. "We need to get you out of these clothes and into your nightdress. You're staying in bed the rest of the day."

Lucinda knew better than to argue with Aunt Mellie's matter-of-fact tone. May as well let her aunt have her way. Besides, a rest might be a good idea to soothe her aching muscles. But she did wish Doc Carter hadn't been summoned.

She closed her eyes, and again the warmth of Jake's arms embraced her. Her heart ached with the story he'd told about his family. He had lost even more than she had.

A commotion at the door roused her. Doc Carter strode across the room.

"Well, young lady, I hear you had a nasty spill. Let's see if there's any damage." Although his face looked stern and foreboding, his blue gray eyes twinkled and put Lucinda at ease.

Aunt Mellie remained by the bed as the doctor conducted his examination. When the doctor sat back and grinned, her worried frown turned to a smile.

"Looks like nothing more than a few bruises and a bump on the head. You should be fine in a day or so, but a little time in bed will help. Get plenty of rest this afternoon, and you should be able to attend church in the morning."

"Are you sure? She was unconscious all the way home."

"Really? That bump doesn't look that serious."

Lucinda's cheeks burned. "I...um...wasn't unconscious all that time."

Aunt Mellie's eyes opened wide, and the doctor chuckled. "That so?" He patted her hand. "Just stay in bed for now. I'll leave something for your aches, but I expect you'll be up and about later this evening."

As soon as he left, Aunt Mellie crossed her arms over her chest. "Now what is this about not being unconscious?"

Lucinda ducked her head. "I was just too embarrassed when I realized I was riding on Jake's horse with his arms around me."

Her aunt frowned and sat on the edge of the bed. "I see. But what about when they put you in the wagon?"

"I figured it would be best to stay quiet until we got home."

Aunt Mellie tilted her head. "Seeing as how you're not seriously hurt, do you want to tell me what happened out there?"

Lucinda closed her eyes to recapture the scene from earlier. "I'm not sure. We were riding along, and I was having such a nice time. I saw Becky and Matt ahead and wanted to join them, so I put my heels into Misty's flanks, and she took off. It felt wonderful, but then suddenly I realized how fast we were going and started to rein Misty to slow her down. About that time she reared up, and I fell backward." Heat flushed her cheeks again, and her eyes flew open. "I hit the ground with a good thump, and the next thing I knew, I was in Jake's arms."

"*Hmm.* Horses can be unpredictable, but you shouldn't have tried riding hard until you were more experienced with our uneven terrain."

"I know that now." The embarrassment vanished as she recalled what Jake had told her just before the accident. She grasped Aunt Mellie's hand.

"Jake and I had the most revealing conversation. Did you know he had a sister who was killed with his aunt and uncle in a wagon accident?"

Her aunt gasped. "No. How awful! We only know that his parents died when he was young. No wonder that boy looks so sad all the time. I'll have to tell Ben." She stood and straightened the covers over Lucinda. "You rest now, and I'll be back in a little while to check on you."

The door closed behind her aunt. Except for a few aches in her arms and legs, her body felt fine. Still, rest never hurt anyone, even if she would rather be up and around.

A tear formed in her eye and slid down her cheek. She had Aunt Mellie and Uncle Ben, but Jake had no one to call family. How terrible to have lost both parents and his sister along with an aunt and uncle. Her grief couldn't compare to his.

After leaving Doc Carter with Lucinda, Ben hurried to the barn. There he found Jake grooming Lucinda's horse.

Jake looked up, worry in his eyes. "How is Lucinda?"

"We'll know more when the doctor finishes his examination."

Jake beckoned him closer. "I wanted you to see this." He lifted Misty's mane and showed Ben the wound. "I think a bullet did it."

Ben frowned and ran his fingers over the spot. "But who would be shooting out on the range?"

"That's what I'm wondering. I heard what was probably a gunshot and something whizzed by my head when I took off after Lucinda. Must have been the bullet that grazed Misty and caused her to act like she did."

Ben's heart thumped. "*Hmm.* I don't like the looks of this. Did you see anyone around at all?" Someone was out on the range taking potshots. His heart filled with anger as well as fear.

"No, sir, but I did have the feeling someone or something watched us and maybe followed us. I thought maybe it was a mountain cat come down this way to hunt."

"Well, a mountain cat wouldn't have fired a gun." His thoughts spiraled like a whirlwind. After Mellie told him about the incidents in Boston before Lucinda left, the only explanation must involve Rudolph Bishop. The idea appalled him, but he had to be realistic. If Rudolph intended harm for his niece, then Lucinda wasn't safe, even here at the ranch.

"Jake, I don't want Lucinda riding alone or being anywhere without one of us. You tell Monk and Hank. I think this may have something to do with her uncle in Boston." Three more men keeping an eye on her couldn't hurt and would ease Mellie's mind.

"Her uncle?"

"Yes, he's angry because he didn't inherit more of his brother's money. If something happens to Lucinda before her eighteenth birthday, then he thinks he'll get it all."

Jake nodded. "I understand. We'll keep a close watch on her."

"Thanks." He turned his head. "I think I hear Doc Carter. I need to check with him about Lucinda." He turned toward the corral then stopped. "I'll tell Mrs. Haynes about this, but don't say a word to Lucinda, Becky, or Matt. No sense in worrying them any right now."

$$\sim\!\!\!\!\sim$$

Jake could understand not worrying the womenfolk. Maybe Ben's explanation was the correct one, and no bounty hunter had come up from Texas. Still, he couldn't be sure.

He completed Misty's care and headed for the bunkhouse. Ben and the doc stood talking by the doc's buggy. Must be good news since they both smiled as they talked. That was a relief.

Jake entered the bunkhouse and headed for the washbasin and pitcher in the corner. The cold water chilled his hands as he washed, but he welcomed the distraction from his thoughts.

Hank and Monk sauntered in. Monk tossed his hat toward the rack by the door, and it landed squarely on a peg and settled there. Jake grinned and dried his hands on a towel. Monk never missed.

The cowboy clapped Jake on the back. "Must have been some ride out there. What happened?"

Jake shook his head. "I don't really know. One minute we rode along talking, then suddenly Miss Bishop took off like lightning struck her." At least that part was true.

"Must not have been too terribly bad. I heard the doc telling

Ben Haynes that she'd be up and around by tomorrow." Hank removed his hat and hung it beside Monk's.

The news relieved him but did not dispel the guilt harbored in his heart. "Still, I feel responsible."

Hank sat on the edge of his bunk. "Did you tell Mr. Haynes about what you found on Misty?"

Monk swung around from the washbasin. "What are you talking about? Was Misty injured too?"

"The filly looks like a bullet may have grazed her and caused her to rear up. I heard a loud crack, then something flew by my head while I chased after them. I told Mr. Haynes, and he wants us to keep a close eye on Lucinda. This may have something to do with family back home—an uncle that might mean her harm."

Hank nodded and winked. "Now that will be easy to do, seeing as how she's something nice to watch."

Jake frowned and clenched his fists. "Just you watch what you say about Miss Bishop. Show her some respect, you hear?"

"Whoa, boy. I meant no harm," Hank said, holding up his hands. "Just an observation; that's all."

Jake turned away, not wanting Hank to see the jealousy that raged in his heart. Firmly, he pushed those feelings down. Right now all that mattered was Lucinda's safety. Jake planned to follow Ben's wishes and not let Lucinda out of his sight.

Mellie stepped onto the porch just in time to see her husband emerge from the barn. "Ben!" She gestured toward him.

He strode toward her. "Stay right there. I was on my way indoors."

She waited until he reached the porch. "I just heard Lucinda's version of the accident, and it wasn't Jake's fault."

Ben nodded and wrapped his arm around her waist. "I didn't think it was after what I saw in the barn."

Mellie stepped back and frowned. "Just what do you mean by that, Ben Haynes?"

"Matt's out with the horses, but where's Becky? I don't want them to hear what I have to tell you."

Mellie's heart jumped. "Now you're scaring me." She pushed through the door into the parlor. "Becky's in with Lucinda."

She slumped in her rocker by the fireplace with her hands folded in her lap. "Now tell me what's going on."

He lowered his voice and Mellie had to lean closer to hear every word. As he spoke, her heart beat wildly in her chest. A bullet? Who could have shot at her children and Lucinda? Then as Ben's words sank in, Rudolph came to mind. "Oh, Ben, do you really think it could be Rudolph Bishop?"

"Wouldn't surprise me, but we have no proof, so we'll just have to watch Lucinda more closely. I told Jake not to let her ride alone and to keep an eye on her even when she's around the ranch."

"That's good, and I'm sure he won't mind the task." Then she proceeded to tell him Lucinda's version of the accident. She leaned back in the rocker when she finished. "So you see, it really is no one's fault."

"Except possibly Rudolph Bishop."

They sat in uneasy silence for a moment. Memories of what Lucinda told her happened just before leaving Boston raced through her mind. Then she remembered the rest of what she wanted to tell Ben.

"Did you know Jake's aunt and uncle also died, as well as his younger sister? That's what Jake told her on their ride this morning."

Ben turned startled eyes toward her. "No. I had no idea. He

did tell me he'd gone to live with an aunt and uncle after his parents died, but he didn't mention a sister."

Tears welled in Mellie's eyes. "She was only a few years younger than he, and she died in his arms. His uncle died instantly, but his aunt didn't pass until a few days later."

Ben shook his head. "No wonder that boy's eyes are so sad."

For a moment they sat together quietly. Such pain and grief for two young people to bear. And now danger too. She breathed a prayer to God, knowing only He could handle such a burden.

Chapter 9

*L*ucinda pushed back the quilt on the bed and dangled her legs over the side. When she stood, no dizziness gripped her, and the pain in her side had disappeared. Bright sun peeked through the lacy curtains and promised a beautiful day for her first visit to the church in Barton Creek.

She dressed and hurried into the kitchen, eager to help her aunt with breakfast. When Lucinda appeared in the doorway, Aunt Mellie gasped. "Child, what are you doing up and about? You should stay in bed all day."

"Oh, Aunt Mellie, Doc Carter said I'd be fine. Look outside. The weather is simply too beautiful to stay indoors, and what better way to get well than to attend church."

Her aunt paused in her cooking to give Lucinda a long, hard assessment. Finally, she smiled. "Well, the color is back in your cheeks, and you look to be all right. Come, give me a hand, and we'll have breakfast ready in no time. I'll tell the others that you and I will be going to church after all."

She ran out to the barn. Lucinda heard her calling Uncle Ben and Matthew. Now that that had been settled, Lucinda set about laying the table.

Becky popped through the back door with the fresh eggs. "I'm so glad to see you up and ready to go. I really didn't want to miss church today."

"Oh, are the pastor's sermons that good?"

Becky's cheeks turned bright crimson. "I guess so, but we have a Sunday school group for our young people, and since I'm going to be thirteen soon, I get to go to it now instead of with the children."

"I see, and is there someone special you want to see?"

Becky grinned. "Well, Bobby Frankston is in the class. He's in my grade at school too. He's already thirteen."

"*Hmm.* That does sound interesting."

At that moment Aunt Mellie returned. She hung her shawl over the hook by the door. "What's so interesting?"

Lucinda exchanged a glance with Becky and recognized the plea in the young girl's eyes. "Oh, I was just commenting on how interesting it will be to meet other people in town. Becky tells me they have a Sunday school before the church services."

"Yes, we do. A place for all ages, from infants to old folks like me. We don't have a large number in any group, but it's a good way to get better acquainted and discuss Bible topics among ourselves. It's a rather new concept for us, but we enjoy it."

Lucinda nodded. "I'm looking forward to going. I've missed attending church."

Matthew tromped in, followed by the other men. Lucinda sneaked a glance at Jake.

Uncle Ben hugged her. "Sure is good to see you so chipper and ready for church this morning."

Jake nodded, his gaze sober. "I'm sorry I didn't catch up to you and grab Misty before you fell."

"It wasn't your fault, and I thank you for taking care of me. I must have given you a fright after what you told me about your sister."

"You did, but then Doc Carter told us you'd be fine." He averted his eyes and sat at the table.

Lucinda bit her lip. Perhaps she'd spoken out of turn in

revealing the bit about his sister. No one else made any comment about it, so she finished her task. Jake still wore his work jeans and a flannel shirt. Her heart fell. Did he not plan to attend with them? Perhaps he would change after eating, but then she remembered he probably didn't attend church anyway. She removed the biscuits from the pan and placed them on a plate.

In a few minutes, the whole group gathered around the table. As Uncle Ben offered thanks, Lucinda added her own silent prayer for Jake.

Still filled with embarrassment from yesterday, Lucinda avoided direct eye contact with Jake. She remembered the feel of his arms around her and how safe she felt. A shudder shook her heart. Her thoughts on the Lord's day should be on more spiritual matters.

After breakfast, Lucinda cleaned the dishes while her aunt and uncle dressed. Becky traipsed into the kitchen wearing a blue dress that set off her cornflower blue eyes.

She helped Lucinda put away the last of the dishes. "I love your shirtwaist. Is that a new style?"

"Yes. They call this sleeve the 'Gibson girl,' and it's what everyone wore back home."

"I saw something like it in a book at the store in town." She reached out to touch Lucinda's skirt. "But you're not wearing one of those skirts bunched up in the back."

"Oh, that's a bustle." Lucinda dried her hands. "I wore them back in Boston, but Mrs. Sutton and I both thought they might be cumbersome for ranch life."

"Well, I don't really like to wear dresses, but Ma says I can't go to church or school in my riding clothes." She furrowed her brow. "Maybe if I looked as nice as you do in a dress, I wouldn't mind it so much."

Lucinda laughed. "Becky, dear girl, you look wonderful

in whatever you wear, and I think one Bobby Frankston will notice you today."

The red rose in Becky's face, but a grin emerged too.

Aunt Mellie returned followed by Uncle Ben and Matt. Her uncle continued on out to the yard. "I'm going out to get the buggy. Jake should have it all ready for us."

Hope rose in Lucinda. Perhaps Jake meant to attend church with them after all. She grabbed her cloak from its peg and slipped it over her shoulders. Of course he wouldn't ride with them. He'd probably be on his own horse.

Disappointment filled her when she approached the surrey. Jake had disappeared. Uncle Ben assisted Becky and her into their seats. Matt mounted his horse, and a few minutes later the family began their ride.

No wonder her aunt and uncle were concerned about Jake's spiritual condition. She had known very few people in her life who didn't attend church. Sometimes she wished her parents' teachings hadn't been so ingrained in her. If they were here, even if they liked Jake, they would not let him call upon her as long as he wasn't a believer.

A bump in the road jostled her, and she pushed thoughts of the cowboy from her mind. The landscape appeared just as forlorn as it had on the day she arrived. Tall trees, with the last of their fall foliage clinging to bare limbs, dotted the landscape. The browns and dusty greens of the land did nothing to relieve the barrenness. Rolling hills graced the horizon in the distance, but here the land lay flat. The wagon followed tracks made from others driving the same trail in the hard-packed ground.

The sun shone down on them and warmed Lucinda's shoulders. The ice from a few days before had melted and disappeared. Another day in God's world to be spent listening to His promises in His house of worship. Her heart sang, and she voiced the words from a psalm she'd read this morning. "This is the day which the Lord hath made. I will rejoice and be glad in it."

Aunt Mellie smiled. "That is a marvelous thought for this morning, Lucinda. Surely the Lord has blessed us abundantly. It *is* a day to rejoice and be glad."

⁂

They drew up to the church with its tall white spire stretching toward heaven. Mellie smiled and waved at her friends. As soon as she alit from her seat, several ladies gathered round. Curiosity rather than friendliness probably motivated their greetings, which should not be surprising, considering how she had bragged and talked about Lucinda for so many weeks.

"Good morning, ladies," Mellie called.

Matt assisted Lucinda from the buggy. Mellie grasped her arm. "This is my niece, Lucinda Bishop, from Boston. She's come to live with us."

Mellie beamed with pride as her friends greeted and spoke with Lucinda. From the corner of her eye, she spotted Becky with two friends. Then two boys made their appearance and swaggered over to the girls. She shook her head. Becky wouldn't be her little one much longer. Mellie prayed Lucinda would be a good influence on the young girl.

Bea Anderson joined Mellie to walk up to the church building. "Your niece is quite the young lady. I spoke with Mary Winters, and we both think Lucinda would be a wonderful person to teach our children, especially our daughters."

"I think that's a lovely idea, but you don't know anything about Lucinda or her ability to work with children."

"Now, Mellie Haynes, you know as well as I am standing here that you've done nothing but brag about her for weeks and weeks. We know she comes from a good Christian background and is well mannered. She's just what our young girls need as an example of what it is to be a young lady. They surely don't have much opportunity to learn proper etiquette and behavior out here. Your Becky is quite fortunate to have Lucinda at the ranch."

Mellie had to admit Bea had been right in her assessment about the bragging and boasting, but Lucinda deserved the praise. Maybe the girl would be a good influence for more than just Becky. Of course the whole matter depended on whether Lucinda would be interested in such an endeavor.

"Why don't you speak with her after the services today? I'm sure if she's interested, Lucinda will do a wonderful job, Bea." Indeed, this may be just the thing to draw Lucinda into life here and help her to feel a real part of the community.

⚜

Jake stood in the barn and stared after the Hayneses as the surrey carried them away. Remorse filled him because once again he had disappointed his boss. Still, Jake didn't feel right going into church. Besides, he'd been lucky not to be recognized the last trip into town, but this time a visit might not fare so well. No, as long as he felt secure here, he'd avoid the town of Barton Creek.

He'd never get away from the guilt of his past. It bore down on him and weighed in his heart like a stone. Reading the Bible didn't seem to help. It only confused him more and emphasized his terrible sin.

The sky overhead shone bright with the sun and a few fluffy clouds. At times like these his heart swelled with something he couldn't quite identify. The death of his family had left a hole that nothing had been able to fill. Not even his attraction for Lucinda lightened the burden he carried.

Jake blew out his breath. It was time to finish his work and get on with ranch business. When he entered the stable, the images from yesterday came back in a stream of pictures. He wandered over to Misty and stroked her mane as he examined the wound.

The salve had done its work. The healing had a good start. He closed his eyes and leaned his head against Misty. He hoped Ben had been wrong about someone trying to hurt Lucinda. He'd rather be the victim of a bounty hunter any day than to have the pretty girl from Boston harmed.

Seeing her dressed for church this morning stirred a longing in him that he didn't quite understand. Girls had never been much of a part of his life. Even the saloon girls the past few years had not attracted him. But Lucinda made him think of his ma and home and all the things he remembered from childhood. An emotion he couldn't describe rose in his heart. It must be what his ma talked about when she had lectured him on girls and love.

Before Ma's death their family had been a happy one. Church had been a regular Sunday activity for them. Since then, he'd turned away from God. He'd never truly listened much to the preacher back then, and the God he knew was just someone who wanted to control lives. He didn't know about any God who loved people the way Ben described.

If this God did love everyone, why had all the people he loved in the world been taken away? Another reason he should stay away from Lucinda. The God he knew about was one of vengeance and would punish him for what he'd done. That punishment might fall on Lucinda or the Haynes family, and he couldn't bear the thought of that.

He strolled back to the bunkhouse just as Hank and Monk rode in from the range. He waved at them, then entered the warmth of the building and removed his coat. A long morning stretched before him, and he wondered what he'd do with it. In the weeks before, chores always seemed to take up the time, but with the colder weather, those had lessened.

Monk pushed through the door, followed by Hank. They hung their jackets beside Jake's and headed for the coffeepot sitting on the pot-bellied stove.

Jake didn't know either man really well, but he did enjoy their company. He filled a tin cup with coffee and joined them when they sat at the table. "Sure is quiet around here with the family gone."

Monk stroked his bristly chin. "Yep. It's like that every Sunday when the Haynes go to church."

Hank wrapped his hands around his cup. "The church in Barton Creek is a nice one. I helped them finish building it last year."

Jake tilted his head and raised an eyebrow. "So why don't you go to church with the family?"

"I'm not much for crowds or sermons," Hank said.

Monk sipped from his cup. "It's been a long time since I went to church. Like Hank here I prefer to be outdoors."

Monk pushed back from the table. "All this talk makes me hungry. Mrs. Haynes said she left some biscuits and jam for us if we wanted something later in the morning. I'm going up to the house to fetch them."

"Sounds good to me. I'll make more coffee." Hank retrieved the container of coffee from the cabinet by the stove.

When Monk left, Hank leaned on the table. "I saw the way Lucinda, I mean Miss Bishop, eyed you this morning. And the way you looked at her reminded me of Ben appraising a steer for its value."

Jake's fist hit the table. "Don't you go comparing Miss Bishop with any cattle. She's one of the nicest people I've met."

"Hey, I meant no disrespect, but you have to admit she's a fine bit of womanhood even if she is seventeen."

Hank's smirk caused anger to burn in Jake's throat, but he swallowed it. "That's just it; she's young and too good for the likes of us."

"If you say so, but I still seen that look in your eye." He shrugged and went to get the coffeepot.

Jake closed his eyes to calm his anger. Anger got him into trouble before, and he wasn't going to let it happen again.

Chapter 10

*L*ucinda fastened her hair with a few hairpins before going out to help Aunt Mellie with supper. The early days of November had flown by, filled with new challenges and opportunities. She had learned to love living on the ranch, and it had produced an inner strength she didn't know was within her. Being busy and occupied helped ease the pain of her parents' deaths. Without a doubt God had brought her here not only to learn to lean on Him, but also to discover new things about herself.

Today Aunt Mellie gave her the task of making the corn bread again. Her baking skills had improved to the point that the men no longer dreaded eating it. Lucinda enjoyed cooking and regretted waiting so long to learn.

Aunt Mellie rolled out dough for the berry pie she planned for dessert. She greeted Lucinda. "Would you check that berry filling there? See if it's sweet enough for your liking."

Becky bounced in carrying a basket of potatoes she'd fetched from the root cellar. She set them on the table. "All my after-school chores are done, and Matt wants to know when supper will be ready."

Aunt Mellie laughed. "That boy and his appetite. All he thinks about is food." She handed a pan to Lucinda. "Better make an extra pan of that corn bread for tonight."

Lucinda tasted the berries. "I think these are just right for the pie. Matt will be very happy." She plopped a spoonful of lard into a black iron skillet. Two pans of corn bread would disappear in a minute with that hungry cousin of hers eating it.

Becky hung her coat and scarf on a hook and grabbed an apron. "What can I do to help?"

Aunt Mellie handed Becky a knife. "You can start by peeling those potatoes you just brought in."

"Oh, I hate that job." But she piled potatoes on the counter and began her task. "Must have been nice to have servants to do things like this for you back in Boston."

Lucinda shrugged. "Maybe so, but I missed out on a lot. I enjoy being in the kitchen with you and Aunt Mellie. Food appeared on our table at mealtime, and I never really gave much thought to how it got there." Even when she had tried to sneak into the kitchen, Cook had shooed her out.

She measured ingredients for the corn bread. "Cook insisted that everyone stay away while she prepared meals. Mama joined her only on Saturdays, when they planned the menus for the next week. Then one of the servants and Mama went to market for the food."

Lucinda poured the batter into the hot, greased skillet. "Mama loved the marketing, and occasionally she allowed me to accompany her to Faneuil Hall and the Quincy Market." She could almost see the colorful array of produce and other items that enticed shoppers with heavenly aromas.

Becky put her potatoes on the stove to boil. "That sounds like fun. We only have Anderson's store here in Barton Creek. Ma gets all our supplies there."

Aunt Mellie crimped the edges of her pie crusts. "Yes, we do, and he carries as much as he can, but I remember going to the market in Boston with my mother, and it seemed there was no end to what was available. Quite different than what we have here."

A short time later the room filled with the aroma of the

baking pastry. Lucinda placed the pans of corn bread in the oven with them.

The men entered with a clamor of conversation and boots clomping on the wooden floor. Matt hung his hat on a hook. "*Hmm.* Smells good in here. I'm so hungry I could eat one of our steers whole."

Aunt Mellie laughed at her nearly grown son. "You say that every meal."

Lucinda removed the pans of corn bread from the stove and placed them on the counter. Jake grinned at her. Her heart jumped, and she dropped her towel. When she bent to pick it up, her hand met with Jake's. A spark of electricity that could have come from the cold shot up her arm, but it came from his touch.

As though he felt the same spark, Jake jerked his fingers away from hers and stepped back. "Excuse me, Miss Bishop." His gaze never left her face.

Lucinda blinked. "Thank you for wanting to help." She turned back to her task. What was happening to her heart?

Uncle Ben wrapped an arm around Aunt Mellie's waist and kissed her cheek. "I think I detect the aroma of berry pie too. No one makes pies and cobblers like you."

A tinge of pink colored Aunt Mellie's face. "I think you may be a mite prejudiced, my love."

Lucinda liked the banter between her aunt and uncle. Their love shone through each word like a beacon. The love she witnessed so often in the Haynes home gave her a new perspective on the emotion, one she didn't quite comprehend.

She mused about God's love and wondered at the power of one simple emotion. Aunt Mellie had been clear in her warnings about Jake's spiritual condition, but Lucinda could no more control her emotions now than she could hold back a river flood. However, she could trust God to take care of her and lead her in the right direction.

During supper, she avoided eye contact with Jake but couldn't help sneaking a peek when she placed the pie on the table. He was handsome in a different way than any boys or men she'd known. His hair touched his collar, his hands bore the calluses of hard work, and his blue eyes and square jaw intrigued her.

Jake reached for his fork. "Would you like to go riding again, Miss Bishop? I promise to take better care of you this time."

Heat rose in her cheeks again. Why did she feel constant embarrassment whenever he was around? However, she liked the idea of riding Misty again. They'd been busy, and the weather had not been cooperative since the accident. "Yes, I believe I would like that."

Becky clapped her hands. "Oh, good. When can we go?"

Uncle Ben pushed back his empty plate. "Maybe tomorrow afternoon. I'll be riding into town tomorrow morning for supplies."

Lucinda leaned forward. "May I go in with you? I'd like to see the town again now that I've been here awhile."

Aunt Mellie nodded. "That's a good idea. We can all go. I'm running short on a few things myself. It's also time to be looking for material to make Becky a new dress for her birthday party."

Becky shook her head. "I want to wear the one Lucinda brought me for my party."

"I thought we'd save that one for Christmas, but if you want it for your party, then we'll make another one for the holidays. Two new pretty dresses for Sundays and special occasions will be nice."

Becky cast a sideways glance at Lucinda and muttered under her breath. "Two new dresses is one too many for me."

Lucinda leaned over and whispered, "I think a certain young man at church would disagree."

Becky's face turned a bright shade of red, but she kept her head lowered. Lucinda suspected the girl didn't want to take any teasing from her brother, but he seemed more interested in dessert.

Teaching Becky the ways of being a young lady might prove to be easier if she wanted to attract the eyes of Bobby. But then, what did Lucinda really know about things like that? Her parents' close watch on her behavior had kept her away from much contact with young men. They had planned to introduce her to society in Boston on her eighteenth birthday. She sighed. The etiquette learned in Boston didn't begin to cover her experiences in Barton Creek.

No one here minded that the utensils didn't match or that they used crockery instead of fine china. So far no one had mentioned social occasions or visiting other families. A trip into town would help in seeing how others in Barton Creek lived.

Matt scooted his chair back from the table. "You ladies enjoy yourselves in town with Pa. I plan to stay here and help with stock. Nothing I need that I can't find right here."

Aunt Mellie laughed. "As long as I leave enough food around, but I do plan on getting a few things for you anyway. You've already outgrown everything I bought in the summer, and you need some warm undergarments for the winter ahead."

Lucinda hid her smile behind her hand when a red flush filled Matt's face. Her young cousin didn't enjoy being a topic of that conversation. She must rescue him. "Maybe we can find material to make another skirt for me. I think I'd like to learn to sew too." Matt shot her a look of gratitude.

"Sewing will be a fine thing for you. We can find all we need at the store." Aunt Mellie stood and stacked a few dishes, then she carried them to the sink. She pumped water into a large kettle.

Lucinda jumped up to help. The time after a meal when they cleaned the kitchen together usually gave her opportunity to talk with her aunt about many different matters, but that didn't seem to be the case tonight. Although Jake and the other two ranch hands left, Ben settled himself at the table to read. Matt and Becky joined him with their schoolbooks. With them so close by, Lucinda didn't raise the questions filling her mind. A full weekend lay ahead, and her time alone with her aunt might not come again until Monday. That would have to do for now.

⚜

On Saturday, Ben hitched the horses to the wagon for the ride into town. He used the excuse of going for supplies, which was true, but his real reason revolved around politics. The results of the recent election aroused his interest. The news should have reached Barton Creek by now. Just a few days since he'd cast his vote, and now he was anxious to know who'd won. Soon a new governor would be appointed by the man elected as president of the United States. They'd also have an election for someone from the Barton Creek area to represent Oklahoma Territory in Congress. Another important step to statehood lay in their representation.

Expansion pleased Ben, but some of the ranchers wanted the land for themselves and resented the farmers who came to plow the ground and grow crops instead of cattle. The economy of the area concerned Ben as much as his own progress. New people coming into the territory and into Barton Creek meant more businesses to open and more money for the ones in existence. He'd never understand why some people had to thwart growth.

Still, growth could also bring problems. Outlaws might find their town more enticing as more people deposited money in the bank. But the real cause for concern came from the farmers plowing up the ground and destroying the natural prairie grasses. Those grasses had survived many a drought and saved the land, but with the land barren, the farmers could find themselves

97

in big trouble if their crops failed and another drought set in. Already he saw the signs of the problems that resulted when prairie grass was turned under for crops. The dust storms had grown worse in the past two years.

Mellie approached with Becky and Lucinda. Becky's face twisted in a scowl. Ben chuckled because his daughter probably wanted to be on Daisy riding the range today and not going into town for new dress material.

His daughter climbed aboard the wagon without his help and plopped down on the side seat built into the bed. Ben shook his head. She'd be a handful for the young men who would be asking his permission to come courting in a few years. Perhaps Mellie was right. Becky did need the gentle ways of Lucinda as an influence. Then a thought struck him, and a laugh bubbled in his throat.

"And just what has you in such good spirits this morning, Mr. Haynes?" Mellie grasped his arm and tilted her head.

He spoke quietly into her ear so the girls wouldn't hear. "Just thinking about how our Becky has influenced her cousin more than we'd anticipated." He held her hand to help her up to the wagon seat while Lucinda joined Becky in the back.

He climbed aboard and clucked at the horses to go.

Mellie turned to glance at the girls. "What do you mean?"

The girls behind him talked and giggled like best friends. Still, he kept his voice low. "Well, Becky's had Lucinda out gathering eggs, riding astride, cooking, and cleaning. And it's not like Lucinda has been able to show Becky waltz steps or the latest fashions or how to receive callers."

Mellie frowned. "You're right, but have you noticed that Becky isn't quite as loud as she once was and that she doesn't just plop down on chairs anymore? Still, it's difficult to expect them to be proper young ladies when everything around them forces them to be so rough."

Ben chuckled. "You have too narrow an idea of what it means to be a lady, my dear. A heart given to the Lord is all that's needed, and thankfully, both our girls have that."

Another giggle erupted from the cousins, and Ben and Mellie shared a knowing look and a smile. Those two were good for each other. The laughter of young folks warmed his heart. Yes, this would be a good day.

⁂

Out on the range, Jake kept an eye on Matt. The boy had a knack for the work. As he grew taller, Matt filled out through the chest and arms. He did as good a job now as any of the other ranch hands. Come next time for taking cattle north, Jake figured Ben Haynes would let Matt go with them.

He envied the boy for his secure, loving life in a family. He wondered again what his own life would have been like if his parents had survived. One thing was for certain: he wouldn't be on the run from the law like he was now.

Matt rode up to Jake's side. "Everything looks good so far. No strays from the Morris herd or from Fowler's."

"Good. We'll be finished early and be back in time to help your pa unload the supplies he bought in town."

Matt laughed. "I bet Pa is more interested in the result of the elections and our new president than he is in getting supplies. He's excited about the idea of Oklahoma becoming a state. 'Course he says that's a ways off yet, but we're headed there." He bent to adjust his stirrup, then continued the conversation. "Pa's been talking about how more people will make Barton Creek a better place to live."

"I believe it will. Texas prospered after it became a state. I like the land around here. I left my uncle's ranch after he and Aunt Josey died. Zeke, the foreman, took it over."

"Why don't you go back and help him take care of it?"

A natural question, but how was he to answer it? "Maybe someday I will, but right now we have your pa's cattle to take care of."

Matt leaned on his saddle horn. "I hope he's right about how we'll grow around here. Sure don't want any range wars like I've heard of in other places."

Jake nodded. Now what did Matt know at his young age about range wars and fence cuttings and cattle rustling? He'd heard tales of such himself but never seen any. Once people started settling into places, land became scarce. Greedy men wanted more than their share and tried to run others out to have it.

Jake cut his gaze to Matt. "Your pa's been telling me about God. Do you think God really forgives people of crimes like that—cattle rustling and range wars?"

Matt didn't hesitate with his answer. "Yes, I do. I don't know why God loves sinners so much, but He does."

A laugh escaped Jake's mouth before he could stop it. Really, what did young Matt know about sin? Growing up with a Christian family and parents who loved him didn't give the boy much opportunity for evil ways.

Matt peered at him through narrowed eyes. "God is in the forgiving business. Doesn't matter what a man has done; God takes care of him. Look at how He's taken care of Ma and Pa all these years."

Why shouldn't God take care of them? They were good Christian people. He couldn't imagine Ben or Mellie Haynes sinning. Matt wouldn't understand the questions rolling through Jake's mind. He'd have to wait and talk more with Ben.

"You know, Jake, we've had some hard times. I remember

freezes and storms that took some of the herd and droughts that claimed them too, but Pa always said God will take care of His faithful children. He was right because we always recovered. And He'll help you." He paused and peered at Jake. "Pa prays for you every night during our family devotions."

Jake jerked his head. Praying for him? Would they be praying for him if they knew the truth? Why couldn't God let him forget the mess he left behind? He couldn't wrap his mind around the concept of God talked about by Ben and Matt. Jake deserved punishment and knew it, but the fear of death filled him more than the guilt of what he'd done.

He'd never go back to Texas.

Chapter 11

*L*ucinda marveled at the signs of activity so absent on the day of her arrival. The once empty streets now were filled with men and women going about the business of shopping, banking, and visiting. Uncle Ben pulled the wagon to a stop in front of Anderson's General Store.

Aunt Mellie alit, using the step on the side of the wagon, and looked up at Uncle Ben. "We'll meet you back here when we complete our shopping. I know you have other matters to attend to, so we'll keep ourselves occupied in the store."

Becky jumped down from the wagon bed, but Lucinda decided to follow her aunt's method of getting to the ground. Uncle Ben clicked the reins and headed toward the livery.

"What are we going to do first?" Lucinda brushed her hand across her skirt to remove spots of dust collected during the ride into town.

"Anderson's will be our first stop. I have a list of supplies. You two take a look at the fabrics and patterns available." Aunt Mellie marched up the steps and into the store.

The bell tinkled overhead, and Mr. Anderson waved a greeting. "Good to see you, Mrs. Haynes. Help yourself. I'll be with you shortly."

The familiar odor of kerosene mingled with the sawdust shavings on the wood floor and the open barrels of pickles, potatoes, and onions. Lucinda grabbed Becky's hand and headed for the back where she could see bolts of fabric stacked on shelves. "Come on. We'll find something pretty for your new dress."

"Humph. Looks like the nice weather brought everyone into town today," Becky said. "I'd rather be outdoors."

"I'm sure you would, but we do want to get a dress ready before your birthday party." Lucinda peered up at the rows of fabric in every imaginable pattern from stripes to solids, prints to checks.

"May I help you?"

She jumped then swirled around to find a young man grinning at her. He wore an apron over his clothes and a pencil nestled above his ear.

"I didn't mean to startle you. I'm Luke Anderson. And you are Miss Bishop, I understand. I'm sorry we haven't been formally introduced, but I do welcome you to our town."

Now she remembered having seen him before. On her first day in town he had been in the store when she came in to buy candy. He stood slightly taller than her in height and stared at her with eyes the color of Aunt Mellie's coffee. She gazed back for a moment before turning to the shelves. "We're looking at dress fabrics for Becky."

From the corner of her eye she noticed the pink in her cousin's cheeks and the look of chagrin on her face. Lucinda hadn't intended to embarrass Becky. She reached out to hug her when Bobby Frankston stepped up.

"Morning, Becky. Miss Bishop."

So that was the reason for the bloom on Becky's face. "Hello, Bobby. It's nice to see you again."

Becky didn't say a word. Lucinda noticed the girl's hands behind her back and her head bowed. "Becky, I'd like to get some of those peppermints and perhaps some chocolate to take home. Would you go up front and pick some out for me? Mr. Anderson and I will discuss fabrics."

Her cousin grinned. "Sure, Lucinda. I'd be happy to." Becky hurried away with Bobby following.

Luke chuckled. "I've seen him staring at her during church a number of times. I think he's smitten."

Lucinda didn't miss the twinkle in Luke's eye. He might be a fun person to have as a friend. After these several weeks, she had not met many others her age in Barton Creek. "I think Becky may feel the same way." The two stood together at the front counter studying the candy jars. "They are cute together."

Luke didn't glance their way, his eyes riveted on Lucinda. "Yes, they are."

Disconcerted by his attention, she reached for a bolt. "I think this one might be a nice color for Becky."

At the same moment, Luke grasped the bolt to help her. His hand brushed against hers. She felt the heat rise in her cheeks and moved her hand away. Had he done that on purpose? From the look on his face, he probably did. He was handsome, but not in the way Jake was. Luke was more like the young men back home, well groomed and clean shaven.

Lucinda unfolded the cloth for a closer look. Her eyes saw the material, but her mind filled with the image of Jake. She remembered the shock she felt whenever his hands touched hers. Nothing like that had happened with Luke. Feelings like those for Jake remained a mystery to her.

"Would you like to see a few patterns, or will you let Becky pick it out?"

Luke's question brought her out of her reverie. "What? Oh yes, Becky will pick it out. After all, it is her dress and her birthday."

She spotted a catalog on the counter. "Do you order goods from that?"

He handed it to Lucinda. "Yes, we take special orders from this. One day we'll expand and be able to carry a larger variety of items, like some of those new stores in the big cities back east."

"I've seen one of them in Boston. Mrs. Sutton took me there when we were buying things for me to bring out here." She flipped through the pages until she found what she wanted. "Could you order one of these sewing machines?"

Luke leaned closer to view the page. "Sure, we can order anything in there. Do you want one?"

"I'm thinking of Aunt Mellie. Her sewing would go much faster with such a machine." She closed the book. "I'll speak with Uncle Ben. It would make a wonderful Christmas present."

At that moment Aunt Mellie called to her. "Lucinda, we've found the pattern. Bring that fabric up here."

Lucinda grabbed the bright blue material and hurried to her aunt. Luke followed close behind. She handed the fabric to Aunt Mellie and stepped back, right into Luke.

His hands held her arms to keep her from stumbling.

At her aunt's knowing smile, Lucinda stepped away from Luke. "Sorry, I didn't know you were behind me."

Luke grinned then strode to his place behind the counter. "No harm. At least you didn't fall." He unwound the cloth and spread it across the counter. "How much do you need?"

While Aunt Mellie finished the purchase, Lucinda strolled over to the front counter where Mrs. Anderson stacked supplies and goods to take back to the ranch. At that moment, the older Mr. Anderson came through the door. He held what looked like a huge chicken in his hands.

"Got your turkey, Mrs. Haynes. He's a good one too. I'll put him in a cage and set him in the wagon."

A turkey? Of course, with Thanksgiving only a few weeks away, they would need a turkey, but a live one? Lucinda had never seen one before. They had plucked dead chickens at the market in Boston, but never a live one. Questions about how it would get from its present state to a dish on the table rolled through her mind. Knowing Aunt Mellie, a lesson on preparing a turkey would be in order, but that was one lesson Lucinda would rather not learn.

⚜

Jake and Matt returned from the range at the same time the others returned from town. Ben Haynes helped his wife with her parcels. Matt hopped down and grabbed the reins of the horses. "I'll take care of these, Pa."

Jake led his horse into the barn, where he and Matt removed the bridles and bits from the team. Matt closed the stall door and secured it behind his horse. "I'm heading back to the house to see what Ma bought in town."

Jake finished mucking the stalls. He reached over to stroke his horse's mane. A briar or two caught in his fingers. He grabbed the curry brush and ran it through the mane. A sound behind him caused him to jump. He turned to find Lucinda standing by the stall.

A hesitant smile formed. "I didn't mean to startle you. Aunt Mellie is busy putting away supplies, and I came out to see Misty."

She stepped forward. "Can you teach me to brush her like that?" Lucinda nodded toward Baron. "I want to get to know her better."

An unfamiliar emotion gripped Jake's heart. Not since Carrie had he seen such sincerity in a request. He clutched the brush harder to still his shaking hand and swallowed hard.

"I'd be happy to do that." He handed her the brush he held and led her to Misty's stall.

Misty nickered and tossed her head, then nuzzled Lucinda's neck.

"She likes you, Miss Bishop, and that's good for a horse and its rider." He grasped her hand and placed it against Misty's mane. "This is how you do it." He pulled her hand down through the hair with a few strokes.

She concentrated on the task. He concentrated on her. Her silky hair was caught in a bunch of curls at her neck by a large blue bow that matched her skirt. As when he first met her, a floral scent filled his nose, and he breathed deeply.

She turned her face to his. Only inches separated them. All motion stopped as they gazed into one another's eyes. What he saw there was so pure and beautiful, he couldn't breathe. He blinked and stepped back. "Did you have a question?" He wanted to groan. What a stupid thing to say.

Her cheeks turned pink. "Umm, no, I think I'd better go back to the house. I can do this some other time." She turned and almost ran from the barn.

He stared after a few minutes. What had just happened? He'd been close enough to kiss her, and how he had wanted to do just that.

The more time he spent around her, the more attracted he became. Her soft voice and mannerisms reminded him of the ladies at church when he was a boy. Lucinda delighted in discovering new things on the ranch, like learning to take care of her horse. Her enjoyment for life gave him hope that perhaps all was not lost in his case.

Then reality set in. He had no future with Lucinda Bishop. Not with the threat of a death sentence hanging over his head. Jake clenched his teeth and pressed his lips together. Then he muttered, "Why would a God who loves people do things like He's done to me?"

"He doesn't do things to people, Jake. We do them to ourselves." Ben leaned against the stall door.

Jake gasped. How much had Ben heard? He took a deep breath and swiveled to face him.

Ben said gently, "Lucinda told me about the loss of your aunt and uncle and sister, in addition to your parents. You've had more tragedy in your young life than anyone should be allowed to bear."

"So why did God do it?" he demanded. "Is He punishing me for something?"

Ben looked solemn. "Of course not. He loves you. Yes, we all sin, and God hates sin, but He doesn't hate the sinner."

Jake looked up at Ben. Could he see the guilt hidden there?

"We do all have to face up to our sins, though." Ben's words were soft, but they cut deep into Jake's soul.

"I suppose so," he mumbled. Then he turned to hang up the curry brush. "Excuse me, sir. I'd better go wash up before supper."

Back at the empty bunkhouse, Jake's first impulse led him to packing his belongings. He stuffed a shirt into one of the saddlebags but abruptly sat down on his bunk. Run. Was that what he'd have to do the rest of his life? Yes; if he didn't face the law now, he'd never be able to stay in one place long. But facing the law would be confessing what he'd done and going back to face hanging.

He had too much life yet to live. He didn't want to die, but what kind of life would he have running away every time the law got close? He shoved the bags aside and sank onto his cot. With head bowed and hands clasped between his knees, he let his past roll through his mind. Running wasn't the answer.

Chapter 12

*L*ucinda yawned once again as she dried dishes at breakfast on Thanksgiving morning. "I had no idea we'd be up this early on a holiday." Indeed, back home she usually slept until the late morning hours on such a day.

Aunt Mellie grabbed her shawl from the hook by the door. "We have to get that old tom ready for the oven. Come on. Ben's fixing to kill him now so we can pluck and dress it."

Lucinda hesitated. Her insides quivered at the idea of killing the poor bird. Still, Becky would be there, as would Matt. She couldn't look like a squeamish coward. She wrapped her own shawl around her shoulders and followed Aunt Mellie to the yard. One more thing she needed to learn about living in the country.

The sight that greeted her was like none she'd ever seen. Matt and Jake chased the turkey trying to rope it in. Hank and Monk stood stationed at two points in case the old bird ran their way. Ben laughed at their efforts, but Lucinda's heart thumped against her ribs. Silently she rooted for the bird.

Becky stomped her foot. "Stop it! Ya'll are scaring him to death."

Matt stopped short and stared at Becky. "What did you say?"

"Um, well, um, I don't think that's the way to do it."

Matt tossed the rope at her. "Here. then. He's all yours."

Becky waited until Matt and Jake moved over to stand by Monk and Hank. She filled her hands with dried corn and sauntered over to the pen, leaving a trail of corn behind her. The old tom began pecking his way to the pen, gobbling up the corn as he went. When he reached the gate, Becky reached down and put her arms around the bird. She glanced up at Matt and her pa.

Lucinda's heart finally slowed to normal. Her uncle and cousin sneaked up behind and slipped the rope down over the turkey's neck. He flapped his wings in protest, but the rope held tight.

Uncle Ben led the turkey over to Hank. An ax dangled from his hand. The men managed to get the turkey laid across a stump in the barnyard. Lucinda suddenly realized the purpose of the ax.

She gasped and placed her fist at her mouth. "Surely you're not going to chop its head off like that."

At Uncle Ben's nod, she covered her eyes just as she heard a squawk followed by a thump. A peek through her fingers revealed a headless bird still flapping its wings.

Oh my. Lucinda staggered a moment before Aunt Mellie's arms steadied her. "So much blood. It's awful." Her stomach churned, and a metallic taste filled her mouth.

"It's a mite easier than wringing its neck like we do the chickens." Aunt Mellie hugged her. "Now our work begins." She gestured toward the barn. "All right, boys, take him in there and let him bleed out, then we'll pluck him."

She directed Lucinda toward the house. "You go on in and get the stove going good. This tom will make a mighty fine dinner for us this afternoon."

Lucinda hurried inside to escape the scene behind her. The laughter and talk from the men reached her ears. The heat rose in her cheeks. They must think her to be a real weakling at being so upset about a turkey. *Some things about living on a ranch I'll never be able to do.*

After the queasiness left, she ventured back outside. The dead turkey, minus its head, sat waiting for its feathers to be removed. Jake held the bird by its feet while Uncle Ben poured scalding hot water into a tub. Then Jake plunged it into the water. Lucinda shuddered again.

Jake glanced up at her and smiled. "He's not feelin' a thing, and it'll make the feathers easier to remove." He yanked the bird out and dropped him into another tub. "Now it's your turn."

Lucinda gasped. "My turn? What am I supposed to do?"

He removed thick gloves from his hands and grabbed a handful of feathers. "You just grab on and pull them out."

Becky leaned over and plucked out a bunch. "Come on; it's easy." She pulled up two milking stools by the tub and sat on one. She motioned for Lucinda to take the other one.

※

Jake swallowed his chuckle at the look of dismay on Lucinda's face. He'd plucked many a turkey in his day, but he could see how the first time would be hard for Lucinda.

Matt pulled up a stool, and the three of them set to the task of plucking. Lucinda sat and watched.

Jake glanced her way. "You know, Miss Bishop, I remember the first time my pa killed a wild turkey for our Thanksgiving. When Pa let that ax come down on the wooden stump, I cried because I loved that turkey."

"Did you really?" Lucinda leaned forward, closer to Jake. Matt and Becky looked on with interest too.

"Yep, I did. Pa explained how God made certain creatures to be sacrificed for human needs. Killing chickens, turkeys, and cows is just His way of making sure we have meat on the table."

"I hadn't really thought of it like that." She reached over and plucked a few feathers from the bird.

Becky punched Matt. "See, I told you it wasn't nice to tease because Lucinda didn't like to see old tom turkey killed." She giggled. "Jake, you'll have to help me think up something to do to Matt for being so in-sen-si-tive."

Jake laughed at her emphasis on each syllable of the word. "That I will, Miss Becky."

Lucinda nodded. "And I'll help too. He's teased me once too often." Her eyes sparkled with mischief.

Matt groaned and Jake grinned. Ever since the day she rode off with that challenge to catch her, Jake saw more and more of the fun-loving girl Lucinda was. Her laughter rang out like music and filled his heart with love.

He grabbed a handful of feathers. "Come on, let's get this turkey finished before your ma comes out and plucks us."

⚓

After the turkey was stuffed and tucked into the oven to roast, Becky went out to ride Daisy while Lucinda set to work helping Mellie with the pies.

Mellie plumped a large pumpkin onto the table. "Come now. We have a nice big pumpkin to clean out and make into pies." As they worked, the aroma of roasting turkey filled the room. A tin basin sat on the table to hold the pulpy mess from the center of a pumpkin. Aunt Mellie thumped the large gourd. "We'll save the seeds, wash 'em off, and then dry 'em. That way, we'll have them to plant for pumpkin next year along with the beans, squash, and corn."

That sounded like a lot of work to Lucinda. Vegetables didn't just show up in the markets. Her experience with flower seeds taught her about growing things. "I always enjoyed the fresh vegetables in the summer. I hope I can help with the garden." A

112

garden as big as Aunt Mellie described would take more effort than a few flowers in a Boston garden.

In less than ten minutes, the pumpkin became only a shell. Two separate pans held seeds and the pulp. Aunt Mellie handed Lucinda a large spoon. "Mash the meat up real good. Then I'll cook it and use it for the pie filling."

Lucinda did as instructed and used all her strength to pulverize the mass of pumpkin. Now would be a good time for her questions. "Aunt Mellie, how did you know you were in love with Uncle Ben?"

Her aunt stopped rolling out dough for a moment and stared through the window over the sink. A slow smile spread across her face. "When he left Boston to return to Kansas, I thought my heart would break because I figured I'd never see him again. I knew he enjoyed my company, but we never spoke of the future. I missed him more every day and wore out the front door checking for mail."

"Did he write to you?"

"Oh yes, often. He described the land where he worked on a ranch, and I wanted to see it. More than that, I wanted to be with him."

"Then how did the two of you get together?" Lucinda paused in her task.

Aunt Mellie wiped her hands on a towel, a faraway look in her eyes. "He wrote that he was coming back to Boston to visit his family and even wrote Papa to see if he could call on me during his stay. Oh my, I was so excited I thought my heart would burst. I think the only reason Papa said yes was because Ben had family in Boston.

"In fact, I think Papa and Mama both thought he'd give up the idea of ranching if he settled down with me. Wasn't to be, though. Ben and I talked of our life together, and when he asked me if I would go west with him, I didn't hesitate in saying yes. I would have and still would follow him to the ends of the earth. Wherever he is, that's where I want to be."

"What did Grandmother and Grandfather Carlyle say about that?" Lucinda couldn't imagine her grandparents being pleased with their youngest daughter going off to the wilds. They had been so possessive of Mama even after she married Papa. Perhaps that had been because Amelia had left them. The last time Aunt Mellie and Uncle Ben had brought Matt and Becky to Boston for a visit, Mellie's parents paid much more attention to the children than their own daughter.

"They weren't happy at all, but both realized if they didn't allow it and have a proper wedding, I'd just run off with him anyway."

Run away with a man? Lucinda didn't think she'd ever be able to do that, but then she didn't have anyone to stop her from marrying whomever she pleased, unless Aunt Mellie and Uncle Ben objected. Her dream of a large wedding might not be appropriate here, especially if she married someone like Jake. Where had that thought come from? She had promised herself to put away any thoughts of that nature.

"You're thinking about Jake, aren't you?"

Lucinda's face reddened. How perceptive her aunt could be. "Yes, I am." She laid down her spoon. "I've never felt this way about anybody before. I don't understand it."

Aunt Mellie wrapped her arms around Lucinda. "My dear, when love comes, it brings emotions and feelings that are difficult to describe. I like Jake, but I don't want you to be hurt if he isn't the man God has planned for you."

Lucinda squeezed her eyes shut to keep tears from forming. "Oh, Aunt Mellie, I know he isn't a Christian. He won't even go to church with us. I can't be thinking of him that way."

"That's right. If he makes any advance toward you, Ben will

have to let him go. As much as we care about him, you are our responsibility, and we will protect you from whatever we feel is not in your best interests."

Aunt Mellie meant well, but Lucinda's heart ached at the thought of Jake being sent away.

⚜

Ben laid down his fork. Another blessed Thanksgiving. He sat here at this table with his family and his workers completely at peace. God was good. His gaze rested on Becky, his little girl and the light of his life. In a few years the young lass who rode like the wind across the prairie and worked beside him as good as Matt would be only a memory. How he wished he could hold back time to keep her on the ranch.

Jake and Lucinda sat across from each other, but there was no mistaking the emotion sparking the air between them. Both he and Mellie had cautioned Lucinda about Jake, but when love takes hold of the heart, no amount of warnings will keep that love from growing. He and Mellie were living proof of that. His love for her had only grown stronger over the years. That love stood on a rock-solid foundation of faith and trust in the Lord.

Under the right circumstances, these two young people could have the same kind of love, but Ben sensed an undercurrent in Jake's life. That boy had something to settle in his past. A relationship with the Lord would go a long ways toward helping Jake to find peace with whatever had happened to cause that haunted look in his eyes. Perhaps in time Ben would be able to help Jake understand God's love.

A question from Hank drew Ben from his thoughts. "Sorry, Hank. What was that again?"

"I just asked how things would be with our new president."

"McKinley will be sworn in after the first of the year and a new governor appointed. Even with the Republicans in office, I don't see statehood coming for at least ten years. Still so much to be done." The election and all it entailed excited Ben with new hope for the territory. "Our country is in good hands."

Hank leaned forward. "With so many new people comin' in, seems like statehood oughta come sooner than that."

Ben shook his head. "No. Those in charge want it to be done right. All parties will have to be in agreement and vote to accept the Constitution. New settlements are being opened and new counties formed every year. Soon the territory will cover close to twenty-four million acres, according to the reports I've heard."

Jake whistled below his breath. "I had no idea Oklahoma was getting that big."

"She's going to be a fine state one of these days, and if the good Lord's willing, we'll all be around to see it happen." Ben grinned and leaned toward Mellie. "Now that we have the politics out of the way, how about some of that pumpkin pie I smelled earlier?"

Mellie pushed back from the table. "I'll have it ready in a few minutes. Come, Lucinda, let's get these men their dessert." She and Lucinda rose and bustled around, cutting pie and handing it out.

As they worked, Jake pressed against the back of his chair and placed his hands palms down on the table. "Sir, I've been thinking about our talks and thought it might be a good idea to visit that church in town and hear the preacher."

Ben swallowed hard to keep from shouting. "We'd be right pleased to have you come with us, lad."

Pure joy shone from Lucinda's eyes for a moment before she hastily dropped her gaze when she caught Ben looking at her.

Matt clapped Jake on the shoulder. "'Bout time you went to

church. I told you we'd been praying for you every night during our family devotions."

Mellie stood by the sink, her hand to her mouth. Ben smiled and nodded at her. Maybe their prayers would be answered soon. What a Thanksgiving this had turned out to be!

Chapter 13

*J*ake loved this time just before dawn when the world awakened and the dark slinked away in the approaching bands of pink and lavender. Birds chirped in the trees to greet the day, and a rooster crowed. Each new morning meant another day with another chance at doing right. This morning he'd do that by going to church. Much as he dreaded it, making up excuses and lying to Ben Haynes bothered him more.

The light glowing from the kitchen window meant the Haynes family was up and about, preparing for the Lord's Day. He'd probably find Ben and Matt in the barn already with the animals. He hurried in that direction to take care of his own chores.

The pungent odor of freshly mucked hay greeted him when he entered the barn. The ping of milk hitting the pail meant Matt was busy. Ben fed the horses nearby. Jake strode over to his own stallion. "Good mornin', Ben. Matt. Looks like it's going to be a nice day."

Ben held out his oat-filled hand to Daisy. "And it'll be even better with you beside us at church."

Jake said nothing, only nodded. He bridled his horse then brushed Baron's mane. All the things Ben told him about God jumbled in his brain with the words from the preacher so many years ago and the verses he'd been reading the past weeks. Nothing seemed to fit. On one hand, God punished people for their sins. On the other, God loved everyone in spite of their sins. Just didn't make any sense to him at all.

Becky appeared at the barn door. "Ma says breakfast is ready. She doesn't want to be late for church this morning, so you'd better hurry if you don't want cold eggs."

Ben wiped his hands on a cloth. "We'll clean up and be right in."

Matt had already set out after Becky. Jake chuckled and closed Baron's stall. That young man wasn't about to let any food get cold waiting on him.

Jake fell into step beside Ben. "I don't have any clothes fit for Sunday-go-to-meeting. Down in Texas, my ma dressed us up for church. Does that matter up here?"

Ben shook his head. "Not a bit. Some folks dress up, but cowboys are a working bunch, and most wear what they have. You'll see."

Another objection forestalled. Well, maybe the preacher could shed more light on some of the concerns plaguing his mind in recent days. Jake hated to keep pestering Ben Haynes with questions even though his boss didn't seem to mind answering.

He followed Ben into the kitchen with Monk and Hank close behind. Mellie finished setting bowls of food on the table and gestured for them to sit. Lucinda poured coffee into the cups but didn't glance Jake's way.

How pretty she looked this morning with her hair gathered in the back with a large, white bow. His mother had always spent a lot of time getting ready to go anywhere. Made him wonder how much earlier the womenfolk here arose each day in order to look so nice at breakfast. He sat across from her again and bowed his head as Ben returned thanks for the meal.

After the blessing, Jake filled his plate with scrambled eggs and all the trimmings, as did the others. Ben started up the conversation. "With the weather so nice this week, I would imagine the Morris family will be coming in to church." He glanced at Lucinda. "They live ten miles or so to the north. It's a long trek for them, but they have a daughter about your age. Her name is Dove."

Becky grinned. "You'll love her, Lucinda. She's part Indian and has the prettiest dark hair and eyes."

Lucinda raised her eyebrows. "Part Indian?"

Mellie passed the platter of biscuits around again. "Yes. Her grandparents came here back in thirty-nine on the Trail of Tears when the Indians were forced to come west to the reservations here in Oklahoma. Dove's mama was born on the Cherokee reservation. Mr. Morris met White Feather on one of his cattle trips and fell in love with her."

Jake's ears perked with interest. He knew Sam Morris but hadn't heard the story about his family before. Back home a man had married an Indian woman and brought her back to town. The community never accepted them, and they finally moved away after many threats against the woman's life. Perhaps things were different here.

Lucinda raised her eyebrows. "But aren't Indians to be feared? They're so savage."

Ben shook his head. "Not these days. Still may be a few groups here and there who rebel, but most are folks just like us."

Becky set her milk glass on the table. "You'll see how nice the Morrises are. They have two sons, John Hawk and Eli Eagle."

Lucinda pondered the names. "Dove, Hawk, and Eagle are all birds. How unusual."

Mellie nodded. "Yes, Emily loves birds of all kinds, so she named her children for them.

"The Morrises are very good neighbors. In warmer weather I visit Emily once a week or so to talk and do our handwork together. You can go with me."

"Oh, I would like that. Mama had a sewing circle that met at our house on occasion. That's how I learned embroidery." She paused then asked, "But I thought you said Mrs. Morris's name was White Feather."

"White Feather is her Cherokee name. She adopted Emily as her English name a number of years ago." Mrs. Haynes handed Jake the platter of bacon.

Jake stabbed a piece and laid it on his plate, then tuned out the conversation and pictured Lucinda in the setting of her home in Boston doing her sewing. What kind of life could he offer? His own would be easier if he cleared his mind of all thoughts of Lucinda, but he feared that would be far more difficult in the days ahead with her so close by.

Ben pulled out his pocket watch. "It's time for us to be going. You ladies finish up whatever you have to do, and I'll have the surrey waiting for you."

Outside, Jake mounted his horse and waited for the women-folk to appear as he fought off the desire to stay behind. He hoped the preacher would shed some light on God and help him understand God's love.

⚜

The idea of meeting an Indian girl roused Lucinda's curiosity, and she gazed around eagerly when they drove into the church yard. Because of the fine weather, more buggies intermingled with farm and ranch wagons. Voices filled the air as people greeted each other, and laughter rang out from the young folks gathered around.

Lucinda considered begging off teaching with the young children and joining the ones her age. Not much opportunity for socializing occurred with so much work to be done and the weather being cold the past month or so. She searched for Mrs.

Anderson. The storekeeper's wife stood on the steps of the little building where the children met. She called out to her, and Mrs. Anderson waved and waited for Lucinda.

The woman shifted the books she held. "What can I do for you this morning, Lucinda?"

"Oh, Mrs. Anderson, might I be excused to meet with the other young people this morning? I do so want to meet some of the others my age in Barton Creek."

"Dear me, of course you can. I hadn't thought about that. We'll miss you, but you do need to get acquainted. You know Luke, and he'll introduce you."

"Thank you. I truly appreciate it. I'll be back with you soon, I promise." She loved the children, but this morning she wanted to meet Dove.

Lucinda made her way toward the group. A beautiful young woman with an olive complexion and black hair stood at the edge of the crowd, not really a part of them. She must be Dove Morris. But why was she standing away from the others? Lucinda hurried to the girl.

"Hi, I'm Lucinda Bishop. Are you Dove Morris?"

Eyes the color of the midnight sky turned to her and widened in surprise. "Yes, I am. Are you Lucinda Bishop? My mother said you might be here."

The group of young men and women silenced. From the corner of her eye, she saw them staring, as if waiting to see what she would do after speaking to Dove. Not one to be intimidated by people her own age, Lucinda extended her hand toward Dove.

"I'm so very pleased to meet you. I do hope we'll become friends. My aunt tells me that she and your mother visit quite often."

Dove's smile filled her eyes with warmth. "Yes, they do."

"Do you meet with them, or are you still in school? I finished last year, so I'm hoping to come with Aunt Mellie to your home.

It'll be so nice to have someone to visit with who is near my age."

Dove frowned and Lucinda stopped. Her babbling on must have embarrassed the girl.

"That would be very nice, Lucinda." Dove said politely. "I should go now." She headed up the steps into the building.

Lucinda turned and found the young men and women now sending glances her way as they continued conversation among themselves. Luke Anderson headed toward her. He smiled and tipped his hat.

"Good morning, Luke." She then marched up the steps to join Dove inside the building with Luke following. Dove was seated in one of the chairs arranged in a semicircle around a table. A man wrote on a board. He glanced around as Lucinda entered.

"Good morning, Miss Bishop. We haven't had the pleasure of meeting yet. I'm Luther Gooding, the Bible teacher. Welcome to our group."

"Thank you. I look forward to hearing your lesson this morning." She sat in the chair next to Dove and smiled.

Luke nodded at the empty seat beside Lucinda. "Do you mind if I take this seat?"

Heat rose in her cheeks. "Not at all. It's good to see you again." She noticed the others taking their places, but none stopped to greet her. That seemed a little strange, but then Mr. Gooding was ready to begin.

She glanced at her new friend. Dove's face bore a peaceful expression. Becky had been right. Dove was a lovely young woman. Perhaps the others were simply too hurried this morning to be more friendly. No matter, she and Dove would become good friends.

Jake sat on the pew behind the Haynes family during the worship service. He'd enjoyed the Sunday school class with hands from other ranches. He hadn't expected to see them at church. They drank coffee, talked, and then listened to a teacher talk about turning water into wine. He'd only half listened, his mind on seeing Lucinda again.

The singing in church stirred memories of childhood. He'd never understood the words much, but the sounds had been both rousing and soothing.

When the preacher stood to speak, quiet settled over the room. Babies slept in their mothers' laps, and even young children sat silently for the moment. Instead of the booming voice Jake remembered from years ago, the preacher began his message in a quiet manner. He spoke of the prophet Elijah and the endless supply of oil for a widow and her son.

He'd never heard this story before. An endless supply of oil? How was that possible? Then the preacher spoke of the endless love of Jesus. The more Jake listened, the more curious he became. Questions rose in his mind. If Jesus loved and forgave sinners, could He love and forgive Jake?

When the service ended, his heart wanted to believe Jesus loved him, but his mind couldn't grasp the idea. Not only had he done an unspeakable evil, but he also had run away from facing the consequences.

Now the only way to really find the truth would be to tell the truth. Jake shuddered. He didn't want to face the consequences of that truth. Fear curled around his heart.

Later in the afternoon, Mellie sat in the quietness of the great room. With Ben napping and the children off on their own, she relished this time on Sunday when she could sit alone with her thoughts. She sighed. With the colder weather, those days would be fewer.

A Bible lay in her lap, and Mellie closed her eyes. The sermon this morning had been good, but the story obscure for those who didn't know the Bible. What had Jake thought of it? Toward the end, she'd peeked behind her and had seen confusion written across his face.

Her mind wandered to Lucinda. It was a good thing that Lucinda had taken the initiative to attend Sunday school with the young people today. Mellie regretted having steered Lucinda to teaching the young children so soon, and she chastised herself for not thinking about Lucinda's need to make friends with others her own age. Of course she needed to meet more young people.

At that moment her niece stepped into the room. "Aunt Mellie, I don't mean to disturb you, but I'd like to talk with you a few minutes."

Mellie smiled and patted the chair next to her. "Of course, my dear. Come sit by me."

Lucinda sat and spread her skirt about the chair. She bit her lip and frowned.

Mellie reached over and grasped Lucinda's hand. "Child, whatever is the matter? You look troubled."

"Oh, I am. I don't understand something that happened this morning."

Mellie said nothing but squeezed Lucinda's hand in reassurance.

Lucinda's lips trembled. "The young people in our class were not friendly at all to me, and they practically ignored Dove. Luke Anderson is the only one who really spoke to us. Am I so terrible?"

The words sent a chill to Mellie's heart. This was one lesson she wished Lucinda didn't have to learn. Although many townspeople accepted Mrs. Morris and Dove, some minds were still closed to the Indians being a part of the community. Mellie weighed her words carefully.

"It doesn't have anything to do with you, my dear. They probably didn't like you being friendly with Dove."

Lucinda gasped. "Whyever not?"

"We live in what was once the home of several Indian tribes. To protect their lands, the Indians attacked homes and towns and wagon trains. Soldiers were sent in to fight them, and eventually the Indians were forced to stay on reservations set aside for them."

"I remember a little of that from talk I heard at home. Do you think they'd ever rise up and fight again?"

Mellie shook her head. "I've no doubt there are some who would still fight if they had the opportunity, but most Indians on the reservations are peace loving."

Lucinda furrowed her brow. "Then why were people so unfriendly today?"

How to explain that? Mellie understood but didn't like the attitudes of some of the townsfolk. "Old memories die hard. Bea Anderson's parents and her brother were killed by Indians when Bea was a child. Somehow she survived the attack, and neighbors found her in her dead mother's arms."

Lucinda sucked in her breath. "Oh my. How terrible!"

"Yes, it was. Others around here have similar stories. They don't know how to trust the red man, as they're called here.

White Feather changed her name to Emily when she became a Christian. Our pastor had no problem baptizing her, but it did disturb some of our church members."

Lucinda blinked. "God loves everybody. That's what I've always been taught."

So as not to disillusion Lucinda, Mellie chose her next words carefully. "That's true, but some just don't see it that way. No matter how free the people of our country are supposed to be, others always find ways to take that freedom away."

"Do you think it will ever change?"

Only God could change a man's heart, and some men simply didn't want that change. Old resentments and prejudices spoke louder than God's voice for too many. "I don't know, my child. I just don't know. I pray it will someday, but we can do our part now by accepting others for who God made them and helping them to find His love."

"Well, I think Dove will be a wonderful friend to have, and I'd like to go with you to visit them."

Mellie hugged her niece. "You are a precious girl, and I'm so thankful you've been taught the true meaning of Christian love. Others may not like your friendship with Dove, but they can't help but like you."

She stood and smiled. "In fact, you might teach them a lesson or two in love yourself. Come, let's fix us some tea."

Lucinda followed her to the kitchen. "One thing I still wonder about. Luke sat down by me and spoke to Dove. Why would he do that if his mother doesn't like Indians?"

Mellie set the teakettle on the stove. "I'd say he's a little smitten with you and was nice to Dove just to be polite. Emily shops at the Anderson's, but Bea won't wait on her. Carl handles all of the Morris family's transactions."

Lucinda sat at the table and folded her arms across her body.

"Well, if Luke wants to be friends with me, he'll have to be friends with Dove too. And so will anyone else."

Mellie said nothing. She loved her niece and didn't want to dash her hopes. Lucinda's attitude may be what the Lord wanted it to be, but would it have any effect on others? Sometimes Christians and their attitudes could be as big a puzzle as any she'd encountered. She reached for the tea box. *Please protect her, Lord. I don't want to see Lucinda hurt.*

Chapter 14

*L*ucinda, Lucinda. Wake up."

Someone shook her arm. Lucinda opened her eyes to narrow slits. Becky stood over her in the dim light of dawn. "What in the world, Becky. It's barely daylight."

"It's my birthday. Remember?"

Lucinda groaned. How could she forget? Becky had talked of nothing else for the past two weeks. "Why do we have to get up so early?"

Becky grinned and pulled back the covers. "Because the longer I'm up, the longer I can celebrate. Besides, we need to help Ma with all the cooking and decorating she needs to do for my party."

Lucinda shook her head and sat up. "All right. I'm awake now. You go on, and I'll be in as soon as I'm dressed."

Becky giggled and scurried from the room. Lucinda pulled dark stockings over her feet, then began her morning routine. How different things were now than a few months ago when she arrived. Nice dresses laid out for her every morning at home had been replaced by her choosing the garments for each day. She even enjoyed wearing the comfortable skirts and shirt-waists. Her new clothes suited her new life much better than the stiff silks and linens in the latest fashions.

She also had fun with Becky's excitement about becoming

thirteen. The young girl had decided her childhood could now be left behind.

Lucinda had come to enjoy Becky's exuberance. The thought of curbing it and teaching her the ways a young lady should behave could wait awhile. Maybe she could remind Becky that the only way to keep from being treated as a child was to act as a young lady. Still, Lucinda didn't want to smother the girl's enthusiasm for life.

She pulled her hair back to her neck and fastened it with a clasp. She would have taken extra time to put it up if she'd been back home, but here she took the easy way.

When she entered the kitchen, Becky stood with her hands balled into fists and resting on her hips.

Aunt Mellie turned from the stove with a twinkle in her eye. "Good morning. Becky here thinks today is supposed to be something special. Wonder what gave her that idea?"

Lucinda tied on her apron. "At least it's Saturday, and you have no school. That's cause for celebration enough. It's too close to Christmas for much else."

She couldn't suppress a grin at the pout on her cousin's face. Becky shook her head. "Oh, no, you've been planning my party all week. I'm not completely deaf and blind."

Lucinda joined her aunt in a good laugh. Friends and neighbors were scheduled to arrive later in the afternoon for the party. "Of course not, but much of the food was done yesterday while you were at school."

Aunt Mellie wrapped her arm around Becky's shoulder. "I know it's hard having a birthday in the winter, but this is a special one, and I do believe the weather will cooperate."

Lucinda removed dishes from the cupboard. Gray skies had grown more pink and orange, and tiny rays of sun shone across the table. If today followed the pattern of the last few, sunshine would fill the skies all day. With mild temperatures, they could expect more people to attend the festivities planned for the afternoon.

After morning chores and breakfast, Lucinda helped Becky with dusting. "We'll have this place shining like a new penny. The dust won't defeat us today."

Becky ran a cloth over a table. "Do you think everyone we invited will come to my party?"

"Oh, I'm sure you'll have quite a crowd here. Didn't your ma invite the parents of your friends too?" Lucinda wiped her cloth across the armoire and admired the shine left behind.

"Yes, she did." Becky twirled around the room. "I really hope Bobby will be here. I like him, and he's nice to me." She paused. "Well, most of the time he is."

Lucinda laughed. "Yes, and I'm sure nothing will keep him from being here—or any of the other boys, for that matter."

The young girl's face turned pink, and she rubbed her dust cloth on an unseen spot. "And they all know what a great cook Ma is too."

Lucinda grinned. "And that reminds me, we need to finish here so we can help with setting up the tables."

She returned to her dusting while Becky put things in their proper places. When they both finished, Lucinda headed for the kitchen to help her aunt. "Everything is shining like new. What do we need to do now?"

"You can help me frost and decorate the cake. And you, Becky, can check with your pa to see what help he needs outdoors."

Becky grabbed her shawl from its hook by the door and scampered out. Lucinda shook her head. That girl did like being out in the sunshine.

The amount of food prepared in the next hour surpassed anything she'd seen except the day of her parents' funeral. Then many hands had prepared and delivered the food, but here Aunt Mellie did it all.

The large table in the middle of the room groaned with the weight of breads, vegetables, and all manner of homemade goods. At the end, Aunt Mellie set out the layers to the birthday cake.

She swirled a white sugar concoction over the layers. Then she separated the mixture into three different bowls and added something to give each a different color.

"What is that? I've seen colored candies and other foods, but we were warned against all food color additives back in Boston."

Aunt Mellie stirred the mixture into a paste—one in yellow, one in green, and one in red. "I use all natural substances, so these are safe. The yellow is from saffron, the red from beet juices, and the green from spinach leaves. They don't add any real taste because of the sweetness of the sugar."

Where and how had her aunt learned all the cooking tricks she seemed to have? Sometimes Lucinda didn't think she'd ever learn it all. Her aunt fashioned a paper cone shaped from parchment, filled it with frosting, and used it to write Becky's name and "Happy Birthday" across the top. In short order, Aunt Mellie completed decorating the cake and stood back to admire it.

"Oh my, it's beautiful. I'll never be able to create something as pretty as that."

"Of course you will. All it takes is practice." Aunt Mellie nodded toward the table. "Can you make a space there for it? We'll clean up the mess and take it all outside when the guests arrive."

The aroma of beef cooking outdoors wafted into the kitchen. Aunt Mellie wiped her hands on a towel. "I believe it's time for us to get dressed for the party. I'll get Becky while you change."

Not quite an hour later Lucinda crossed the lawn to greet guests already mingling there. Becky pushed past her and ran out to find her friends. The Morris wagon arrived, and Lucinda hurried over to speak to Dove. This was going to be a most fun day, especially since the unseasonably warm weather permitted the party to be outdoors. People in Boston would think it a spring day with the temperatures in the high fifties.

＊

Jake stood to the side out of the way. Becky and her young friends laughed and teased each other. Sadness gripped his heart. She reminded him so much of his sister, Carrie, and how she loved life. Her thirteenth birthday had been one of fun and festivities just before Ma became ill and died. Since then, he'd had no time for such frivolity and no desire for it.

Lucinda strolled across the yard with Dove. The two girls spread a blanket across the grass under a bare oak tree and sat together. Jake couldn't take his eyes off the young women. Both were beautiful in their own ways. Lucinda's paleness and light brown eyes contrasted with Dove's darker skin and the almost black eyes of her Indian heritage.

The young women leaned toward each other, and the sound of their giggles reached his ears. Oh, to be seventeen and have no real cares or worries in the world. Both girls had families who loved them and took care of them. He longed for a small portion of what they had in the way of love.

Suddenly the hairs on his neck prickled. He jerked around, but only family and friends of the Haynes milled about. Something didn't set right. Although it had been well over a month since the shooting, his vigilance hadn't slackened. He still watched Lucinda like a hawk.

He strolled over toward the corral area where Monk and Hank tended the wagons and horses. After another look around the area, he spoke to the men. "Say, you two know most of the people around here. Have either of you seen anyone you don't recognize as being from Barton Creek?"

Monk scratched his beard. "Can't say that I have. Why?"

Hank turned from securing one of the teams. "I'm not as familiar with everyone as Monk, but I did see someone I didn't recognize a little earlier. He was sitting on a horse by the side of the road just looking this way. I don't know if he rode in or not."

"What did he look like?"

"Don't rightly remember, except he wore a black coat and hat. His horse was dark too, and the saddle had a little silver tooling on it. Is there a problem? You thinking about Misty's gunshot wound?"

"Yes. I just have that feeling something's not right. You know Mr. Haynes told us to keep an eye on Lucinda, and I aim to do just that."

Hank pushed back the brim of his hat. "You don't think someone would try anything with a crowd like this, do you?"

Jake shook his head. "I don't know, but it's better she's safe than for us to be sorry later. You two keep your eyes and ears open, and I'll walk around to see how things are. Just don't let Lucinda out of your sight."

Hank squared his hat. "Sure. We don't want anything happening to her. I hope you're wrong about trouble. Too nice a day for it."

"No day's a nice day for trouble." Jake strode away and headed out behind the stables. He paced the outside edges of the area around the house and barns. With all the wagons and horses here today, he'd not be able to pick up any tracks he didn't recognize. He must warn Ben Haynes.

His boss talked with several men by the spit, where they were turning the skewered beef.

"Mr. Haynes, may I speak with you a minute?"

Ben waved to his friends and joined Jake. "What's the problem, son?"

Jake relayed his speculations and the search results. "I don't like the idea that some stranger may be watching us."

Ben stroked his chin. "I trust your instincts after what happened to Misty. We'll have to be more careful today and not let Lucinda be anywhere alone."

"I agree. Monk and Hank are keeping an eye out now. We'll take turns."

"That's good. I'm sure the three of you can handle it." A frown crossed Ben's face. "Let's not say anything to Mellie. Don't want to worry her with all she has to do with the guests here. I'm going back over to take care of the meat. If anything comes up, let me know. I'll be keeping watch too."

After Ben rejoined his friends, Jake searched for Lucinda. Luke Anderson had joined her and Dove by the oak tree. Jake's heart skipped a beat. He recognized the look on Luke's face. It mirrored the way Jake felt whenever he saw Lucinda. He breathed deeply. Better for her to be courted by a young man like Luke who could give her a future than one like himself, who had no future.

Still, jealousy crept into his heart, and he strolled to where they sat.

Lucinda glanced up at Jake and smiled. "I'm glad you could join us. Dove and I were just talking about what a lovely party this is and how good all the food smells."

"That it does. Mrs. Haynes is a great cook." He couldn't help but bask in the warmth of her eyes.

At that moment a voice called out that the time had come for Becky to open her gifts.

Everyone gathered as a group near the front porch where the presents sat piled, waiting for Becky.

Jake remained close by Lucinda while the gifts were opened and everyone exclaimed over them. Why couldn't he settle down and relax with the others? He clamped his teeth together. Nothing would happen to Lucinda today. Not if he could help it.

Chapter 15

Jake adjusted the cinch on Baron's belly. Misty nickered in her stall. "Be patient. I'll get to you in a minute." The filly pawed the ground as though she anticipated the outing ahead.

Ben Haynes had asked him to accompany Lucinda to the Morris ranch this morning. Since the day he sensed danger a week ago, the men on the ranch kept even closer watch on Lucinda. Maybe it all had been his imagination, because as suddenly as it had it come, the sensation had disappeared. But he hadn't imagined the sound of the bullet that wounded Misty.

He strolled to the horse and patted her nose. His hand stroked the neck where she had been wounded. Only a small scar indicated anything had happened to the horse.

He threw Lucinda's saddle up over Misty's back. With only a week until Christmas, Lucinda had requested the ride to visit Dove. He completed Misty's care and led both horses outside. Ben and Lucinda approached him in a heated discussion. He stopped, but couldn't help but overhear their words.

"I still think the sewing machine would make a wonderful gift for Aunt Mellie. Our sewing would go so much faster with a machine." Lucinda's mouth set in a firm line.

Ben shrugged. "No doubt it would, my dear, but like I said, it's not something we can afford right now. Besides, it'll take several weeks if not months for it to be ordered and shipped."

Lucinda shook her head. "But I can get it for her. Mr. Sutton will wire the funds to my account here."

A muscle in Ben's jaw twitched. "Lucinda, I know you want to help, but we're not going to let you use your money like that. When the time is right, and funds are available, I'll be pleased to get that machine for Mellie. Until then, you'll have to make do with your hands."

Jake stepped behind the horses to avoid embarrassing Lucinda. From the set of her jaw, she wanted to argue further. She had a stubborn streak, but that was natural seeing as how she was kin to Mellie Haynes.

"Is Misty ready?" Lucinda stood with hands on her hips.

"Yes, we're ready when you are."

She grabbed the reins and turned on her heel. "Good. Let's go." She swung herself over Misty's back and settled in the saddle. She pulled the reins and headed out.

Ben shrugged and lifted his hands in the air. "Women. Who can understand them?"

Jake shook his head and mounted Baron. He spurred his horse into a fast trot to catch up with Lucinda. When he reached her side, he remained silent, preferring to let her take the lead. His senses went on full alert. If anyone followed them today, he'd know it.

Finally Lucinda slowed to a leisurely walk beside him. "I must apologize for my behavior. I let my anger with Uncle Ben spill over on you, and I had no right to do that."

"Apology accepted, Miss Bishop." Not that he needed one from her, but he had no desire to embarrass her by saying so. She appeared much more relaxed when she turned and smiled at him.

"Please, call me Lucinda. We're not in Boston, and Miss Bishop is far too formal for friends."

"If you say so, Miss—I mean Lucinda." The name rolled off his tongue. He wanted to be more than a friend, but he'd keep his distance out of respect for her and the Hayneses.

They rode in comfortable silence for several minutes, with Jake aware of every movement and sound around them. Lucinda had no idea that danger may be following her, and Ben had warned him not to tell her. On his own, he would have done just that so she could be on alert herself. But Ben Haynes was boss, and whatever he wanted, Jake would do.

She lifted her face toward the sky. "Looks like our bout of nice weather is going to be over soon. With Christmas coming, snow would be nice. We always had a white Christmas in Boston." She turned her attention toward him. "I know it's hard to think about your family, but what was it like on your ranch?"

How much should he reveal? Her eyes were so honest and trusting, he had to tell her the truth. "We had a spread much like the Rocking H down in the south part of Texas. Lots of big ranches down that way. I went on my first cattle drive when I was fourteen, and I knew that was the life I wanted."

"When did your mother take ill?"

"Right after my fifteenth birthday. Carrie and I went to school and helped at home the best we could. She didn't last but a few months. Then when Pa died, I was too young to take over, and that's when my aunt and uncle came." Somehow talking about it with Lucinda wasn't as painful as he thought.

"What happened to your home?"

"Uncle Earl sold it and put the money in a bank. I suppose it's still there."

"Oh, maybe in a trust like my parents did for me in their will. Why don't you go back to claim it or have it sent here?"

He didn't answer. She didn't need to know the truth. If there was a chance for them to be together, then he'd have to tell her.

"Have you any plans after you turn eighteen?" That would get the conversation on safer ground until he could figure out what to tell her.

Lucinda grinned. "Well, I don't really have anything planned yet. Depends on what happens the next few months here. I may go back east and finish my schooling. I think I might like to be a teacher."

"Would you stay back east to teach when you finish school?"

Her eyes lit up, and she lifted her head toward the sky. "I do believe I'd like to come back here. Aunt Mellie and Uncle Ben are my family now, and Becky and Matt are like a brother and sister to me. Uncle Ben talks about Oklahoma being a state someday. You know, I think I'd like to be around when that happens. It sounds exciting."

"If you do return to Barton Creek, the students will be lucky to have you for a teacher."

Her laughter rang out. "I don't know about that. We'll have to see what happens. If you're still around, you can help me if the big boys get too rowdy."

He smiled at her. Nothing would please him more, but he could make no plans for the future until he settled his past.

A few minutes later they arrived at the Morris spread.

Dove ran out to meet them when they rode into the yard. "I'm so glad you're here. I've run into a problem with my stitching."

Lucinda alit from Misty and handed the reins to Jake. "I'll take a look. I imagine we can fix it." She glanced back at Jake. "I do hope you don't mind waiting for me. Uncle Ben insisted that I not ride back home alone."

Jake tipped his hat back on his head. "Don't mind at all, Lucinda. I'll take care of the horses and visit with the boys in the bunkhouse. Just let me know when you're ready to leave."

"Thank you. I'll do that." Then she hooked arms with Dove and strolled toward the house.

Her smile wrapped itself around his heart as it had so many times in the past weeks. Once again the beauty of the two girls struck him. Some lucky young men would claim them as brides, and probably in the not-so-distant future. Under different circumstances he could picture himself as being one of those young men.

He blinked and shook his head. He had to quit daydreaming and face reality. Lucinda Bishop could never marry him. He'd never marry anyone.

❧

Lucinda followed Dove into the house. Although more rustic, it was every bit as big as many of the fine homes she remembered in Boston. She'd heard Uncle Ben mention that Mr. Morris was one of the most successful ranchers in all of Oklahoma Territory. They even had a washroom with a bathtub like the one the Bishops had in Boston.

"Good morning, Mrs. Morris. I do hope you don't mind my coming over here so close to Christmas. I wanted to knit a shawl to be a surprise for Aunt Mellie, and I've had a hard time doing it at home without her finding out."

Mrs. Morris smiled and set a tray laden with a teapot and cups on the table. "I'm glad you could come. Dove needs help with the embroidery. I can knit and crochet, but embroidery still challenges me."

Dove held up her handwork. "See, my satin stitches aren't smooth at all, and my French knots are awful."

Lucinda examined the piece. It reminded her of her own first attempts at needlework. "This can be easily fixed. I'll snip out the threads here, and we can try again."

"While you girls take care of your projects, I'll be in the kitchen baking. If you need any help, just let me know."

As soon as Mrs. Morris left the room, Dove leaned toward Lucinda. "I see Jake accompanied you this morning. He's so handsome."

Heat rose in Lucinda's cheeks. "Yes, he is. And he's a very nice young man with a tragic past. He lost all his family."

"Oh, I'm so sorry to hear that. No wonder you two are attracted to each other. Both of you lost your parents."

Lucinda gulped. Dove had noticed too. Did that mean others besides her family also saw the feelings she had tried so hard to keep hidden? She'd have to be more careful in the future. "He's just a friend. We can talk to each other about things like that."

Dove poured a cup of tea and handed it to Lucinda. "If you say so, but I've seen him staring at you with more than a glint of friendship in his eyes."

The teacup rattled on its saucer. She grasped it with her free hand to keep from dropping it. Surely Dove had to be mistaken. "You're just seeing things. Besides, he isn't a believer, so I can't even think about him in any way but as a friend."

"But if he were a Christian, things would be different?"

"I…I don't know. I do like him." How would she feel? Emotions churned inside, but she squared her shoulders and nibbled a sugar cookie. She leaned toward Dove. "Is there a young man you're interested in at church?"

Dove shrugged. "Not really. The only two who are really our age are Luke Anderson and Martin Fleming. But Luke is as smitten with you as Jake is, so that leaves Martin for me, I guess."

"I think Luke is just being nice. In fact, he seems to be nice to everyone, including you." Dove's cheeks reddened. "But that's all he's doing with me, being nice. Besides, Martin's handsome in his own way, although he is a little thin. But he's pleasant to be around."

Lucinda peered at her friend. "Do I detect feelings for Luke?"

Pink colored Dove's cheeks. "I do like him, but it's a hopeless cause with his mother's feelings toward Indians. I doubt any young man in Barton Creek will want to court me."

"Oh, Dove, that can't be true. You are much too pretty to be ignored." Despite her words, Lucinda feared the truth in Dove's words. The boys may be attracted but would think twice about courting her.

What about Luke? She'd have to be even more careful with her actions and words in Luke's presence in public to discourage him. She didn't want to add anything to further the notion that he may be her beau. Luke would be great for Dove. Oh dear, things with men could get so complicated.

After they finished their tea and cookies, the girls chatted amiably over their handiwork for the next few hours.

Lucinda held up the shawl. "I think it's all done now. It's a good thing too because I must be getting back. I've already kept Jake from his chores long enough."

Mrs. Morris joined them. "I see you're finished. Let me wrap it for you so Mellie won't know what you've been working on."

Lucinda pulled on her heavy jacket and picked up her gloves. "It's been such a good visit, Dove. If I don't get to see you before, have a merry Christmas."

Mrs. Morris returned to the room and handed over a parcel wrapped in brown paper. "Here's the shawl for your aunt. I know she'll be proud to wear it."

Lucinda hugged Mrs. Morris. "Thank you so much. I think Aunt Mellie will be truly surprised."

"I'm glad you could come. Visit again soon. And tell your aunt and uncle I said merry Christmas."

Jake waited for her outside. He helped her mount her horse, secured the bundle for her, then swung up onto Baron.

She rode beside him on the way home, searching her mind for how to reach out to him and tell him of God's love. Finally she said, "I can't stop thinking about your losses. I thought I had lost everything when I lost my parents, but you…"

He didn't answer for a moment, but then he turned his darkened eyes to her. "I can't understand how God could be so cruel as to take the ones I loved most away from me."

His words sent slivers of pain through her heart. How could she explain? She breathed a prayer for guidance. "God isn't cruel, Jake. Things do happen that cause pain and grief, but God grieves and suffers with us. He knew the hairs on our head and the number of the days of our lives before we were even born."

"But why would He let us suffer so? My ma was in such great pain before she died. I'll never understand that."

"I know it's hard. At first I didn't want to believe Mama and Papa were gone, but God gave me comfort and peace. He never left me alone."

Jake shook his head. "I sure feel like He's left me alone. God must not like me to let all these things happen."

"No, that's not true. God loves you now and always will. He loved you enough to have His Son die for you. You have to believe that."

His laugh carried derision and unbelief. "Yeah, He surely loves all the bad things I've done and died for them."

What bad things could he have done? She'd seen only good in him. "There's not anything so bad that God can't forgive it."

"Even drinking and gambling?"

"Yes, even that." Although she had not known any men who did such things, those activities didn't suit the Jake she knew.

A cloud seemed to descend over his face as though he hid

some secret. She wished he'd tell her more about himself, but she was afraid to know what he might be hiding.

"I do know one thing, Jake. God has a purpose and a plan for our lives. I think of all the wonderful things I would have missed if I hadn't come here. Even though I still miss my parents, God knew exactly what He was doing and what I needed. He took care of me."

"Is that what puts that peace in your eyes that I see?"

"Yes, it is, and you can have it too. Try it, Jake. Trust in God, and let Him help you. He won't let you down."

Again he rode in silence for a few moments. He stopped his horse and leaned forward, resting his forearms on the horn. "You've given me something more to think about, Lucinda." He paused, then a grin lighted his face. "I'm sorry for the reason you had to come, but it's good that God sent you out this way."

This time his words made her heart sing. Maybe she wouldn't leave at all. Barton Creek and the people she'd met were becoming more like home every day. "You know what, Jake? I think maybe this is where I belong."

"I reckon it might be." He nudged his horse back to move on up the trail.

He wanted her to stay on the ranch, and although it shouldn't, the idea pleased her. Now she truly looked forward to Christmas and his being a part of the celebrations.

Chapter 16

On Christmas Eve Jake joined with the family to decorate the tree Ben had set up in a corner of the great room. Flames danced bright orange and gold in the fireplace, and the love in the Haynes family shone as brightly as the glass ornaments Mrs. Haynes pulled from their boxes. Lucinda stood beside him weaving strands of popped corn through the limbs.

Since that day coming home from the Morris ranch, she had not spoken more than a few words with him. Being close to her now with the scent of lavender every time he breathed caused his insides to shake like leaves in the wind.

Matt scrambled to the back side of the tree to help. When he stretched out his hand with the popcorn strand, both Jake and Lucinda reached for it at the same moment. His hand hovered over hers for a moment, the warmth from it coursing up his arm straight to his heart. Her cheeks reddened, but she didn't pull away.

Her brown eyes appeared luminous in the light from the kerosene lamps, and at that moment he realized his love and would do anything to protect her from danger, even give his own life.

For the first time he began to understand what Ben and Lucinda had tried to help him see about a man who loved people so much that He was willing to die for them.

The idea overwhelmed him, and Jake moved his hand and

stepped away from her to place the strand up higher on the limbs. Verses he had read ran through his mind. Things Ben and Matt said now made sense. He breathed deeply. He'd never smell the fragrance of pine again without thinking of this moment.

The look in Jake's eyes as he gazed at Lucinda worried Ben. The boy's love glowed as brightly as the flames of the candles on the table. Ben wanted the best for the two young people who had come to mean so much to him, but such a chasm separated them. Mellie may not agree with him, but he had to do something to keep the two apart, at least until he could talk more with Jake about his spiritual condition.

Mellie strolled in bearing a tray laden with steaming cups of hot cocoa. As the others gathered around to grab the chocolate and a few cookies, Ben picked up the family Bible from which he always read the Christmas story. He opened it to the Book of Isaiah and wrote down a few words, then marked the passages with a bookmark. He'd have Lucinda do the reading tonight.

Ben joined in drinking the cocoa and munching on Mellie's Christmas cookies. After a few minutes, he set his cup down and motioned for Lucinda to follow him to the doorway.

Lucinda's green dress brought out the auburn highlights in her hair. She favored her mother to the point that if Ben hadn't known better, he could be speaking with Amanda Carlyle Bishop instead of her daughter.

He swallowed the lump in his throat. "My dear, I want you to read the Christmas story for us tonight. You're a new arrival and special new member of our family, and I think it would be fitting for you to lead us." He handed her the Bible. "I noted a few verses in Isaiah. Read them first, then the story from Luke."

Lucinda grasped the Bible. "But Uncle Ben, don't you always do this?"

He covered her small hands with his own rough, callused ones. "Yes, but this Christmas Eve I believe you should have the honor."

She hesitated only a moment before nodding. "I'll read the story for you because you have done so much for me." When she read one of the verses he had chosen, Lucinda looked up at him with a sparkle in her eye. "Oh, this is one of my favorites and so appropriate for tonight."

Ben patted her arm. "I know you'll do a wonderful job. Come, let's join the others."

They made their way back to the family gathered near the fireplace. Ben picked up his mug of cocoa, and his gaze settled on Mellie. He needed no words to convey his love for his wife. Tonight would be special, and she, as so many times in the past, understood and returned his silent message with a pleased expression and a sparkle in her eye.

⤝

Lucinda's stomach churned with doubt. Would she be able to read the story as effectively as she knew her uncle could? At his signal, she opened the book and began reading from the ninth chapter of Isaiah, verse six: "For unto us a child is born, unto us a son is given: and the government shall be upon his shoulder: and his name shall be called Wonderful, Counsellor, The mighty God, The everlasting Father, The Prince of Peace."

Lucinda held the place with her finger. "This is the prophecy that told us of Jesus's birth many hundreds of years before He came." She peered at her uncle. "Uncle Ben has asked me to read from another part of Isaiah. It tells us why Jesus was born." At first she had been puzzled by her uncle's choice, but now she

148

realized what he had chosen would be directed toward Jake.

"God had a purpose for Jesus's human birth. He grew as a man and experienced the same things as other men. He knew the reason for His coming. Isaiah told us about it too. In the fifty-third chapter of his book, verses five and six, Isaiah wrote, 'But he was wounded for our transgressions, he was bruised for our iniquities: the chastisement of our peace was upon him; and with his stripes we are healed. All we like sheep have gone astray; we have turned every one to his own way; and the Lord has laid on him the iniquity of us all.'"

❧

Jake stood away from the group as Lucinda read. Her words pierced his heart. The child had been born just as the prophet had said. Angels heralded His birth. That part he knew from all the years of celebrating Christmas. What he had not been able to understand before became clear to him in that moment.

A door in his heart opened. This man Jesus loved him enough to die no matter how bad his sin had been. *O Jesus, forgive me for not understanding, forgive me for not believing You could love me, and forgive me for what I've done. I want You to be a part of my life now.*

Although peace filled his heart, a burden still weighed it down. Lucinda finished reading and closed the Bible. Ben prayed, and Jake squeezed his eyes shut. What was he supposed to do now?

Tell the truth, and trust Me to take care of you.

Jake's eyes flew open. Who had spoken to him? Everyone around him sat with heads bowed listening to Ben's prayer. He thought his heart would burst with the desire to make his life right. It had to be God speaking. He had no choice but to obey.

As soon as Ben uttered his "amen," Jake faced him. "Mr. Haynes, I need to speak with you a moment. In private."

Ben's eyes held love in them. A lump formed in Jake's throat, and fear wormed its way through his veins. What would Ben say when he learned the whole truth? Would scorn replace the gleam of happiness?

When they were out of earshot of the others, Jake inhaled deeply and let his breath out slowly. "I understand what you've been trying to tell me, and I asked Jesus to forgive my sins tonight."

Ben clapped him on the shoulder. "Jake, son, that's wonderful. It's what Mellie and I have been praying for all these months." He turned to lift his hand to the others.

Jake grabbed Ben. "No, wait. I have to tell you more. It may change how you feel about me."

Ben peered at Jake but remained silent.

"I killed a man down in Texas." There, he'd said it.

After the first shock of disbelief flashed across his face, Ben said simply, "Tell me about it, son."

Jake recounted the whole story. "I had been living out on my own for several months but always had Aunt Josey and Uncle Earl to come home to. After they and Carrie died, my life had no meaning or purpose. I was seventeen and without a family, so I left the ranch under the care of the foreman and took out on my own.

"I drifted around about a year making money playing cards and working in a stable or two in different towns. I was pretty good at cards, but one night about a year ago I got into a card game in a saloon down in Rio Alto, Texas. I shouldn't have been in a place like that, but I needed money. The poker game seemed like a good place to get it. The problem came when I saw one of the men cheating. He had an extra card, and I caught him putting it in his hand. When I called him on it, he drew a gun, but I was younger and faster and shot first. He fell backward with blood staining his chest."

Ben nodded. "What did you do then?"

"I ran. I got on my horse and headed north and didn't stop until I was far away. I don't know if they sent a posse after me."

Ben's lips set in a grim line. "This does need to be resolved, so what do you propose to do now?"

Facing what he'd done might cost him his life, but now that Ben knew the truth, complete peace filled every part of his being and lifted the weight in his heart. God would take care of him. "Sir, I must return to Texas and face the consequences of what I've done."

"Yes, you should. I can't condone what you did, but I love you like my own son, and I will try to help you." Ben paused before he continued. "Let's go into town and talk to the sheriff. He can give us a better idea of what to do from here."

His hand grasped Jake's shoulder again. "Right now, though, we have Christmas to celebrate."

Ben turned to the group still sitting around the fire. "Jake has some wonderful news. He's a new believer tonight. What better gift could he give Jesus than his life?"

At first, everyone sat in stunned silence. Then Mellie jumped up and ran to hug him. Tears spilled from her eyes. "Oh, my dear boy, how we've prayed for just such a thing."

Over her shoulder his gaze locked with Lucinda's. A light shone where he had never seen it before. It gave him hope like he'd never known. Monk, Hank, and Matt shook his hand, but Becky grabbed him and hugged him.

Joy filled his soul. Tonight and tomorrow he'd bask in his newfound faith. But soon he'd have to put that faith to the test.

Chapter 17

*O*n Christmas Day, everyone feasted on ham, sweet potatoes, and all the trimmings. After the large afternoon meal, Jake wanted only to retire to the bunkhouse for a nap, but he stayed to have more time with Lucinda.

Her golden brown eyes fairly sparkled as she spread her skirt to sit near the fire. Her smile meant more than it ever had now. "I'm so happy for you. Your decision last night is the best gift of the day for all of us."

Jake swallowed hard. He wanted to remember every minute with her when he made the long trip back to Texas. "Thank you, Miss Lucinda. If I'd known how good it'd make me feel, I'd a done this a long time ago."

"Peace like no other fills your life when you become a believer." She furrowed her brow and leaned forward. "You do understand that bad things can still happen, don't you?"

He knew more than Lucinda could ever guess. "I do, but now I know God will take care of whatever comes." If it were not true, he'd never be able to make the trip back to Texas.

Lucinda handed a cup of hot mulled cider to Jake and smiled. "I made plenty of cookies for everyone, and I promise you they are not salty but quite good if I say so myself."

Jake bit into one, and to his delight, the cookie tasted sweet with a hint of cinnamon. Perfect in his estimation, just like the girl who baked it.

Ben joined them and drew on his pipe, then let the smoke drift upward as he exhaled. "Tomorrow Jake and I are going into town on some business. We'll leave after breakfast."

Mrs. Haynes leaned forward. "Ah, it's Saturday, and I could use a trip in to replenish supplies. I want to see the Christmas decorations one more time too."

Jake's breath caught in his throat. How would he explain his mission if the women tagged along? He wouldn't be able to bear the expression on Lucinda's face when she learned of his fate from her uncle.

To Jake's surprise, Ben accepted his wife's request. "Tomorrow looks like it'll be a fine day for a ride into town. You can visit with your friends, Mellie."

Mrs. Haynes clapped her hands. "That means we can also check on the plans for the special services at church on Sunday." She glanced toward Jake.

Before she could speak again, Ben cleared his throat. "That's fine, Mellie, but we can talk of that later." He beckoned to Jake. "I must have a few words with you. Let's go out to the barn."

With dread in his heart, Jake followed Ben. Had Ben changed his mind about tomorrow? Would his boss make him go to the sheriff alone? Questions churned in his mind, and his courage weakened.

When they entered the building, Ben stopped. "Son, I know what we agreed to yesterday, and I intend to keep my promise and go with you, but there's something else you need to do." He paused a moment. "You have to tell Lucinda yourself what is going on and why you won't be coming back with us."

Jake's heart fell to the pit of his stomach. Every ounce of courage drained away. "I...I can't do that. I don't want to see the look on her face."

"I know, but if you don't, she's going to be hurt even more. I can't let that happen."

"What will I say?" Fear filled him, and he longed for the peace and serenity of this morning.

"The weather is good today, so ask her to ride with you. God will help you know when the time is right, and He'll give you the words to say."

"What if she doesn't want to go out this afternoon?"

Ben laughed. "Oh, she will, she will." He strode back to the house.

Jake walked over to Baron and stroked his mane. "Well, old boy, we're going for a ride." Before he reached for his equipment, he bowed his head against the horse. "Lord, I know this is the right thing to do, but I'm scared. I haven't known You long enough to understand how to handle my problems."

Trust Me. I will not forsake you or leave you.

Lucinda spoke at his side. "Jake, Uncle Ben said you wanted to see me."

He swerved around. She wore her riding clothes. "Lucinda! How long have you been here?"

"Not long. I saw that you might be praying, and I didn't want to disturb you."

He swallowed hard. "Oh." He pulled Baron's cinch tight. "Since the sun is out, I thought you might want to ride with me. I have some things I need to tell you."

How quickly her smile would change when she heard his story.

"I changed into my riding outfit in hopes you'd want to do that. You finish Baron, and I'll saddle Misty."

Lucinda hurried to Misty's stall and reached for the bridle. "I love this horse. Thank you for picking her for me. She's perfect."

Jake joined her to lift the saddle from its perch. "With your training back east, I thought you two would fit. I'm glad I was right." He hefted the saddle over Misty's back, then stepped away to let Lucinda finish the task.

Awhile later they rode by the creek. The icy water rippling in its course soothed his nerves. The only sound came from the *clip-clop* of the horses' shoes on the hard-packed ground. Late afternoon sunshine warmed their backs.

Lucinda raised her eyes toward the sky. "I've grown to love this country. There's so much space. Back home houses are crowded close together, and the streets are narrow. The only trees grow in the parks and out in the country. Here it seems like I can see hills, flatlands, and trees that go on forever."

"It's a grand country all right, but I do miss the hills of central Texas where I grew up." He had to muster up the courage to speak soon. In a short time the sun would set, and he didn't want to ride back in the dark.

He pulled up on his reins. "Let's stop here for a minute and walk." He dismounted and helped her down. Jake held the reins of both horses lightly. He wanted to take her hand in his but restrained himself.

They strolled in silence a few yards before Jake cleared his throat. "Lucinda, what I have to tell you is hard, but you need to hear it from me. Mr. Haynes asked me to tell you."

Her eyes opened wide with a touch of fear. He longed to take her in his arms and hold her but instead clenched his fists at his sides. Then the story spilled forth up to the point of the shooting. Fear changed to disbelief as her hand covered her mouth.

"So, you see, Lucinda, I killed a man, and I'm turning myself in to the marshal in Barton Creek."

☙

Lucinda's heart thumped. Killed a man? Why hadn't he said anything before now? She stepped back. "I don't understand. You killed someone?"

He then told her what happened after the shooting. Her anger grew not toward Jake but toward the circumstances that led him to commit murder. Then her love for him bubbled to the surface, and she threw her arms around Jake's neck. She buried her face in his chest. "Oh no, this can't be true. Not now." Then just as suddenly she stepped back. Heat filled her face. How could she have been so brazen? She raised her eyes to gaze into his, surprise clearly displayed there.

His jaw tensed, and a vein pulsed in his neck. A deep sorrow settled into his blue eyes. "I'm so sorry, Lucinda. I know what I did is a great shock, and I should have told you long ago. I didn't want anyone to know that part of my past. But now I couldn't live with myself if I didn't go back and face my crime. I'd be living a lie."

She understood but didn't want to accept his words. She bit her lip before responding. "God did forgive you, and surely Uncle Ben can put in a good word for you, seeing as how you're a Christian now. He can make it right." And she believed that with all her heart.

He didn't answer but turned and walked a few steps away. She ran to his side and grasped his arm. "I know you must face the consequences of your actions, but it's so hard."

"That I know, and that's the reason for the trip tomorrow."

The sadness in his eyes took her breath away and broke her heart into slivers. He spoke the truth, but her body ached with the thought she may never see him again after tomorrow.

"Please let me go with you into town. I don't want to say good-bye at the ranch."

"That's up to your aunt and uncle. If they think it's wise, then all right. Just don't get your hopes up."

He hadn't yet said he cared about her. Lucinda fought back the tears filling her eyes. She gazed at him and let all the love she'd garnered in the past few months shine through her eyes. "If you're leaving, then I want you to know how much I care about you and what happens to you."

Jake reached out his arms and gathered her close to him. Her head rested under his chin, and his breath stirred her hair. Tingles of electricity coursed through her body. Tears streamed down her face.

"Lucinda, I never thought I'd find a girl like you. It's almost like a cruel joke."

If Jake hadn't given his heart and life to the Lord, he wouldn't be leaving her. But even as that thought filled her mind, she recalled the promises of God she'd read over and over again. She stepped back and grasped Jake's hands.

"God has a plan in all this," she told him, earnestness filling her words. "He told us that all things work out for good for those who love Him, and you and I love Him. He's going to make it right. He's never let me down, even when Mama and Papa died. We have to trust Him."

"I will try," Jake said. But doubt and fear colored his voice.

Determination boosted her faith. "Jake, you're coming back to us. I believe that with all my heart. I'll never stop praying for you. Remember this, every morning when you wake up, I'll be here on the ranch praying for your safety."

He pulled her close again. "Knowing that, I can face anything they do to me."

They stood quietly for a few minutes. She listened to the

steady rhythm of his heart and memorized the beat. She wanted to remember every detail of this time and place.

Finally Jake released her. "The sun's going down. Time to go back. We don't want them to worry about us."

The trip seemed much shorter than the one to the creek earlier. Lucinda rode as close to Jake's horse as safety allowed. She memorized every feature of his face so that when she prayed, it would be there for her.

⚓

Mellie paced across the porch. Where were those children? They'd been gone nearly an hour. She still couldn't believe what Ben told her earlier. Jake couldn't have killed anybody on purpose. It had to be an accident or something. Maybe the boy didn't remember it all as it really happened. Maybe he'd made a mistake.

She peered toward the horizon and spotted the two riding in. "Ben, they're coming." She didn't wait for him but hurried out to the corral to meet them. Ben ran across the yard to join her.

They stood in silence, her hands clasped firmly in Ben's. When Jake and Lucinda stopped their mounts, Mellie ran toward them. As soon as Lucinda stepped down from Misty, Mellie grabbed her in a tight hug.

"I'm so sorry this happened." After a moment she stepped back. "Come, let's go inside out of the cold. They'll tend the horses."

She turned to Jake and swept her fingers across her cheeks to wipe away her tears. What could she say to this boy she had grown to love like a son? She grasped his arm. "We love you."

Ben took hold of Misty's reins. "I'll take care of Misty. Jake and I need to talk some more."

Mellie kept her arm around Lucinda as they entered the house. While Lucinda and Jake were out riding, she'd told Becky and Matt the news about Jake. Now they grabbed Lucinda and wanted to hear more about Jake.

Mellie tied on her apron and proceeded to heat the milk to make cocoa. She had to keep busy. This would be one Christmas the Haynes family would never forget.

Chapter 18

*T*he trip into Barton Creek took no more than the usual time, but to Jake, it had never been shorter. Lucinda sat in the wagon with her aunt and cousin while Ben drove. Matt, Hank, and Monk rode alongside. No one talked, but the silence spoke louder than any words they could have uttered.

Last night Ben had warned Jake that he must cut off all contact with Lucinda until his situation was resolved. Every minute with Lucinda only made the reality more painful. The quicker he turned himself in, the sooner he could be out of her life. She deserved much more than he could ever offer her.

He stared at Lucinda's rigid back. The turmoil in his heart fought with the peace of his soul. His love for her threatened to tear him apart, but he set his mind on the only thing that could see him through the days ahead, his newfound faith.

Although he longed to hold Lucinda in his arms one more time, perhaps even to kiss her, he must not let his thoughts go in that direction. Temptation to do that loomed last night, but he couldn't bring himself to hurt her further than she had already been. A few weeks ago he would have blamed God for separating him from those he had come to love, but now he understood God's love and protection sometimes brought heartache. Like his having to leave, but for that he had no one to blame but himself. God hadn't put the gun in his hand or caused him to pull the trigger. He was forgiven, but he still must face the consequences of what he'd done.

Lucinda must have sensed his thoughts as she cut a glance toward him. Tears glistened on her cheeks. He turned away, not able to cope with the feelings conveyed by that one look. He swallowed back the grief rising in his throat.

The buildings of Barton Creek appeared on the horizon. Only minutes remained before he'd be sitting in a jail cell.

When they reached the main street, Ben stopped the wagon. He stepped down and motioned for Jake to do the same. His feet hit the hard-packed ruts, and he breathed deeply. Matt, Hank, and Monk dismounted and joined Jake in his walk to the sheriff's office. Jake didn't look at Lucinda again, but her face would be etched permanently in his mind.

When they walked through the door, Deputy Claymore stood and stretched out his hand. "Good morning, Ben. What brings you to Barton Creek today?"

Ben grasped Claymore's hand. "Morning, Micah. My friend Jake Starnes here has a problem."

Jake cleared his throat. "I shot and killed a man down in Texas. I'm here to turn myself in."

The deputy scratched the stubble of gray-streaked whiskers on his chin, and he peered at them. "Jake Starnes, you say?" He shuffled through a stack of papers on his desk. "I haven't seen a warrant or a wanted poster come across my desk. When did this happen?"

"About nine months ago in Rio Alto along the Colorado River. We were in a card game, and one of the men was cheating. I shot him before he could shoot me. I ran out of there before they could get the law on me. Name of the man was Henry Girard."

Claymore grabbed the keys from their hook by his desk. "Marshal Derreck won't be here until next week, but if what you say is true, you have to be under arrest until then." He grasped Jake's arm, but compassion filled the lawman's eyes.

Ben shook his head. "You could release him to me, and he could stay with us until then. He's like part of our family."

Jake cut in. "Let's get this done. Lock me up now, and I'll wait here for the marshal." He couldn't return to the ranch. This jail is where he belonged.

The deputy jangled the keys. "I have no alternative except to put you back there. Follow me." He led the way to the cells and opened one. He moved back and waited for Jake.

Monk and Hank stood behind their boss. Jake set his jaw for this one last moment with them. "Thank you for all you've done for me. I'll never forget how you took me in as a stranger." He glanced at his two friends. "And thank you for showing me the ropes and being patient while I learned."

Monk twitched his mustache. "Didn't take much learning for you to get the hang of things. You already knew most of it."

Hank clamped his hand on Jake's shoulder. "We'll miss you. And I'll watch over Miss Lucinda for you. We'll keep her safe."

Finally he turned to Ben. He found nothing but love shining in the man's eyes. "I'm so sorry to disappoint you and cause your family this grief. I can't begin to thank you for all you've done for me."

Ben grasped his shoulder. "No need to, son. We love you and will never stop praying for you."

That promise and the one from Lucinda were all he needed to keep him headed in the right direction. He shook hands with Ben, who nodded, then turned and left with Monk and Hank.

How different Jake's life would be now if he had met them last year, before this all happened. Jake stepped into the cell.

The door clanged shut, and the key grated in the lock. Deputy Claymore dangled the ring on his fingers. "Ben Haynes must think a lot of you, young man. He likes people, but not many merit the loyalty of that rancher." He turned and headed back to his desk.

Jake sank onto the cot in the corner. His hands drooped between his knees. Ben Haynes had been good to him. His biggest regret at the moment was that he had let down the man who had become like a father. He hated the disappointment he'd seen in Ben's eyes Christmas afternoon, and Mellie's concern sent more pain to stab his heart.

Both of these paled, however, with the realization of Lucinda's love for him. Joy and pain melded into a regret he would never forget. With her image engraved on his heart and the Lord riding with him, he'd face whatever waited in Texas.

⁂

Lucinda followed Aunt Mellie into the general store. The tinkling bell above the door reminded her of the first day she arrived in Barton Creek. So much had happened in the few short months since then.

Mrs. Anderson greeted them with a wide grin. "Good morning, Mellie. Didn't expect to see you in town today. Figured you'd be home resting after a big day yesterday."

Aunt Mellie moved to the counter and spoke in tones too low for Lucinda to hear. She turned to gaze out the window and down toward the jail. What was happening there? Her heart ached to see Jake again. The days ahead looked as bleak as those just after her parents' death.

A voice from behind called her name, and her shoulders jerked. She turned to find Luke Anderson with a small brown bag in his hand. "Merry Christmas, Miss Bishop." He offered her the bag. "I remembered how you bought peppermints the first time you were here, so I thought you might like these."

His gesture touched her. She grasped the candy bag in her hand. "Thank you, Luke."

"My pleasure. Will you be in church tomorrow?"

"Yes, most definitely." Praying for Jake in church as well as at home would be a priority in the coming weeks.

Aunt Mellie waved to her. "Come, Lucinda. Help me select materials for a few sewing projects."

"Excuse me, Luke. I must help Aunt Mellie."

"Of course. I'll be looking for you tomorrow." He stepped back and returned to the task of restocking a shelf.

She joined her aunt at the counter for sewing supplies. She selected yarn and fabric for sewing during the days when the weather prohibited outdoor activity.

Her hands made choices, but her mind lingered on Jake and what would happen to him now. She knew little of the laws concerning punishment for a crime like murder, but judging from last night's talk, death most probably awaited Jake in Texas. The black cloud of uncertainty cast its shadow on her heart.

The bell tinkled again, and Lucinda gathered up materials for purchase. Uncle Ben waited at the counter. The dire expression of sadness on his face caused her to drop her sewing supplies.

He stepped toward her then stopped. "He's down in jail," he told her in a low voice. "The marshal can't take him to Texas until sometime next week."

Lucinda's hand covered her mouth. "Oh." She grieved to think of Jake all alone in the jail cell. "May I see him?"

"That's not a good idea. It wouldn't be proper, and it will only make parting more difficult." He reached for her hands.

Lucinda shrank back then fled outside. Wagons and buggies filled the streets with townspeople going about their business as usual. Any other day the sound of people calling greetings to her and the general hubbub of activity would have interested her, but at this moment nothing mattered but seeing Jake one more time.

She glanced over at the marshal's office. Her throat tightened, and all air squeezed from her lungs. Jake sat inside that building in a cell. A deep breath helped, but she still gasped for air. As much as she wanted to move, her feet wouldn't cooperate. Seeing him like that would make matters worse. Instead, she must concentrate on those last moments together by the creek and then his final words before he went back to the bunkhouse last night. They were forever engraved on her heart.

I love you, but we both know my future is not in Barton Creek. I don't know when or if I will ever return, and if I don't come back, I want you to promise me that you will go on with your life here.

Lucinda had finally promised, but her heart would go on loving him no matter who she might meet in the future. Tears blurred her vision. The chill in her soul came not from the temperature but from the despair settled there. She had always imagined murderers as evil, mean persons, but Jake didn't fit that at all.

The bell jangled behind her. Pain coursed through her veins, a pain no medical relief could cure. Uncle Ben stepped up behind her and placed his hands on her shoulders. "I'm sorry. We tried so hard to keep you from being hurt."

She turned to him. "Why is God being so unfair? Why did He let this happen?"

Uncle Ben held her close and patted her back. "I don't know. I just don't know. We can only cling to His promise to work things out for good."

She wanted to believe him, but for the moment, she couldn't see how anything good could come from Jake being in prison, facing death.

Chapter 19

*J*ake hunkered down in his saddle to warm himself against the cold wind blowing across his back. Mr. Derreck, the federal marshal riding with him, hadn't said much since they left Barton Creek before dawn this second day of the New Year. What a way to start the year 1897. Derreck didn't seem too happy with this first task of the New Year either. Being a month or two away from his other duties must be what bothered the lawman.

The handcuffs on his wrists fit tightly under his gloves. At least he had on gloves. If not, his fingers would be frozen by now. He rested his hands on the saddle horn. Broad shoulders, square jaw, and piercing eyes all marked the marshal as someone not to be fooled by any tricks or escape attempts. Not that he planned any. He was through with running.

A blast of frigid air whipped the hair at his neck and sent a freezing chill under his collar. The creak of the saddles and the clop of horseshoes against the hard-packed ground broke the silence.

At least the weather should improve once they entered Texas. Down in the hill country, winter temperatures remained above freezing the majority of the time. But then, Texas weather never followed a plan. A balmy day could become freezing overnight without much warning.

The scene from the fateful evening of the shooting came back more often now that he was headed back to face the outcome of his actions. He had never seen a gunshot wound in a man before, and the sudden, ever-growing burst of red from the man's chest had terrified him.

The marshal slowed. "This will be a good place to stop and rest from the cold for a few minutes. The rocks and that alcove will protect us." The marshal swung down from his mount and waited for Jake to do the same.

Jake's feet hit the frozen ground with a thud, and he steadied himself against his horse. A few minutes later he sat against a rock with his knees pulled to his chest and his arms draped across his legs. As the marshal predicted, the wind didn't whistle or blow as hard in this spot.

The lawman slapped his hands against his arms and rubbed them. "We'll stay here and give the horses a rest." He squatted down beside Jake. "Son, the deputy back in Barton Creek tells me you are a new Christian."

Jake peered from under the brim of his hat. "That's right."

"That's good. I've been a believer myself for close to twenty years. You'll have people praying for you, and that's always a good thing." Marshal Derreck stood and tilted his head toward a group of trees nearby. "I'm going to relieve myself, then you can do the same after I come back. I trust you won't try to escape, but to make sure, I'm taking the horses with me."

Jake could only nod. "I'm not going anywhere." Even as tall as Jake was, the man stood several inches taller and outweighed Jake by a good amount. Size made no difference. He didn't plan to run.

This journey might take longer than he figured with the weather slowing them down. The longer it took, the more time he'd have to think about Lucinda. The love in her eyes on that last night at the ranch gave him comfort and heartache at the same time. How could something so wonderful hurt so much? He'd never been in love, but how else could he explain the emotions of the past week?

Marshal Derreck returned. "With the weather like it is, it may take us a week or so longer than what I thought. Those hills down around that area won't be easy to navigate if there's snow or ice."

After Jake relieved himself, they mounted their horses and set out toward Texas. A picture of Lucinda reading the Bible on Christmas Eve came to mind. He closed his eyes, remembering how the flames from the fireplace cast red highlights into her hair as she spoke. Her hands cradled the Bible with reverence, and she spoke with a tenderness he hadn't heard since his mother told him bedtime stories as a babe. That's the picture of Lucinda he wanted to carry with him always.

Lucinda awoke with a start, the winter dawn reaching its fingers of light into the room. She lay in the silence, her mind rushing ahead to the events of the day. Jake was on his way to Texas with the marshal. She squeezed her eyes closed to shut out the image, but it only intensified.

Silent tears coursed their way down her cheeks. She did nothing to stop them or wipe them away. How could she face a New Year without Jake? Only God could see her through the dark days ahead.

Lucinda turned over in the bed and hugged her pillow. She refused to think about those last Sunday who had muttered in disgust when Uncle Ben had asked the congregation to pray for Jake. She'd pray every day for him as long as she had breath.

In the quiet of the early morning, Lucinda reached for her Bible and sat on the side of the bed. She opened it for her morning devotions.

The pages parted on her lap to the Book of Matthew. Her eyes opened wide as she read the scripture in Matthew chapter twenty-one, verse twenty-two. It seemed to leap off the page. "And all things, whatsoever ye shall ask in prayer, believing, ye shall receive." She sucked in her breath. A promise from God. She must believe that everything would be all right. This promise would be hers from this day on.

Daylight grew brighter in the room. Lucinda closed her Bible and straightened the covers on the bed before heading to the kitchen to help her aunt. Though her heart weighed heavy with grief, hope slid in to ease the worry.

During breakfast, no one mentioned the empty chair where Jake usually sat. Her aunt and uncle spoke very few words, but even those were stilted and terse. She found nothing to say herself.

Monk pushed his chair back. "I'm going to the barn." He stood and stared straight at Lucinda. "We all miss him. Let's admit it then get on with our chores." He turned on his heel and strode from the house.

Uncle Ben dropped his napkin to the table. "He's right. We'll continue to pray for Jake, but we must go on with our life here on the ranch."

Becky sniffed and jumped up to take her plate to the counter by the sink before she left the room.

Lucinda sat still for a few moments as Hank and Uncle Ben said a few words to Aunt Mellie. They continued on outside to start their day. Lucinda waited for Aunt Mellie to speak, but she kept silent. Finally, Lucinda stacked plates left on the table and placed them with other dishes on the countertop.

She worked in silence beside her aunt. Tears filled her eyes as they did Aunt Mellie's. Words would not come.

Aunt Mellie wiped at her eyes with the corner of her apron. "Enough tears. Let's get on with our work. Like Monk said, we miss him and that's that." She worked the handle of the pump with a little more energy than usual.

Lucinda began washing. "We must believe that somehow God is going to work out all of this. Jake told me to think ahead to my future and not about him, but that will be so hard."

"Maybe so, but the boy is right. That is what you must do." Aunt Mellie blinked her eyes. "Well, I'd better get the saddlebags ready for the men."

With Becky off visiting a friend for the morning, Lucinda did both their morning chores. Dove had promised to come for a visit, and Lucinda looked forward to the time with her friend and their sewing projects. Not that she expected to get much done in that department, but having her best friend by her side would take away some of the loneliness creeping into her heart.

Dove and her mother arrived in time for the noon meal. After they ate, Dove and Lucinda sat near the great fireplace in the main room and sorted through the threads in the sewing basket. Aunt Mellie and Mrs. Morris worked together in the kitchen. The blues and purples appealed to Lucinda today, and she selected several lengths to begin a new project.

Lucinda threaded her needle with blue strands. "I found a Bible verse this morning, and I believe it with all my heart. It said that whatever we ask in prayer, believing, we shall receive. I'm going to embroider that as a sampler and hang it in my room as a reminder to pray for Jake."

"I know that verse. It's a good one. Are you praying for his return?"

Lucinda picked up a wooden hoop. "Yes and no. I'm praying for God's will to be done, but I'm also praying that God's will is for Jake to return."

Dove placed her hand on Lucinda's arm. "And what if he doesn't come back?"

The words pierced Lucinda's heart. "I...don't know. I prefer not to think of that now." But no matter how hard she tried, the thought was always there in the dark edges of her mind.

Dove did not reply. She picked up her needlework and began stitching.

Lucinda bit her lip. If she believed that Jake would return someday, then God could make it happen. If He didn't, she would still trust the Lord in everything. With the New Year, a new phase of her life had begun, and this time too would be in God's hands.

<hr>

When the lunchtime dishes were done, Mellie heated water for tea. "I'm so glad you're here today, Emily. Things were a bit gloomy at breakfast this morning."

"I can imagine they were." Emily laid aside her sewing. "I still can't believe you had him here all this time and didn't know about his past."

"He's been like another son to Ben and me. Such a sad background too." Mellie filled the tea ball and set it in the boiling water to steep while she arranged cups and saucers on a tray. "He came to us after he hired on to help Ben with the drive last season. We only learned about his losing his family a month or so ago. Then on Christmas Day he told us the rest."

"Well, we can only pray for him now."

Mellie nodded and poured tea. Someone knocked on the front door. She excused herself to answer it. Lucinda and Dove still sat leaning toward each other as though sharing secrets. The sight brought a smile to Mellie's lips. What a good idea it had been to invite Dove and Emily for a visit today.

She opened the door and gasped in surprise. "Oh, Charlotte,

I wasn't expecting more company. Do come in. Emily Morris and Dove are here."

Charlotte Frankston's nose rose upward. "No, thank you, Amelia. I just came to say that I for one cannot understand how you could have let a murderer live with you for the past months. Why, he could have killed you all in your sleep."

Mellie's heart pounded. *Lord, help me hold my tongue.* "Oh, Charlotte, I don't think so. What happened to Jake was just a set of unfortunate circumstances."

"Still, it's not proper for a Christian family to harbor a criminal like that. It gives our entire town a bad name."

Mellie swallowed hard and clenched her teeth. With every bit of courtesy she could muster, she said, "I'm sorry you feel that way. I had hoped we could count on your prayers for Jake during his journey to Texas."

"Humph. He's going back to get what he deserves. If I'd been in church instead of home seeing to Bobby's cold, I would have let my feelings be known. Good day, Amelia." Charlotte Frankston's skirt swished about her feet as she turned to leave. At the edge of the porch she stopped and turned back to face Mellie. "I don't think it's a good idea for Becky and my Bobby to be friends under the circumstances."

With those parting words, Charlotte Frankston climbed back into her buggy and turned her horses toward town.

Mellie's mouth gaped open. What did that have to do with Jake being here? She bit back the words that threatened to leave her mouth. The nerve of that woman. Being the wife of the town's most prominent citizen didn't give Charlotte Frankston the right to be judge and jury for everyone else.

Emily's hands crossed at her throat. "Was that Charlotte Frankston? She sounded so angry. I couldn't help but overhear."

Lucinda gripped her needlework. "Oh, Aunt Mellie, how could she be so cruel?"

Mellie shook her head and closed the door. "I don't know. We've been friends since the first day we met in Anderson's General Store the day after I moved to Barton Creek."

She headed back to the kitchen and sat with a thud at the table. What caused some people to behave in such a way as Charlotte had? And then to involve the children was just plain cruel.

Emily placed her hand on Mellie's arm. "I'm so sorry that happened. Charlotte and Bea haven't been friendly to me, but I never dreamed Charlotte could be so venomous to someone like you, dear Mellie."

Mellie sipped her tea. The warm liquid calmed her nerves, and the anger subsided, but the hurt remained. How many others felt the same as Charlotte? She tried to remember who had murmured against Jake at the church services. Having even one friend voice her feelings in such a spiteful way created an ache in Mellie's heart. What else could go wrong this day?

Then another knock on the door sounded. She furrowed her brow. "What now?"

Lord, give me strength for whatever lies ahead. She arranged a smile on her face and opened the door. Shock ran through her. Ben's maiden aunt stood on the porch. "Aunt Clara! What in the world are you doing here in Oklahoma?"

Mellie stared at the plump woman before her. Of all people to show up on her doorstep in January, she least expected Ben's aunt Clara from Kansas City.

The woman cocked her gray head toward Mellie. "Well, are you going to invite me in? It's freezing out here."

"Of course, of course. I'm sorry. You just surprised me." Mellie stood back for the woman to enter. One of the young men from the stables in town unloaded trunks and boxes from his wagon. Mellie stared at all the baggage. Aunt Clara directed the boy as to where to put the trunks and boxes.

Lucinda stood close to Mellie. She kept her voice low. "And I thought I had too much. How long does she plan to stay, and who is she?"

Mellie shook her head. "Clara Haynes, Ben's maiden aunt who lives in Kansas City, or at least she did."

Clara marched over to the fireplace. She pulled on the fingers of her gloves to remove them. "At last, warmth. I didn't know you lived so far from town. Goodness me, it took forever to get here."

She nodded at Emily and Dove. "Well, Amelia, are you going to introduce me to your guests?"

"Oh dear, pardon my manners. It's such a shock to see you. Aunt Clara, this is Emily Morris and her daughter, Dove." She reached an arm around Lucinda's waist. "And this is my niece from Boston. She's come to live with us. Lucinda, Emily, Dove, this is Clara Haynes, Ben's aunt."

Aunt Clara unfastened her cloak. "It's nice to meet you, Emily, Dove." She held out the garment and looked around for a place to hang it.

Lucinda stepped forward. "I'll take that for you. It's a pleasure to have you with us." She carried the garment to the hall tree by the front door and hung the cloak over a peg.

The mound of luggage sat stacked by the door. Mellie wished Ben were home. Where would they put Aunt Clara? "Why didn't you let us know you were coming?"

Clara sat down and arranged her skirts. Her round face glowed red from both the cold and the heat from the fireplace. "I would have if you had wire service in this place. I had no idea Ben had moved so far out in the country. Why, I expected wild Indians to attack our wagon at any moment."

Mellie's jaw tightened. "Emily is Cherokee."

Aunt Clara raised her eyebrows. "Is that so? Well, you're dark like them, but you certainly don't look like the savages we saw back in the old days in Kansas." She turned to stare at Lucinda.

"I remember you from one time when I visited my sister in Boston. You were just a little thing then. What are you doing way out here in the middle of nowhere?"

Lucinda's cheeks turned pink. "My parents died, and Aunt Mellie and Uncle Ben are my guardians."

"Really? I'm sorry to hear that. They were lovely people." She glanced toward Mellie. "Our Ben always was one to take care of strays and orphans."

Mellie breathed deeply. With Aunt Clara around, they would know no peace and quiet. The only word she could think of at the moment to describe the elderly woman was fussbudget.

What would Ben think of her sudden arrival? Neither of them had seen Aunt Clara since they left Kansas six years ago. "Did something happen in Kansas City to cause you to travel this far in the middle of winter?"

Aunt Clara waved her lace handkerchief. "Oh no, my dear, I've been lonely this past year since the death of my brother. With all the children grown, I didn't have much reason to stay around, so I decided to visit my nephew in Oklahoma Territory. I packed up enough to stay with you for a while. Of course I had no idea you already had family with you. I thought I'd be here for Christmas but didn't quite make it. I do have gifts for everyone."

"That's all right, Aunt Clara. We have plenty of room." But where could they put the older woman? Matt would have to move to the bunkhouse. She prayed he'd be cooperative. Then another thought occurred. Why hadn't Clara gone to Boston to visit her sister there? She and Aunt Alice had been close until Clara moved to Kansas to live with Ben's mother and father as missionary and teacher and to help take care of Ben and his brothers and sisters after his mother's death.

Mellie blew out her breath. They'd handle this somehow. "Clara, would you like a cup of tea?"

Clara removed her bonnet and shook her silver-gray curls. "No, thank you, but could you show me where I may take a respite? It's been a long trip, and I'm somewhat weary."

"Um, yes, of course." She drew Lucinda aside and kept her voice low to keep Clara from hearing. "Show her to your room until I can take care of making a place for her."

Lucinda nodded. "Yes, ma'am." She held out her hand to Aunt Clara. "If you'll follow me, I'll show you where you might refresh yourself."

Clara smiled. "How sweet of you." She peered at Lucinda. "Why, you look just like your mother with your height and dark hair. I'm really sorry about your parents. Bless their souls."

Lucinda led Clara from the room. "Uncle Ben and Aunt Mellie have been very good to me." She glanced back at Mellie and winked.

Mellie almost giggled aloud but caught herself. Lucinda may be just what they needed to keep Aunt Clara occupied. As sweet as the woman was, she had a tendency to be somewhat nosey and outspoken and repeated herself often.

Mellie turned to Emily and Dove. "I'm sorry for that little reference a few minutes ago. Aunt Clara means well, but sometimes she speaks before she thinks."

Emily laughed and waved her hand. "Oh, I understood. She had no way of knowing we are Indian, and she drew from her own experience."

"You're being kind, but after she gets to know you, she'll be fine. However, I do remember her having a few unpleasant encounters with Indians as a young woman."

"Yes, and those memories die hard, as I'm learning from things that have happened to some of the citizens of Barton Creek."

Lucinda returned. "Aunt Clara is on my bed. She said she needed a little nap before dinner."

Mellie jumped up. "Oh my! Supper! I almost forgot about it."

Emily hurried over for her coat. "It is getting late. Come, Dove. We must get home ourselves and take care of supper for our menfolk too."

Lucinda and Dove hovered to the side and whispered between themselves. Mellie escorted her friend to the door. "Thank you for coming over today. It made things much easier for us. Of course we had no idea we'd have the excitement that came along."

"I'm glad we can be here for you and Lucinda. But with the weather getting colder, I don't imagine we'll make the trip again before the weekend. We'll look for you at church on Sunday."

Mellie stood with Lucinda at the door for a few moments after the women left, but the cold drove them back to the warmth of the hearth. Mellie headed for the kitchen. "At least I have a cobbler already prepared. Desserts are one thing Clara loves."

She stopped and stared at the stack of luggage still in the parlor. "But what in the world are we going to do with all her things?"

⚓

Before dinner that night, Lucinda helped prepare Matt's room for Aunt Clara while he moved his things to the bunkhouse. His attitude amused her. When Aunt Mellie had mentioned it, Matt beamed and said he looked forward to living out there with Hank and Monk. Probably thought it made him more of a man. At sixteen and six feet two inches, he did look like a man. The move would do him some good, as well as clear a place for another relative.

Lucinda smoothed the bedspread and stepped back to let Uncle

Ben and the others bring in Aunt Clara's trunks and valises.

Uncle Ben set down one trunk. "I can't imagine what persuaded Aunt Clara to come west, especially in the winter. Boston is the much more logical place for her. She could have gone all the way by train."

"From talking to her, I believe she just wanted to see how your life out here is. It's really bad in Boston this time of year."

He patted Lucinda's shoulder. "You're right. I didn't think about that. Where is the little lady now?"

"I believe Becky is entertaining her with some tales of what ranch life is like. Do you suppose I should be calling her Aunt Clara too? It's not like I'm blood kin to her."

"I'm sure that will be fine." Then he winked. "She'd have let you know if it wasn't. Aunt Clara does speak her mind. Now let's go have supper."

Lucinda nodded. She'd have to remember that about Aunt Clara. In her experience, limited as it was, frankness in speaking one's opinion could lead to hurt feelings and misunderstandings. She prayed this would not happen with Aunt Clara.

Much to Lucinda's surprise, Aunt Clara accepted Monk and Hank at the dinner table. At first the older woman raised her eyebrows as though to question why the help ate with the family, then she shrugged her shoulders and bowed her head for the blessing. Seated next to her, Aunt Mellie appeared to relax. At least there'd be no misspoken words at supper.

After the meal, Lucinda found herself in the parlor seated by the elderly lady and Becky. Uncle Ben stood near the fireplace preparing his pipe for his evening smoke.

They had opened Aunt Clara's gifts before dinner. Now she clasped her hands in her lap. "I'm sorry, my dear, that I didn't have something for you. If I'd known you were here, I would have brought a gift." She tilted her head toward Uncle Ben. "I must say Barton Creek surprised me. It is somewhat smaller than I expected, but then I really did not know what to expect. I've seen a lot of different things in my years, but this is nothing like Kansas City. "

Lucinda smiled and leaned toward Aunt Clara. "I didn't know what to expect either. Being accustomed to Boston, the primitive feel of the town made me wonder if I had done the right thing by coming west. Now I love Barton Creek and its people."

Aunt Mellie picked up her knitting. "And we're very happy to have Lucinda with us."

Aunt Clara peered at Lucinda. "You are of courting age, are you not?"

"Yes, ma'am. I'll be eighteen in a few months."

Aunt Clara sat back with a satisfied grin. "I thought as much. Seems to me the young men in this town would be scarce." She pursed her lips. "Amelia, how do you ever expect this young lady to get married without any eligible young men around? And that goes for Becky too. I just might have to take them back to Kansas City in the spring to find them suitable mates."

Uncle Ben almost choked on his pipe. "Clara, that's absurd. Becky is barely thirteen. Plenty of time before we need to think of marrying her off. As for Lucinda, I think that is a decision she will need to make for herself."

Becky planted her fists at her waist. "Besides, there are plenty of boys at my school. Bobby Frankston and I are good friends, and I—" She stopped short, and her cheeks turned bright pink.

Lucinda squelched the gasp in her throat. Aunt Mellie's jaw clenched, and her knuckles turned white as she gripped the knitting needles tighter. Her aunt hadn't said anything to Becky about Mrs. Frankston's visit. Lucinda's heart pounded at the thought of telling her cousin she might no longer have a friendship with Bobby. Distaste for Mrs. Frankston and her obnoxious behavior earlier in the day rose like bile. She'd do everything she could to make the news more bearable when Becky found out.

Aunt Clara apparently did not notice the silence from Lucinda and Aunt Mellie. "Why, that's wonderful, Becky." She sat back and tapped her chin with a plump finger. "One thing I do not understand. Why did you choose to be called Becky? Rebecca is a perfectly fine name. At least you didn't ruin it completely by shortening your middle name to Sue instead of Susan."

Becky's eyes opened wide. Lucinda hastened to address Aunt Clara to cover her cousin's embarrassment. "I think everyone has a shortened name. It does save time when you want to call someone."

"Humph, then why aren't you Lucy instead of Lucinda? It is because you are a properly bred young woman and know the rules of society." Aunt Clara raised her eyebrows.

At that moment Lucinda wished with all her heart she had allowed Aunt Mellie to call her Lucy. Now Aunt Clara might think she wanted to be better than other family members.

Aunt Mellie rescued her. "No, that's not the reason. Lucinda had many adjustments to make, and we didn't feel a name change necessary."

Aunt Clara merely "harrumphed" again. Outspoken barely scratched the surface of the woman if her behavior tonight was an indication. If she was like this with family, what might she be with others? Surely she realized how personal some of her comments were. Lucinda swallowed hard. *Oh my, what would Aunt Clara think if she knew about Jake?*

Jake? She hadn't thought about him since this afternoon. With so much going on and Aunt Clara's arrival, she'd had no time to think about where he might be. Lucinda stood. "If you don't mind, I'd like to be excused. I'm rather tired this evening."

Becky jumped up to join her. "Me too. I'm going to bed." She kissed her father and mother good night.

As much as she'd rather be alone, Lucinda understood why Becky wanted to leave. She wrapped her arm around her cousin's shoulder. "Good night, Uncle Ben, Aunt Mellie, Aunt Clara."

Becky plopped on her bed when they reached their room. "Having Aunt Clara here is going to be interesting, to say the least. I barely remember the last time I saw her."

"She is rather blunt with her opinions, isn't she?" Lucinda turned back the covers on her bed.

"That's a polite way of saying she's rude." Becky pulled off her shoes, then unbuttoned her dress.

Lucinda kept quiet and prepared for bed. This evening had been rather mild compared to the ranting this afternoon when Aunt Clara discovered the house had no private room for personal necessities. The picture of Aunt Clara using the necessary building out by the barn brought a giggle to her throat. Of course, with the cold weather, the family used the chamber pots set aside for that purpose in each bedroom.

With the lights finally out, and Becky quiet, Lucinda's thoughts turned to Jake. He certainly wouldn't meet Aunt Clara's standards for a beau, but that didn't matter to Lucinda. She hugged her pillow.

No matter what happened with Aunt Clara, Mrs. Frankston, or anyone else, she would love Jake and pray for him to be safe. And God would bring him back to her if that was His will.

Chapter 20

*T*oday was Sunday, and once again they would have to face the congregation at church. How many would remain loyal to the Haynes family and pray for Jake? Lucinda sighed and dressed in her warmest skirt and shirtwaist.

In the kitchen Aunt Clara sat at the table in her finest.

"Good morning, Aunt Clara. I trust you slept well."

The older woman picked up the blue floral Spode china cup before her. "Yes, I did, even though the wind howled most of the night. I suppose you become accustomed to hearing it."

"Yes, I hardly hear it now." The sight of the flowers on the cup reminded Lucinda of her mother's Italian Blue pattern. Mama and Aunt Mellie had chosen their patterns in Boston when they married. Aunt Clara must be special since Aunt Mellie used the china only on holidays. Aunt Mellie handed her an apron.

"Is your tea satisfactory?" Aunt Mellie held the pot, ready to add more to Aunt Clara's cup.

"Oh, yes, quite." Aunt Clara narrowed her eyes at Lucinda.

"Is that what you plan to wear to church?" Then she leaned back. "Of course, it's probably different out here. But I still like to dress up for services."

Lucinda bit her lip to keep from laughing. Hadn't she felt the same when first arriving in Oklahoma? She knew exactly what Aunt Clara thought. Before Lucinda had opportunity to reply, Becky returned with the eggs, and preparation for breakfast began.

This morning Lucinda didn't miss the raised eyebrows again as Hank and Monk joined them for breakfast, but Aunt Clara smiled at them and nodded her head in greeting. She might not approve of the help eating with family, but at least she curbed her outspoken comments. For a change, Aunt Clara said little during the meal. As soon as she laid down her fork after the last bite, she pushed back her chair. "If you'll excuse me, I must finish preparations for church."

Uncle Ben leaned toward Aunt Mellie. "I wonder what Clara will have to say about our little church."

"No telling, but let's pray for the best." She began stacking dishes for cleaning. "Come, girls, let's get this chore done. We don't want to be late."

After the dishes were done, Lucinda retrieved her cloak and bonnet from the pegs by the door. "Is there anything else I need to do so you can get ready?"

"No, dear, it's all done." Aunt Mellie wiped her hands on a towel then hung her apron on its hook.

Aunt Clara padded in and beamed at Lucinda. "You look lovely, my dear. That hat is most becoming."

"Thank you, but it's really a bonnet. Nothing like your beautiful chapeaux."

Aunt Clara patted her curls under the black velvet hat secured with a pearl hat pin. A large feather waved from the side. "I do hope it's warm in the church. I dislike having to keep my cloak on."

No doubt she wanted to show off her city finery before the women of Barton Creek. Lucinda grasped Aunt Clara's arm and guided her out to the waiting buggy. Uncle Ben had added side curtains to help ward off the cold air. Aunt Mellie and Becky hurried to join them. Uncle Ben assisted Aunt Clara into the backseat and nodded to Becky. "You'll sit up front with your ma and me."

Becky frowned but obeyed. Lucinda winked at her cousin. "At least you'll be quite warm between them."

"But it's more fun in the back talking to you." She climbed up and plopped herself beside her mother.

Uncle Ben hoisted himself into the driver's side. Matt joined them on his horse. Aunt Clara tucked the blanket about her and bobbed her head, the feather dancing with the movement.

"I'm certainly glad to see my nephew values the Lord's Day and makes sure his family is in worship. I worried about that out here in a territory. Wasn't sure you'd even have churches in this place."

"Oh, we have a fine church and a wonderful preacher." Lucinda settled back for the trip and let Aunt Clara expound on the glories of Kansas City.

In the churchyard, everyone hastened to leave the buggy to seek the warmth inside. Lucinda and Becky headed for the building where the younger people met, and the others entered the sanctuary.

Conversation buzzed as she opened the door. Suddenly all talk ceased, and eyes turned in her direction. She knew they must have been talking about Jake. Heat rose in her cheeks.

Dove placed a hand on Lucinda's arm. "We were just talking about Jake and where he might be now." Her dark eyes held welcome warmth.

Lucinda removed her cloak. "I don't have any idea how far Jake could have traveled, but I'm certain the Lord is looking after him."

Heads nodded, and conversation picked up again. All but

Caroline Frankston spoke to Lucinda. The girl, the same age as Matthew, sat with hunched shoulders.

Before the teacher called for their attention, Lucinda slipped to Caroline's side. "I understand, and I don't blame you. Just remember that Jake is God's child and needs our prayers."

Caroline sniffed and nodded her head. "Thank you. Mother can be so stubborn. I really will pray for him." Then her eyes brightened. Matt had entered the room. He sat down behind them, and Caroline's cheeks fairly glowed. Lucinda bit her lip. Another Frankston-Haynes connection to be broken.

Lucinda hugged Caroline before turning her attention to the Bible lesson for the day.

The teacher said, "God keeps His promises. He's given us too many to think about in one morning, but remember this. He tells us He will never forsake us. He will always be with us."

The words comforted Lucinda's soul. God's promises belonged to Jake as they belonged to her. She would cling to that until the day Jake either returned or they received word otherwise.

⚓

The first day on the trail back to Texas went by without incident. Sunday morning dawned with a sharp bite of frost. At least the marshal had been kind in finding a warm place to stop for the night, even if it had been a jail cell. Of course that may have been more for his own good rather than Jake's, but he appreciated it all the same.

Although no snow had fallen, the ground was frozen solid, making the ride precarious. The horses fought to keep solid footing as they approached rougher terrain.

Marshal Derreck stopped at the edge of a small town. The white steeple of a church stood out in the outline of the buildings. "It's the Sabbath and time to worship. We're going to church."

185

He dismounted and helped Jake from Baron, then unlocked the handcuffs. "I don't believe you'll need these inside. I figure you won't try anything during church, and we don't need any questions. When the service is over, we'll be back on the trail."

"Yes, sir, and I thank you for including church in our journey." He massaged his wrists with his gloved hands.

"Couldn't do it any other way. Most folks consider it rather foolish to take the extra time and with a prisoner to boot, but I prefer to believe my prisoners can benefit from the words of the preacher."

Jake climbed the steps and slipped into the back-row pew with Derreck. A few heads turned to stare. Derreck tipped his hat and then removed it, and Jake did the same. Simple in style, the whitewashed walls and plain furniture emphasized the beauty of the polished wood pulpit. Peace filled Jake's heart.

After the service, they didn't wait around to greet the pastor or speak with any members. Marshal Derreck pulled Jake in front of him and strode from the church. Jake mounted Baron, and Derreck fastened the cuffs once again.

The marshal did turn to wave at a few of the members who exited the church and stared after them. Jake nodded toward several who waved. He wondered if they would have been as friendly if they'd known he wore handcuffs and was guilty of murder.

"We've a longer ride ahead of us because of the weather, but we'll stop in for worship wherever we find a town with a church. I've seen you reading your Bible at night. Keep doing it, and you'll be all right."

Jake figured God to be big enough to be wherever His children were. How would the Haynes family be greeted this morning? Surely everyone in town knew about his circumstances. He prayed no one would blame or accuse Ben because of his kindness.

Dove would remain Lucinda's friend no matter what others might say or do. The Indian girl's loyalty ran deep, and Lucinda would need it in the days ahead.

᪣

After the services, Mellie cringed and clenched her teeth at the sight of Charlotte Frankston. Charlotte and Bea Anderson had sent piercing looks of accusation her way all through the services.

As the two approached, Aunt Clara tugged at Mellie's sleeve. "Who are those women? They look bitter enough to sour every creek around here."

What an apt description, but before Mellie could answer, Charlotte stood before them. "Good morning, Mrs. Haynes. I see you have a guest."

Mrs. Haynes? What happened to Mellie? She breathed deeply and pasted on a smile. "This is Ben's aunt Clara Haynes, visiting from Kansas City."

"Oh, I see."

Mellie bit her lip to keep from laughing. Charlotte's nose actually twitched when she spoke. Mellie grasped Clara's arm. "She'll be here through the winter, and we're delighted to have her."

Bea Anderson joined them. "Well, I must say she's much better company than that Jake you've had recently. Letting a murderer live with you and not even telling anyone about it. Why, he could have killed all of you in your sleep, or any of us in town for that matter."

Mellie's blood rose, and heat filled her face. Bea was worse than Charlotte to speak in front of Aunt Clara. The poor woman's mouth gaped open with shock written all over her face.

Charlotte and Bea turned on their heels and, with a toss

of their heads, hurried off. Aunt Clara grabbed Mellie's arm. "What are they talking about? I heard the preacher praying for someone named Jake, but I had no idea he had anything to do with your family."

"I'll tell you on the way home." Just at that moment, Becky ran up and threw her arms around Mellie.

Mellie hugged her daughter tight and glanced over Becky's shoulder. Bobby Frankston stood near his family with a forlorn look on his face. Mellie stiffened when Charlotte grabbed her son's arm and shoved him up into their buggy. Caroline slumped in her seat as Matt strode toward his family with clenched fists.

Becky raised a tear-stained face and peered at Mellie. "Ma, Bobby said he couldn't be friends with me anymore because we let a murderer live at the ranch."

Mellie hugged her tighter. "His parents don't understand about Jake like we do. As far as they're concerned, he killed a man and is evil."

Becky pressed her head against Mellie's shoulder. "It's just not fair. I didn't do anything."

Matt swung a leg over his horse. "Quit your whining, and get in the buggy."

Mellie bit back the scolding words for Matt. He hurt as much as Becky.

Aunt Clara clucked her tongue. "Dear me, this sounds more sinister than I thought. What were you thinking to let a killer live with you?"

Mellie assisted Becky up onto the front seat. "It's not like that at all. Here comes Ben. I'll explain everything on the way home."

Lucinda hurried across the yard and climbed up to her place without a word. Mellie climbed up to her seat. If Aunt Clara didn't understand about Jake, Mellie just might be as outspoken as the older woman.

When they rode out of town, Aunt Clara crossed her arms. "Now tell me just what is happening around here. I've never seen such goings on at church before."

Mellie took a deep breath. "We had a young man hired on to help Ben and the others with the trail drive. He seemed so sad and lonesome that Ben asked him to stay on for the winter. The boy wasn't a Christian, so Ben and I told him all about God. At Christmas he gave his heart to the Lord. He's really a sweet boy, but he was lost and confused. After he accepted Jesus, he told us about an incident in Texas."

When Mellie finished the story, Aunt Clara sat with her lips in a firm line for a few minutes before speaking. "I know everyone thinks I'm nosy and a bit blunt, so I'll just speak my mind now. I don't understand why you haven't told me before now, but it seems to me that when a child comes to the Lord, that's a time for rejoicing. God's in the forgiving business. I'd say it took a great deal of courage for him to own up to his mistake and be willing to go back and face his punishment."

Lucinda's face brightened, and she hugged Aunt Clara. "Oh, thank you. I know you'll pray for Jake's soul. He's so...so...I don't know how to explain it."

Aunt Clara's eyes narrowed, and a slight grin graced her lips. "I see, and I take that to mean the young man means a lot to you. Looks like we're due for some heavy prayer sessions."

Mellie's eyes filled with tears of thanksgiving. Precious Aunt Clara. For all her meddlesome talk, she understood. She could only imagine what would have happened if Aunt Clara had known about Jake when Charlotte and Bea made their comments. Now that would have been something to remember.

Ben clicked the reins to speed up the horses. "I always knew you were the wise one in the family, Aunt Clara, and you just now proved it to me."

"Well, thank you, Ben. But if you ask me, some people around this town need to learn what it means to treat each other with brotherly love and kindness no matter who or what they are. Sometimes Christians can be the cruelest when one of their own is hurt. I never understood that and still don't."

Mellie shook her head. Truer words she hadn't heard in a long time. With Aunt Clara on her side, Mellie decided that whatever Charlotte or Bea had to say would slide off her shoulders like snow on a warm roof.

But how could she explain such behavior to Becky? Aunt Clara's words would help, but she knew her baby's heart hurt with the rejection from her friend. Matthew would be all right, but Becky needed a little extra measure of love. She wrapped her arm around Becky and hugged her close.

Mellie shivered; winter had set in. She prayed for Jake's safety in the bitter weather. Her heart ached as any mother's would for a son.

Lucinda and Aunt Clara sat huddled against the cold with their heads close and low words being exchanged. Despite her first misgivings, Aunt Clara may prove to be the best thing for the family in the days ahead. She had more sides to her than a hexagon, and each one revealed a new attitude. Indeed, the plump little woman from Kansas City just might set the town of Barton Creek on its ear.

Chapter 21

*O*ver the next four weeks, bitter cold set in, and Lucinda's
teeth chattered as she readied for another day of chores.
Her black woolen stockings added some warmth to her legs, and
she pulled on her shoes. She dreaded going outdoors for chores
this morning, but work must be done despite the weather.

Aunt Clara sat at the kitchen table sipping tea, now her
morning ritual. She smiled when Lucinda entered the room.
"Ah, good morning, my dear. It's a cold morning for gathering
eggs. Becky just now left for the henhouse."

Lucinda reached for her heavy shawl. "She's quicker than a
fly avoiding a swat at a picnic. One of these days I'll beat her
getting dressed." Goodness, when had her speech become so
casual? A year ago she'd never heard half the sayings she now
used regularly.

Aunt Mellie laughed. "Not until she has as much to do to be
ready to face a day as you do."

Heat rose on Lucinda's cheeks. She did spend extra time on
her hair and other grooming. "True enough." She wrapped the
shawl about her head and shoulders. "I'll be back shortly." She
closed the door behind her and raced for the henhouse. The
freezing air burned her face. It reminded her of her first day
here. At least the wind didn't blow as hard today as it had then.

The hens cackled when she opened the door to step inside.

Becky glanced up from her task. "Not many eggs this

morning, but enough for breakfast. I had hoped for enough for Ma to bake a batch of her cookies."

Lucinda picked up a basket. "Well, if I were a hen, I don't think I'd want to make the effort to lay an egg on such a cold morning." She slipped her hand under the golden red hen before her and pulled out a nice-sized egg. Sometimes the hens didn't want her hand in the nest and either squawked or ruffled up their feathers, but this morning the little red hen simply turned her head to stare at Lucinda with a beady eye. "Sorry, girl, but our men like their eggs for breakfast."

She gathered only two more before Becky stepped back and announced, "I think that's it." She pulled her shawl tighter about her shoulders. "I'll race you to the house."

Before Lucinda could react, Becky bolted through the door and ran to the house. That girl. Where did she get so much energy? Lucinda let out her breath then followed her cousin, holding her basket close to her chest. No need to take chances and lose one of her eggs.

Later at breakfast, Aunt Clara greeted Monk and Hank with a cordial smile. She seemed to understand the roughness of life on a ranch, but she still clung to her manners and raised an eyebrow on occasion when she, Matt, or Becky made a mistake. But to her credit, Aunt Clara didn't admonish them.

Conversation flowed around her, but Lucinda's thoughts were elsewhere. Because of the weather, church had been neglected for the past four weeks, and she missed it. At least Becky and Matt appeared to accept their situations with the Frankston family. But what would happen when they were able to attend church again? Uncle Ben believed warmer days were not so far away. Perhaps spring did come sooner here than it did in Massachusetts.

How was Jake faring in this weather? Lucinda prayed he and the marshal had traveled far enough south to escape the icy temperatures. Surely they would find a warm place to camp at night.

Her appetite fled, and she shoved food across her plate. Uncle Ben pushed back from the table.

"Wrap some of those hot bricks in cloth. We may not make it back by noontime, and a warm meal will do us well. I'm taking Matt with us this morning. We need an extra person." He retrieved his coat from beside the door.

Aunt Mellie nodded. "I'll have everything ready in a few minutes." She addressed Becky. "I think this will be a good day for you to stay home."

Her cousin's countenance brightened considerably. "Oh, thank you, Ma. I can read the books Aunt Clara brought me."

"After you help Lucinda, then you may read or perhaps practice your stitching."

Lucinda raised her hand to her mouth to hide the smile forming. House chores and stitching, two activities Becky didn't particularly care to perform. Lucinda would make sure the time went by faster this morning. She rose from the table to help her aunt with preparing the saddlebags for Uncle Ben. Becky sat with a glum expression.

Aunt Clara reached over to pat Becky's arm. "Now, now, dear. With the four of us, we should make quick work of all the chores. After a little work on your sampler, we can sit by the fire, sip tea, and read. That would be a lovely way to spend an afternoon."

A smile erased Becky's frown. "You make it sound like fun. I'll go tend to the beds now." She scampered from the room.

Uncle Ben opened the back door. "The clouds look full of snow. We may be in for a heavy storm. I want to get plenty of feed out for the cattle, but we should be back by early afternoon if not sooner."

Aunt Mellie wrapped one last brick and placed it atop the food in the leather pouch. "I'm all finished with this. Best you get on with your work. Please don't stay out too long."

Uncle Ben kissed her cheek. "We won't." He nodded to them. "You ladies stay warm." Then he strode through the door.

Lucinda plunged her hands into the soapy water to wash dishes. She hoped Ben and the others would be all right. She voiced a prayer for them as well as for Jake.

❧

Ben led his men to the range lands. Monk drove the wagon loaded with extra hay for the cattle. The wind had slowed, but the temperatures hovered around the freezing mark. Last year he'd had the foresight to build feeders for his herd. Long troughs with a slanted cover would hold enough feed to keep the cattle from starving for a few days. After that, the weather would take its toll if they couldn't get back to replenish.

The snow flurries began when they completed filling the second bin. With three more to go, they had to hurry to complete their task before the ever-increasing snowfall became a blizzard.

"Pa, when we get this one filled, Monk and I will ride ahead and start the next one."

Ben shook his head. "No, we'll get done faster if we keep a steady pace."

Matt shrugged but followed orders. The snow fell harder, and the wind howled around them. Ben herded his stock toward the feeder, where they huddled under the partial shed.

By the time they reached the last feeder, the snow fell in blinding sheets. Ben dismounted and filled the trough with Hank's help. They pulled the last of the hay from the wagon. "This is the last one. Monk, you and Matt get on back to the house and tell Mellie to have a pot of hot soup ready for me and Hank."

"Yes sir, Mr. Haynes. Come on, Matt." He clicked the reins and turned the team back toward the ranch.

Matt tied his woolen scarf over his hat to cover his ears and secure his hat, and then he followed the wagon. Satisfied his son would be protected, Ben leaned over to pitch more feed into the trough.

He worked side by side with Hank for the next five minutes as they completed their task and made sure this part of the herd stood by the feeder. The snow swirled furiously, and the wind howled. The world around them lay white in every direction. Nothing could be seen except driving snow and a few feet ahead.

Ben moved his horse closer to Hank's. "I don't see the wagon's tracks. Snow's already filled them."

Hank examined the ground more closely. "At least we know what direction to take."

Ben pulled the extra blanket from his saddlebags, thankful now he'd thought to have them all carry an extra one. He wrapped it around his shoulders, and Hank did the same with his.

They rode in silence for what seemed to be an eternity, but Ben knew it couldn't have been more than ten minutes. They were at least another half hour from home with the wind blowing and the snow so heavy. He felt numbness in his feet and hands even though heavy socks and gloves covered them. The wool scarf Mellie knitted for him slipped from his nose. He pulled it back up and realized his breath froze against the cloth.

Hank's shoulders hunched inward, and he pulled his blanket tighter, but he managed to stay close. Pure misery filled his eyes. Maybe they should try to find a shelter from the icy wind and wait for the storm to pass. Ben peered through the blinding snow. An outcropping of rocks should be around here somewhere.

Ben reached over to grasp Hank's arm and gestured for the young man to follow him. Ben pulled his hat low on his forehead. They wouldn't make it back unless they found shelter.

A few minutes later, the formation of boulders and rocks

appeared. Ben headed toward it and motioned for Hank to follow. An indention not quite high enough for a man to stand, but large enough to shield from the wind, gave some relief.

Under the shelter, Ben removed the scarf covering his face and brushed off the ice formations.

"In all my years on the range, this is the worst storm I've seen. Don't believe it ever got this cold when we were in Kansas. I hope the horses will be protected." Ben wrapped the scarf back around his neck.

"Being from down south, I never seen this kind of snow myself. Right now, I feel like I'll never be warm again," Hank said.

Ben opened the saddlebags they had used at noon. "These bricks aren't warm now, but we do have food left. We can stay here until it slows up some. Matt and Monk will bring back help when we don't return on time." He prayed the two of them made it home safely.

Hank's teeth chattered, and his body shook. "Ben, I'm so cold. Do you think we'll make it through this?"

Ben pushed the boy back further into the indention against the rocks. "We will. We're healthy and strong, and God will take care of us." He had to believe that, but sometimes just believing it didn't mean that was God's plan.

Ben offered Hank a biscuit and piece of ham, and then he ate some himself. How he wished they had a contraption to keep food warm. Hot coffee would taste mighty good at this point. He inspected the remaining contents of the bags. A few pieces of beef jerky remained, as well as two more biscuits. That would do; they could eat snow for water.

Hank finished his biscuit but said nothing. He pulled his knees up to his chest and wrapped the ends of his coat around them. Ben sat next to him to provide extra warmth for both. The wind continued to howl and whistle through the cracks between the rocks, but they were still sheltered from the worst of it, and no snow fell on them. The cloth he had spread for them to sit on offered some comfort, but they would soon be soaked from the moisture.

Ben sat as close as possible to Hank and stared at the opening of their crude shelter. As long as the daylight lasted, they would be safe, but if night fell without the storm letting up, or someone finding them, he feared for their lives. The temperatures would plummet even lower, and they would need more protection than they had. Ben's head drooped against his chest.

He had no idea how long they sat in the small space, but silence surrounded them. Ben raised his head to listen more closely. The howling wind had stopped. He reached out to shake Hank. No response. Ben shook him again. Ben scrambled to pull off his glove and check the boy's neck to check for a pulse. His fingers felt a thread of a beat.

If he could get the boy on his horse, maybe they could find the way to the ranch. He pulled his glove back on and realized both his feet had no feeling at all. Frostbite: one thing he had hoped wouldn't happen.

He tried to stand, but his feet wouldn't hold him, and he fell back down. Someone had to come soon, or Hank would die. Although Ben hated the thought of Matt and Monk or anyone else being out in this weather, they were his only hope. He searched through his pack and found one more blanket. He wrapped part of it around Hank and huddled close. A slight feeling of warmth flowed over Ben, and his eyes grew heavy with sleep.

He jerked awake. No, he couldn't go to sleep. That meant sure death, but at the moment it took every ounce of strength to keep his eyes open. His eyelids grew heavy but had no strength to fight back. His mind filled with images of Mellie. Warmth flowed over him as he remembered the wonderful years they had spent together. No better helpmate could he have than Mellie. At least she would have Matt if he didn't survive this venture.

⤚

Mellie fretted about the kitchen. The wind moaned through cracks around the windows, and the snow outside brushed against the panes, piling in the corners. She hated February for its unexpected storms. Ben and the boys should have been home by now. She prayed her husband would walk in soon.

A commotion at the back door grabbed her attention. Matt and Monk stumbled through. Her breath caught in her throat. They looked half frozen. She reached out for her son.

Monk slammed the door behind him and clapped his hands together. Snow clumped on his shoulders and on the brim of his hat. "Ahh, this warm air feels good."

Matt stood as in a trance. "Where is your father?" Mellie demanded. "Is he right behind you?"

Monk's mustache drooped with the frown on his lips. "No, ma'am. He and Hank stayed to fill the last feed trough. He sent me and Matt back with the wagon."

Mellie gasped and fell against a chair. Ben was still out there somewhere. Of course he'd wanted to see his stock taken care of properly, but at what expense?

Aunt Clara handed Monk a cup of warm coffee. "It's not too hot, so it won't harm your frozen insides. Drink it slow and come warm up by the fire."

Monk accepted the cup and wrapped his hands around it. "Mighty obliged. Soon as I get into dry clothes, I aim to head back out and make sure they're all right. They might have lost their way in the blinding snow."

Mellie nodded, but her heart pounded against her ribs. Matt had already headed to the bunkhouse to change. Lucinda and

Becky hugged each other by the stove, fear clearly printed on their faces. Aunt Clara sat, silent for once, but her lips were moving as if she were praying.

Mellie squared her shoulders and spoke to Monk. "I don't want you to go back out, but I know you must for Ben's sake and for Hank." She waved toward the stove. "Lucinda, get more bricks and heat them. They'll need the extra warmth."

Monk thanked her, then opened the door to head for the bunkhouse. Mellie leaned against the door to close it tight against the wind. "We must make sure they have plenty of clothing layers and heavy socks."

In a daze, she hurried to her tasks of filling a tin pot with hot coffee. She didn't know how long it would stay hot, but long enough to warm their insides for a little ways.

She refused to think about what could happen to Ben and Hank if left to the mercy of the elements. With her head bowed over the sink, Mellie offered up a silent prayer for her husband's safety and for the welfare of her son and Monk.

In a few minutes, Monk and Matt pushed through the door again, then shut it. They were bundled up with extra layers of clothing and wool scarves about their necks and tied over their hats.

"I'm hoping they made it as far as the rocks. We found them last spring, and they make a sort of cavelike structure that'll shield them from the worst of it." Monk grabbed the bag Mellie held out to him. "We'll look there first."

Mellie rubbed her palms against her apron. "How long do you think it will take you to reach them?"

Monk rubbed his chin. "Longer than it took us to get here. At least an hour there and back."

"We'll have things ready when you return." She embraced Matt. "Be careful. I hate for you to be going back out, but find your pa." She handed him a blanket wrapped around warm bricks and a packet of food. "Put these extras in the wagon. They'll help when you find them."

"We will, Ma. We will. Pa's going to be OK."

She hugged him once again. He'd grown into a man without her ever realizing it. He stood tall and strong, ready to brave the freezing temperatures to find his father. Love and pride in both her men swelled in her breast as she blinked back tears.

Matt grasped the bricks close to his body and headed back outside.

When the door shut behind the two men, Mellie turned to her family. "Time to have us a prayer meeting before we get things ready for their return."

※

Ben's head sagged against his chest. He shook it and opened his eyes. He thought he heard his name called, but as he listened, silence greeted him. He figured it must have been the wind. Worry filled him over Hank. The boy didn't look good. Ben checked Hank's pulse and still felt the weak beat in the boy's neck. Ben settled back against the wall of the rock.

His head lolled with the drowsiness, but again he heard his name. He leaned forward to listen and this time heard his name clearly. When he tried to stand, his legs wouldn't hold him, but he yelled, "Here we are."

The call came closer, and Monk's body appeared in the opening. Never had a bushy-faced man looked so good. Ben held up his hand. "I knew someone would come."

"Let's get you two outta here." He shoved his hands under Ben's armpits. "Matt, come give me a hand with your pa."

Strong hands lifted him, but his feet stung with a thousand needles. They dragged him to the wagon and together pushed him up into it. They covered him with blankets and hurried back for Hank.

A few moments later Hank lay beside him. Ben pushed his body close to Hank's to give added warmth. The silence fell about them with an eerie quality. The wagon jerked, then began to move. The only sound now was the crunch of the wheels through the snow.

"Pa, we saw the horses headed back to the barn. We followed their tracks partway and figured this had to be where you found shelter."

Although his feet and hands tingled, the frostbite had not penetrated deep. Now if only Hank's was as mild. He couldn't see through the heavy layers whether the boy still breathed or not, but God had provided and protected them thus far.

All desire for sleep now gone, Ben peered up at the gray-white sky above him. No more menacing dark clouds hung around. The storm had passed.

Mellie would have everything ready for them at home. The thought of her waiting got him through the worst of this ordeal. Between the Lord and his Mellie, he'd survived.

Soon the wagon stopped, and Matt turned to his father. "We're home, Pa."

Ben raised up on one elbow to see over the edge of the wagon. Mellie and Lucinda ran from the house.

Mellie clasped her hands and lifted them toward heaven. "Thank You, Lord. Thank You."

A few minutes later both Ben and Hank were in the warmth of the house. Mellie and Aunt Clara had dealt with frostbite before and knew exactly what to do. They instructed Matt to place them on the rug away from the fire. She had warm blankets ready to wrap them in after removing the damp outer clothing.

Aunt Clara handed Ben a cup filled with tea. He wrapped his hands around it and let the soothing liquid warm his insides.

Hank still lay without moving, wrapped in a blanket. Mellie had removed his coat and the scarf wrapping his face. Her fingers probed for a pulse. The look in her eyes told Ben that Hank was alive. Relief washed over him like a flood. *Thank You, Lord.*

Mellie bent over Ben. "Now, it's time for you to be in bed. I don't want to take Hank back out in the cold to the bunkhouse, so we'll make a place for him here in the house."

Aunt Clara picked up the discarded garments. "He can have my bed. I'll go in with the girls."

Lucinda nodded. "Becky and I can sleep on my bed, and Aunt Clara can have the other. We'll take turns checking on Hank during the night."

"Good, that's settled. Monk, Matt. Help me get your father to our room, then you can take Hank to Aunt Clara's."

Ben's hands had warmed, and the circulation returned with the redness that accompanied it. He knew that blisters would form within the next twenty-four hours, but that was good. It meant the frostbite had not gone deep enough to impede circulation.

Supported between Monk and Matt, Ben hobbled to his bed. Mellie let him get settled, then leaned over to kiss him.

"Ben Haynes, you had me scared half to death."

Ben held her hand against his face. "I kept seeing your face and praying. I knew the Lord would take care of us. We'll probably lose some of the herd anyway, but we'll still have a good one."

"You did everything you could to protect them. We'll get by, whatever happens with the cattle."

Ben furrowed his brow. "Did the boys take care of the horses? They're half frozen themselves."

"Yes, soon as they brought you and Hank in, they went back

out and warmed the horses in the barn. Monk seems to think they'll be fine. He'll make sure they're bedded down before he goes in for the night."

Ben felt drowsy again. "That's good. I think I'm ready to sleep now. Go take care of Hank."

She kissed his cheek again, then tiptoed from the room. Ben breathed deeply to let sleep overtake him, but he sensed a presence standing by the bed. He opened his eyes to find Aunt Clara.

"Oh dear, I didn't mean to wake you."

"I wasn't quite asleep yet. Thank you for giving up your bed for Hank."

"*Pshaw.* 'Tis the least I can do for the poor boy." She placed her hand on his arm. "I remember you as a child when I first came to live with your family in Kansas. I still see that little boy in you. You were always concerned about your pets just as you were concerned about your herd today."

"And it almost cost me my life. I won't be so foolish again." Next time he'd remember his family first.

Chapter 22

Jake and the marshal rode in silence through the freezing drizzle. North of them the storm carried snow, but now it fell just short of being sleet. Marshal Derreck mentioned a town a few miles ahead where they would seek shelter for the night. Then it would be only a few days before their destination. Derreck had been right. It'd taken almost four weeks for them to travel this far with the bad weather and having to stay in a town or two for several days to get out of the worst of the weather.

The thought of death didn't grieve or frighten him as much as it had months ago. What did frighten him was why God had sent Lucinda into his life only to take her away again. He couldn't understand that part of God's working, but Lucinda had told him to remember that God worked all things for good. That hadn't happened for him so far.

The faint outline of buildings appeared in the distance. Marshal Derreck turned in his saddle, leaning on his saddle horn. "Just so you know. I wired ahead from the last town and asked the sheriff to check with the law in Rio Alto for me."

Jake furrowed his brow. "Why would you do that? I told you what happened."

Derreck pulled on his reins. "I've been going over your confession in my mind, and it's raised a few questions—questions I decided to have answered. We should know something by nightfall."

Jake grasped his saddle horn as Baron followed the lawman. Although the weather was warmer now during the day, as the sun set, the temperatures would fall, and cold set in. He hoped they'd be in the next town before that happened.

A gust of wind brushed across his neck. At least the wind didn't blow like it had in the past few days. The trees through which they rode offered a little protection from the occasional bursts from the north.

In the late afternoon they rode into town. A sign swinging in the wind announced the sheriff's office. Another day closer to his fate, Jake didn't bother to examine the buildings or his surroundings. One town was like another down here.

Derreck slowed his horse. "We'll stop in and talk with the law. See what he may have found out."

The lawman dismounted and secured his horse. Jake swung down from Baron and followed him inside. The only difference in this jail from the others he'd seen was that big white stones comprised this one instead of clapboards or red bricks. They stepped inside to a large room with two desks, a rack of guns, and a center door open to reveal the cells beyond. He looked forward to a night on a cot instead of the bare ground.

A balding man sat behind one of the desks. When he saw the two men, he stood.

Derreck pushed up the brim of his hat. "Evening. You the sheriff?"

The man behind the desk stretched out his hand. "Sheriff Logan. You must be Marshal Derreck."

Derreck grasped the offered hand. "Right, and this is the prisoner I wired about, Jake Starnes."

"Haven't found out anything yet. I sent my deputy down to Rio Alto, but it'll take a day or two before he's back. They don't have wire service down there." He reached for the ring of keys by his desk. "Suppose you want to put him up for a night or two."

"Possibly. I need to check with your wire service here for an answer to one I sent back to Kansas. Both of us will make use of a couple of your cells for tonight."

Logan's eyes opened wide. "We have a right decent hotel. No need for you to put up here."

"We'll be fine. Is there a place I can find a meal and a place to get a shave and maybe a bath?"

The keys jingled as the sheriff pointed to his right. "Down yonder toward the stables is the barber, and he has a bathhouse there. On down a few doors is Mrs. Parsons's boarding house. She serves a good spread. I'll take care of your prisoner for you. You just tell Mrs. Parsons that Sheriff Logan needs a meal down here for a prisoner. She usually brings mine, so she can bring one for the boy too."

"Thank you. I'll do that." Derreck unlocked Jake's cuffs. "I don't think you'll need these for a while. Go on in and make yourself as comfortable as you can, and I'll make sure you get something to eat."

Jake rubbed his wrists where the metal had chafed them. If only they could be off forever. He followed the sheriff to one of the cells. At least it was warm and dry. He sat on the cot provided and rubbed his hand across the rough blanket. The sheets looked clean. A hot meal and a warm bed were an unexpected blessing.

He reached into the saddlebag Derreck had placed by the door of the cell and grabbed his Bible. Now would be as good a time as any to read what God had to say to him today. He opened it and began reading Paul's letter to the Philippians. But he had a hard time concentrating. Jake's heart ached with foreboding. What if something had happened to Lucinda? He prayed for her safety, but peace wouldn't come. How he longed to be with Lucinda at this moment. He laid back and closed his eyes.

The aroma of apple pie awakened him. For a moment he was home, but reality set in. He sat up on his bunk and shook his head. A plump, little woman stood outside the cell holding a napkin-covered basket. "I'm Mrs. Parsons, and I've brought your supper. The marshal said he'd be back shortly."

The sheriff unlocked the door, and Jake grasped the basket. "Thank you, ma'am. I'm much obliged. The food sure smells good." His stomach rumbled, reminding him of how long it had been since his last good meal.

The sheriff escorted Mrs. Parsons back to the front. Jake sat on the edge of his cot and uncovered the basket to find fried chicken, potatoes, and apple pie. He even detected the fresh-baked smell of rolls. This would be a real feast. He bowed his head and gave thanks.

After he devoured every crumb, Jake wiped his hands on the checkered napkin.

Marshal Derreck ambled in. "Hope your supper was as good as mine. I understand her other meals are just as good."

Jake grinned. Another meal like this would sit with him for a few more days on the trail. "She's a mighty fine cook."

The marshal unlocked the cell and stepped inside. "I have some news for you. When Sheriff Logan's man returns, he will go on with you to Rio Alto. The answer I was expecting came, and I have to return to Kansas to take care of another matter."

Jake's spirits plummeted. He'd grown to like the marshal and dreaded going on to Rio Alto with a stranger. But then, he had no say whatsoever in the matter. Right now, he was anxious to return to the scene and get everything over with, no matter what the outcome would be. "I'm sorry you have to go back. How long will I stay here?"

"Not much longer. Probably a day; maybe two at the most."

Jake stretched forth his hand. "I'm mighty obliged for the

treatment so far on this journey. You've helped me more than you know."

Derreck grasped Jake's hand. "Young man, you've been a blessing to me. I've seen many killers in my days as a lawman, and you are the least likely one I've ever met. I pray things will turn out well for you in Rio Alto." He paused then said, "I have a lawyer friend I've asked to help you. He's looking into the incident in Rio Alto too."

A lawyer? Hope sprang into Jake's heart. Then his spirits fell again. When a man was guilty, he had to pay for the crime. And he knew he was guilty.

Chapter 23

*L*ucinda sliced carrots and added them to the soup simmering on the stove top. The aroma of chicken and vegetables in the black cast-iron pot filled the room. "*Hmm.* This smells good enough to cure any and all ailments," she told Aunt Mellie.

Only a few days had passed since the snowstorm. All Uncle Ben and Hank had to really show for their mishap in the snow were blisters on their hands and a few on their feet. Doc Carter had left a salve for those in case it was needed, but he said to leave them alone and let them heal themselves.

Lucinda added a pinch of salt to the soup. "I do hope Hank won't try to get up too soon. He needs this extra day to rest and get back his strength."

"Yes, he does," Aunt Mellie agreed. "I'm glad Ben is experienced and knows the importance of taking care of himself after nearly freezing to death. God certainly guarded them. All we have to worry about now is infection if those blisters don't heal properly."

Aunt Clara swept into the room, her skirts rustling with each step. "Well, those boys are all settled on clean sheets and have fresh nightshirts." She peered into the soup pot. "This smells delicious. Hope you made enough for all of us."

Aunt Mellie laughed. "We made plenty. We'll all have a bowl at noontime."

Aunt Clara settled at the table. "Too bad Monk won't be back to eat with us."

"Oh, he has plenty to eat with him. I packed his bag extra this morning. He'll have a tough job checking the entire range for any cattle we lost in the storm."

Lucinda furrowed her brow. "Do you think it'll be very many?"

"I don't know, dear. Ben lost more than a few the last big storm. I suppose the loss will be as much or more this year."

Aunt Mellie opened a cupboard door to make a list of supplies she needed. "Lucinda, you and I need to ride into town and pick up some things at Anderson's. Aunt Clara can stay with the men."

"Do you really need enough to fill the wagon? I can go in and pick up what you need, then meet Becky and Matt after school. They can help bring home the supplies too."

Mellie checked her list. "Well, that will be easier on us, as I don't like to leave Clara alone with both men to tend to."

Aunt Clara patted her gray hair. "Not that I couldn't do it, but from the way I've seen you handle a horse, dear, I do believe you would do fine, and the weather is much nicer today. Besides, Ben prefers Mellie when he needs something."

"Then it's settled. I'll ride in with your list. Matt and Becky can help bring things home." But the real reason for her desire to go into town had nothing to do with groceries. She wanted to speak with Deputy Claymore.

After their noon meal, Lucinda set about to make cookies for afternoon tea. Matt would appreciate them with a cup of hot cocoa when he arrived home. On second thought, she should make a double batch.

"Aunt Mellie, are there enough raisins left for the oatmeal cookies?"

"I believe so. Let me check." She searched through the pantry and found a tin of the dried currants. She opened it and peered inside. "Just enough for today. This is something else to add to the list."

After their tea, Lucinda changed into her riding clothes and headed out to the stables to saddle Misty. Being cooped up in the house during the foul weather made this outing even more enjoyable. The weather for February was as changeable as the seasons, and today the sun shone through a cloud-filled sky. She looked forward to being outdoors and on her own.

⚜

Mellie went in to see about Ben. He sat propped up in bed reading his Bible. "It's good to see you sitting up."

"I feel like coming in to eat with the family tonight. I've been confined to this bed long enough."

Mellie laughed. "We'll see about that." She pulled up the sheet and inspected his feet. The blisters appeared to be healing well. "I'll let you up if you wear those soft slippers Aunt Clara made for you. No need to aggravate those sore spots."

He grinned and pulled at her arm. "Thank you for your approval." He lifted his nose in the air. "Do I detect the smell of some of your oatmeal cookies?"

"Yes, Lucinda made them, and they're quite tasty."

"Tell her to bring me in a few. I could stand a little something before supper."

"I would, but she's gone into town for a few supplies I need. She'll be back with Becky and Matt after school." Mellie straightened the covers. Ben's hand gripped her arm, an expression of alarm on his face.

"You didn't let her go alone, did you?"

She stared at the strong clasp of his. "Ben, you're hurting me.

211

Yes, she'll be fine. The weather is clear, and it's not anywhere near freezing now."

He dropped his hand. "I'm sorry, but you know we said we'd not let Lucinda go anywhere alone."

Mellie bit her lip. She hadn't thought about that today. In fact, nothing had happened for so long that she believed the threat to have passed. "I'm sorry. I didn't even consider any trouble for her. I'm sure she'll be fine. She's going straight to town then meeting Matt and Becky at the school. They'll ride home with her."

"Then we must pray she makes it into town safely." He furrowed his brow. "I believe Rudolph Bishop is quite capable of making arrangements for an 'unfortunate accident' to claim our Lucinda. And it wouldn't surprise me any at all if your sister's death wasn't an accident."

Mellie sucked in her breath. He had voiced the very thoughts she'd had, but hearing the words aloud brought fear to her heart. Why hadn't she thought of the danger for Lucinda before letting her take off all alone? "Oh, Ben, nothing must happen to her. It would be my fault."

Ben grasped her hand and shook his head. "Lucinda will be all right. Don't worry."

His words were meant to reassure, but they failed to convince her. She had put Lucinda in harm's way.

❧

The buildings of Barton Creek appeared on the horizon. Lucinda would have plenty of time to get the supplies Aunt Mellie needed and see Deputy Claymore before meeting Matt and Becky for the ride home. One thing she didn't miss about Boston was the slush and dirty streets after a big snow. Here the sun bathed the land and very little snow remained. Only a few patches survived the warm rays. She might never get accustomed to the quick changes in the weather.

Misty's ears twitched and then stood straight up. She bobbed her head. Lucinda leaned forward to soothe the mare. "It's all right, Misty. We're going into Barton Creek. You've been there before. Soon we'll see Daisy and Becky."

At the store, Lucinda dismounted. Inside, Bea Anderson stood near the wall shelves with a customer. She glanced in Lucinda's direction but didn't acknowledge her presence.

Lucinda furrowed her brow, then remembered the woman's actions at church a few weeks ago. Dismayed, she gripped the list in her clenched fist. How could a Christian woman be so closed-minded?

Luke appeared from the storeroom. "Hello, Lucinda." He glanced past her shoulder. "Did you come in alone?"

"Yes, Uncle Ben is still laid up recovering from frostbite, so I'm running errands for Aunt Mellie." Lucinda relaxed at his friendly manner. Luke must not share the sentiments of his mother.

"Well, then, how can I help you?"

She smoothed the paper on the counter. "This is the list Aunt Mellie made of things we need. When they're packed up, I'm going to meet Becky and Matt. They'll help me take the things home."

Luke grinned. "I'll be happy to get these for you." He headed for the shelves along the side wall. "Tell me what happened to your uncle. He had frostbite, you say?"

Lucinda related the story as Luke set a few cans and tins on the counter. When she finished, he shook his head. "That could have been really terrible. I'm glad he's doing well."

"Yes, and if the weather is warm enough, he plans to be in church on Sunday. As strong as he is, I'm not sure we could do much to hold him back."

Luke tallied up the cost of her supplies. "Yes, we've missed you these past weeks." He looked at her quickly, then glanced down, speaking casually. "I don't know if you've heard, but we're having our annual box-supper social in a few weeks. I was wondering if you plan to attend."

Lucinda bit her lip. "I believe Aunt Mellie mentioned a social of some kind. Exactly what is it?"

A warm smile spread across Luke's face. "Well, the young ladies of the congregation fix up suppers in decorated containers, and then the men bid on them to help raise funds for the church. Of course, the married men always know what their wives fixed, so the fun is when we single men have to decide which girl made each box or basket and bid on the one we think was made by the girl we want to eat with."

"Oh, that kind of social." Lucinda didn't think she wanted to participate in anything like the box supper just yet.

"I would count it a great honor if you allow me to accompany you. Martin Fleming and I would ride out to bring you and Dove into town. Then if I'm so lucky to get your box and he wins Dove's, we can eat together."

"Oh, what happens if someone else gets my box?" Dismay filled Lucinda. She hadn't counted on something like this.

"I don't think that will happen." A grin spread across his face. "We fellows usually pick the right boxes and get our bids."

How could she say no and still be polite? With only a few boys their age around, refusing the offer would be rude. She had suffered through a few times when her parents arranged an escort for a social event even though she hadn't wanted to go. Mama always said to refuse such an invitation was an affront to the person offering. Nice young ladies could endure one evening in order to be seen socially.

"Lucinda?"

"Oh, I'm sorry, Luke. My mind was elsewhere for the moment.

So much has happened in recent days." She paused. "I'll consider your offer." That sounded vague, but at least she hadn't said yes or no. Aunt Mellie could advise her as to the best course of action.

"Thank you. I'll wait for your answer." He rang up the bill. "Is this to go on your uncle's account?"

"Yes, please." She checked the list once more. All the supplies were there. "I'll be back in a while to pick up the parcels."

"I'll have them ready." Then he grinned broadly. "And I do hope your answer is yes."

Lucinda pasted on a polite smile and hurried out the door. She made her way to the law offices down the street. When she entered the building, Deputy Claymore jumped to his feet.

"Good afternoon, Miss Bishop. What can I do for you?"

"I...I wanted to inquire as to whether or not you had heard from Marshal Derreck."

"Not yet, and I'm not supposing I will. We don't have a telegraph here, remember?"

She had quite forgotten that in her desire to know of Jake's welfare. "Do you have any idea where they might be?"

The deputy strode over to a large map covering one section of the wall. He scanned it for a moment before pointing to a spot. "I'd say they're about here, allowing for the weather and all."

Lucinda peered at the place marked by Claymore's finger. She couldn't quite make out where it might be in relation to where the two men were headed. "How much longer do you think their trip will be?"

The deputy rubbed fingers along his chin line. "Don't rightly know for sure. Depends a lot on the weather. I'd say they should be just about there."

"Thank you." Her heart grew heavy when she left the deputy behind. So little time left to pray.

After she met her cousins, they picked up the supplies and

loaded them into the saddlebags. On the ride home, Becky chattered about the upcoming social event at church and the fun they would have. Lucinda was silent, dreading the thought of hurting Luke's feelings. She really didn't want to go, but how could she in all politeness turn him down?

Suddenly a crack rang out, then a searing pain ripped through Lucinda's shoulder. She screamed at the same moment Becky did and fell from her horse. The sky appeared hazy as she lay on her back. When her hand touched the pain in her shoulder, she felt something wet and sticky.

Matt shouted at Becky. "Go get Doc Carter. Lucinda's been shot!"

Then her world turned black.

Chapter 24

ellie rushed into Doc Carter's office with Ben close on her heels. She had tried to get him to stay behind and rest, but when he heard Becky say Lucinda had been shot and was in Doc Carter's office, nothing could hold him back. "Where's Lucinda?"

Doc washed his hands at the basin in the corner. "She's in the other room, sleeping. I gave her a touch of laudanum for the pain."

Ben grabbed Mellie's hand. "How bad is she hurt?"

"The bullet went through soft tissue and muscle only without striking a bone or vital blood vessels. Very clean shot."

Mellie gasped and slumped down on one of the hard chairs in the office. "Rudolph Bishop. I know he's behind this." He could have hired someone to come after her. The very idea sent blood rushing to her head.

Ben turned to the doctor. "When can we take her home?"

"After I'm sure she's stable and can be moved with no harm. It'll take a little while for the wound to heal, but she's fine otherwise."

"Good," Mellie said. "Aunt Clara is making sure everything is ready at home. I must send Matt and Becky to help her." Matt had disappeared as soon as they hit town, and she hadn't seen Becky. "Where are those two?"

As if in answer to her question, the two young people opened the door. Deputy Claymore followed them into the room.

Becky rushed to her mother. Her words tumbled out. "Oh, Ma, I was so scared. We were just riding along talking when we heard this loud noise just before Lucinda screamed and fell off her horse. Her shoulder was covered in blood."

Mellie breathed deeply and hugged her daughter. "I know. It'll be all right."

Deputy Claymore cleared his throat. "I've been out to where the shooting happened. It doesn't look like an accident. Since neither Becky nor Matt remember seeing anyone about, I searched the area around the trees and found trampled grass and some hoof prints in the slushy snow and mud."

Ben crossed his arms at his chest. "We have reason to believe that a relative from back east is behind the shooting, but we don't have any way to prove it."

Claymore rolled his hat between his hands. "Why don't you come on down to the office and tell me more about this relative."

Ben nodded and turned to Matt. "You stay here with your ma and Becky until I get back. When Lucinda wakes up, we can see about taking her home with us."

Doc Carter held up his hand. "Wait a minute, Ben. Becky told me about the frostbite. Let me check you and make sure you're healing properly."

Mellie jumped up. "Please, Ben. I didn't want you coming with me, but I knew nothing could stop you, so it's just as good a time as any to make sure Clara and I did our jobs well."

Ben shook his head but grinned. "If you don't mind waiting, I'll humor my wife and let the doc examine me. Won't take long. I'm fine." He followed the doctor behind a screen in the corner.

Deputy Claymore said, "Miss Lucinda was in my office shortly before she went to meet Matt and Becky. She was asking about young Jake. I'm sorry I didn't have any news to give her.

Of course, I'm not going to have any until the marshal returns. I sure hate to see her grieving his absence when he's not likely to be coming back."

The deputy was right. As much as they wanted to believe in Jake's return, the likelihood of that happening grew more remote with each passing day. Too much time had passed since his departure. Mellie lamented again that the town had no telegraph service as yet.

With Lucinda's birthday coming soon, the time had come to start thinking about her future. Still, if she knew her niece, that young lady would resist any attempts at getting her mind off Jake. And now she had her niece's physical well-being to worry about too.

Ben appeared from behind the curtain. "Clean bill of health, my love. Doc here says everything's healing well."

"He's right, Mellie. You and Clara did a fine job of treating his blisters. No infection at all."

Mellie breathed a sigh of relief. That one compliment bolstered her confidence in her nursing skills. "Then that means Hank will be mending properly too."

Ben pulled on his coat. "Let's go, Claymore. We can talk more down at the jail."

He stopped at the door. "Don't wait for me. If Lucinda awakes before I return and is all right, go ahead and take her home." He glanced at Matt. "You drive the wagon, and I'll ride your horse. I need you to check with Monk when you get back to the ranch. He's been out checking the herd again. We need to know exactly how many we lost."

Matt stood. "Yes, sir, I'll take care of it."

Becky sat on the floor beside Mellie, lost in her own thoughts. She stroked Becky's hair as Doc Carter busied himself with cleaning instruments and putting away supplies. Then he disappeared into the room where Lucinda lay. When he returned, a grin creased his face.

"Miss Lucinda is doing well. If you'll make sure the wagon is ready for her, we can carry her out."

Mellie jumped from her chair. "Praise the Lord. Let's get our girl home."

Matt jumped to his feet. "I'll get the wagon." He raced to the door.

"Make sure the padding is doubled and the quilt covers it." Mellie turned to the doctor. "Now what do I have to do once we get her home?"

While he explained about cleaning the wound and changing the dressing, Becky slipped into Lucinda's room. She left the door ajar, and Mellie watched from the corner of her eye as her daughter stood by Lucinda.

Matt returned, and he helped Doc Carter get Lucinda to stand.

She stumbled. "Sorry, I still feel a little light-headed."

Doc Carter patted her arm. "You will for a bit. Just be sure to do whatever your aunt tells you, and you'll be healed in no time. I stitched up the wound, but even though the bullet didn't do much damage, you'll be sore awhile."

Lucinda only nodded. The two men led her to the wagon. Mellie wrapped her arm around her niece's waist and guided her outside. "Stay close by on Daisy," she told Becky. "Don't go galloping off on your own." She didn't need anything else happening to her family.

"I won't," Becky promised.

Mellie gazed down the street before climbing up into the wagon seat beside Matt. His horse stood tethered to the post by the doctor's office for Ben to ride home. At that moment,

Ben appeared and waved. A young man with a badge walked toward them.

"Mr. Haynes asked me ride out to the ranch with you. He decided it might not be safe yet."

Mellie nodded. She trusted her Ben to take care of them.

Matt and Doc settled Lucinda in the wagon bed. In a few minutes they began their journey home. Now that the danger had passed, Mellie's eyes blurred with tears. How close her family had come to losing two members in the past week. *Thank You, Lord, for sparing their lives.*

⚘

Lucinda awakened in the darkness. She tried to turn over, but the pain burning her shoulder stopped her. Then she remembered— something had hit her shoulder, and she'd fallen from Misty.

Everything that happened remained a blur. The only clear thing in her mind was the throbbing pain from her wound. Who could have done this to her?

She squeezed her eyes shut and tried to visualize the afternoon. The images came in clear until she fell from Misty. After that she remembered nothing until she woke up in Doc Carter's office with Becky standing beside her. A vague memory of being put into a wagon came to mind. That must be how she came to be in her own bed.

The door creaked, and a sliver of light broke the darkness. Aunt Mellie stood in the doorway.

"I'm awake. Come in." Lucinda tried to rise up on her good arm, but pain racked her body.

"I have a spot of herb tea if you feel up to it." Her aunt approached the bed with a light in one hand and a teacup and saucer in the other. She set the lamp and tea on a table and leaned down to help Lucinda sit up.

"Mama always said herb tea could cure many ailments. Maybe that's what I need now. My shoulder does hurt. In fact, my whole body aches." She winced at the movement in her effort to sit up. With Aunt Mellie's support, she finally sat upright.

Aunt Mellie held the cup while Lucinda sipped the tea. Its warmth soothed her nerves, and she relaxed.

"Doc Carter says you'll be fine. He even said you'd be up and about in a day or two."

Lucinda blinked her eyes. Her cousins. "Are Becky and Matt all right? They didn't get hurt, did they?"

Aunt Mellie set the cup back on the bedside table. "No, no, my dear. They're fine. Ben spoke with Deputy Claymore, and he's investigating the incident."

Lucinda breathed deeply and sank back on the pillow. "That's good. It would have been terrible if they'd been hurt too. I can't understand what happened. I remember Doc Carter saying something about a gunshot."

Aunt Mellie pursed her lips and furrowed her brow. She said nothing for a few moments. Then her mouth relaxed. "I may as well tell you what we suspect so you'll be extra careful. We think your uncle Rudolph is behind this."

The name sent a shiver through Lucinda. She had pushed all thoughts of him from her mind. She hadn't wanted to think that he might even be responsible for the accident that took her parents' lives. "Do you believe he'd come all the way out here to hurt me?"

Aunt Mellie shook her head. "No, but I believe he's truly capable of sending someone to do his dirty work for him."

Such behavior was beyond the realm of Lucinda's comprehension. She'd always been part of a loving and caring family. Her mind couldn't wrap itself around such a foreign notion. In light of what had happened this afternoon, she would need to be more careful. "I won't ask to go anywhere alone. But then, Matt and Becky were both with me when it happened, so perhaps just being with someone else isn't enough."

"Your uncle and I have discussed that. We believe if adults are with you, this man won't be as likely to try something like this again. I imagine he felt quite safe with only Becky and Matt as your escorts." She reached down to smooth the quilt and then pulled up a chair.

Aunt Mellie pursed her lips. Lucinda knew the look. Her aunt had something to say that Lucinda might not like. "This is as good a time as any to discuss your future. You know Ben and I will do everything we can to protect you until your birthday in a few months. We won't let you become a recluse and be afraid of going out."

Lucinda didn't intend to do that, but she sensed more to what her aunt said than the actual words. She had to be thinking about the box supper. "Aunt Mellie, Luke asked to be my escort for the church social coming up in a few weeks."

Aunt Mellie's eyebrows arched in surprise. "He did? Now that's an unusual turn of events. When did this happen?"

"This afternoon when I was purchasing the things on your list, he mentioned taking me and going with Martin Fleming and Dove."

"Now that sounds like a fine idea. You and Dove can prepare your food and decorate your boxes together. We'll hide them well, so Martin and Luke won't know which ones are yours when it comes time for bidding."

Lucinda didn't want to dampen her aunt's enthusiasm, but she couldn't help but think of Jake. It hadn't been that long since they'd said good-bye, and she didn't want to give up on him. Doubts about encouraging Luke also worried her. She had never purposely led a young man to think she cared about him, and she didn't intend to start now.

Aunt Mellie caressed Lucinda's hair. "Now, Lucinda, we haven't heard a word from Jake. We have no way of knowing what has happened to him. As much as I love the boy, we can't spend the rest of our days looking for him to come back. Whatever the Lord wills, we have to accept."

God may be with him and watching over him, but Jake needed friends with flesh and blood to support him and help him. But that was impossible. "I'll still pray for Jake until we hear with certainty what has happened."

"I'll accept that, but you think about making some young man happy at the social. It is a fund-raiser, you know." She stood. "I'll leave you to rest now. If all goes well, you should be able to attend church services Sunday. Ben is quite anxious to go since we haven't been there in a month."

"I'd like that." Then she remembered sleeping arrangements. "Aunt Mellie, wait. Where will Becky sleep tonight? I don't think I could take her moving around with my shoulder being so sore."

Aunt Mellie laughed. "We've already thought of that. Hank is going back out to the bunkhouse. Aunt Clara will move back to her room, and Becky will have her bed back. Don't worry about us. You get some sleep. I'll tell Becky to be quiet when she comes in."

The door closed, and darkness claimed the room once more. Lucinda lay still in the bed, her eyes staring up toward the ceiling. She didn't want to give up on Jake. Her faith still stood strong, and she prayed for his safety.

She mulled the situation over in her mind. Maybe the answer for Luke's invitation would come in the light of the morning. Tomorrow would be soon enough to think about such things.

Chapter 25

*J*ake sat on the edge of his cot, his head bowed and hands clasped between his knees. Three days since Marshal Derreck had brought him here. Time to think and wonder more about what would happen to him in Rio Alto. The marshal left to return to Kansas, so now Jake could only wait and speculate. Severe rainstorms delayed the return of the deputy from Rio Alto. But today, no rain meant his journey would resume.

The cell had grown less comfortable and more confining. The sheriff did provide good food but made no attempt to be friendly. The only time he spoke to Jake came when Mrs. Parsons arrived with meals. Having someone to talk to or even to listen to would help the boredom that set in. Idleness only gave him more opportunity to think about what lay ahead.

The sun cast striped beams through the bars on the cell window above him. The remains of breakfast sat on the tray at his feet. A pair of boot-clad feet stopped at his cell. He raised his head to see a tall man in a tan coat. Sheriff Logan stood behind him.

"Jacob Starnes?"

The stranger's voice rang with authority. Jake swallowed hard. "Yes, sir, that's me."

The man removed his hat. "I'm Mac Daniels. Marshal Derreck and I are friends from way back. He asked me to look into your case and accompany you to Rio Alto. I'm your attorney."

His attorney? Jake grasped Mr. Daniels's outstretched hand.

"It's nice to meet you, but I can't afford a lawyer."

"That's not a concern. I've been paid, and we're off to Rio Alto."

This made no sense. "Why did you take my case? I plan to plead guilty because the man's dead."

Sheriff Logan unlocked the cell door, and Daniels stepped inside. "You let me worry about that. We'll talk about it on the trail."

Logan handed Jake his belongings. "My deputy will go with the two of you to Rio Alto to make sure you reach the sheriff there. Not that I don't trust Mac here, but I have to be careful."

Jake nodded, picked up his Bible and hat, then shouldered the knapsack. "Fair enough. This is all I have. I'm ready to go."

He followed the deputy and Mac Daniels outside, where once again he felt the cold, hard steel of handcuffs snapped around his wrists. He turned and looped them over his saddle horn and hoisted himself onto Baron. Daniels secured Jake's bag to the saddle. Soon he'd be back where all his troubles began.

Deputy Roberts reached over for Baron's reins and led them out of town. The horses plodded through the streets thick with mud from the heavy rains. Storms to the south had delayed the deputy's return, but now the skies overhead shone bright and cloudless.

When they reached the edge of town, Jake turned and looked back. People made their way through the mire to go about their daily lives. If only they realized how lucky they were to be free and running errands or tending to business.

"Mr. Daniels, what did Marshal Derreck tell you about me?"

The lawyer gazed at him for a moment before answering. "The whole story, and I'm to make sure you get a fair trial."

"A fair trial? Isn't this what lawyers call an open-and-shut case? I don't understand. I know what I did, and I'm not denying it."

"Yes, you did kill a man, but didn't you tell Derreck the man pulled a gun before you shot him?"

"Yes, sir. I called him a cheat, and he pulled out his gun, but I was quicker and shot him first." He'd been over the story so many times in his head and couldn't erase that scene from his mind.

"Then it seems to me you shot in self-defense. There may be a few men who witnessed the killing and will testify to that effect."

Jake's heartbeat quickened. "I didn't kill him on purpose, but I had no other choice. I didn't want to be shot myself."

The lawyer nodded. "That's what I mean, son. We're going to plead not guilty because of self-defense. You could be a free man in a few days."

The words were there, but Jake couldn't wrap his mind around their meaning. He'd thought of his guilt for so long that nothing else had occurred to explain what happened. If Daniels believed in Jake's innocence, then perhaps the new sheriff would too. Hope crept into his heart to take root.

Deputy Roberts shifted around in his saddle. "Don't matter what lawyer talk you use, he's my prisoner and my responsibility until he's safely in the jail at Rio Alto."

Daniels simply nodded and said nothing.

A million thoughts scrambled themselves in Jake's brain. Why had God let this happen? If he'd known he could claim self-defense, he would never have fled. He could have been on his uncle's ranch and living as a free man all this time. He thought of all he had lost by running away.

But then he remembered what Lucinda had told him, that all things worked together for good for those who loved God. Realization dawned. God had taken the killing and used it to bring good into Jake's life. If he had not run, he would never have met the Haynes family and would never have known Lucinda.

No matter what happened now, God controlled it all.

Contentment and peace flowed over him like warm spring rain, washing him clean of all guilt and doubt.

⚓

On Sunday, Lucinda breathed the fresh air, thankful to be outdoors again after several days in the house. The gold cross atop the church steeple glistened in the morning sunshine as they rode into the churchyard. Several members rushed to greet them. Luke Anderson appeared by the carriage and offered his hand to help Lucinda down from her seat.

She smiled and held out the hand on her good arm. The right one rested against her chest, supported by a sling Aunt Mellie devised to keep the arm immobile. Her feet touched the solid ground, but Luke continued to hold her hand. Heat rose in her cheeks. What would others think?

Luke crooked her hand onto his elbow. "I was so sorry to hear about your accident. Does it hurt much?"

At that moment Charlotte Frankston passed them. She stared daggers at Lucinda then said, "Luke Anderson, I would think your mother taught you better than to associate with people who harbor criminals. Why, that murderer is probably the one who shot at Lucinda. Serves the family right." She sniffed, raised her nose to the air, and sashayed toward the church.

Luke let go of Lucinda's hand and covered his mouth to smother a laugh. "I always knew Mrs. Frankston was a snob, but that was too much."

"Luke Anderson, this is no funny matter. Of course it was rude, and seeing her like that wasn't nice. However, we mustn't judge her like she judged us."

Luke composed himself, but the twinkle remained in his eye. "You're right. I apologize."

Dove joined them. "Oh, Lucinda, I'm so glad to see you and

know you're all right. We were so worried about you." Then she nodded toward Mrs. Frankston. "I couldn't help but overhear. That was rude."

"Yes, but I can't let it upset me because I know it's not true." Lucinda linked arms with her friend, leaving Luke on her injured side. "Uncle Ben is thankful for your father sending some of his men over to help Monk while he and Hank were laid up."

Dove walked beside Lucinda. "My dad and your uncle are good friends and willing to help out each other. Mr. Fowler from the ranch on the other side of us isn't so friendly. He even tried to round up some of our cattle, claiming they were his, but he couldn't cover up Pa's brand."

"That's terrible. I heard Uncle Ben talking about some trouble with a man named Fowler. I'm glad the Rocking H brand is hard to do over."

Luke shook his head. "Some men are too greedy for their own good. Come, it's time for Sunday school."

She followed Luke and Dove into the classroom as she pondered his words. Greed. That's what had gotten Jake into trouble and what fueled the anger in Uncle Rudolph now. She vowed at that moment to never let the love of money fill her with greed. Instead, she would put her inheritance to good use.

※

After church, Mellie searched the yard for Lucinda and Becky. She spotted her niece strolling their way with Luke. He didn't hold a candle to Jake, but he and Lucinda made a nice-looking couple. She hoped Lucinda would realize life after Jake did exist.

The young couple stopped by the buggy. Becky hitched herself up beside Mellie. "I think Luke's as smitten with Lucinda as Jake was."

Mellie's gaze rested on her niece and Luke. He assisted

Lucinda on board. Becky was right; the look in the boy's eyes clearly showed his feelings for her niece. He bowed, waved at Mellie, then turned and headed for town.

Before Mellie could ask about the box social and Lucinda's response to Luke's invitation, her niece leaned forward.

"I'm so sorry for what happened earlier. Luke shouldn't have laughed about it."

Aunt Clara patted Lucinda's arm. "That's quite all right my dear. I enjoy seeing Charlotte get in a tizzy."

Mellie frowned at Clara. "I couldn't believe my ears. She tried to humiliate us all with her comment to Luke and then that one about the shooting."

Lucinda shook her head. "We can't do anything about people who have their minds set. Let's forget them. We know the truth." Then she smiled. "Aunt Mellie, I took your advice and accepted Luke's invitation to the church social. Dove is coming to our house that day to decorate our boxes. You'll have to help me plan what to cook."

Mellie grinned. "That's wonderful. We can make plans this afternoon if you like." Lucinda would have fun, and maybe eventually she'd forget about Jake, although Mellie hadn't been able to do that herself.

Ben sat beside her, his eyes clouded with sadness. A comment caught in her throat. Her husband mourned the loss of Jake as much as Lucinda did. Even Matt talked about missing him. He'd been with them less than a year, but they had loved him like their own. Mellie swallowed hard. They must look to the future and forget the past.

Chapter 26

The trip to Rio Alto took two days, and Jake spent Sunday at the jail there. The next few days the officials made work of assembling a jury and calling witnesses, and by Thursday, Jake sat in the makeshift courtroom in the hotel dining room, awaiting his fate. Three men he remembered from the card game testified on his behalf. Their words raised new hope in his chest. The first two had told virtually the same story as the man before the judge told now.

"On the night we played poker, this young man, Jake Starnes, had won two pots. On the third one, the deceased, I mean Mr. Girard, raised the ante and then won. After he won two rounds, we dealt another hand. I noticed Jake here watching the man real close like. Just before Girard declared victory a third time, young Jake here accused him of cheating. Girard drew his gun, but young Jake here was faster. Both fired a round, but Jake's hit the mark."

The judge peered at the witness. "And what did Jacob Starnes do?"

The man scratched his beard. "Well, I guess he ran away like the others said. One minute he was there, and then he wasn't. Just like that, he disappeared. I guess none of us paid any attention to him, 'cause when Girard fell, two aces fell out of his coat."

The judge nodded. "Thank you, you may return to your seat." He turned his gaze toward Jake.

Mac Daniels rose. "Your Honor, in light of the testimony of these eyewitnesses, I ask this case be dismissed."

The judge peered at Jake. "Looks to me like you're a decent young man, and I hope this incident has taught you a lesson about sitting in saloons and playing poker with men smarter and older than you."

Jake's insides trembled with a mix of dread and anticipation, but he looked the judge square in the eye. "It has, Your Honor. I plan to return to Oklahoma and marry a young lady there. No more card playing or saloons for me."

The judge pounded his gavel. "Case dismissed. Don't let me see you in my court again."

Jake sank into his chair in stunned silence. Just like that, he had freedom. His throat choked up, and he blinked his eyes. Daniels clapped him on the shoulder. "It's all over. Now you can head back to Oklahoma."

Jake grasped the lawyer's hand. "I don't know how to thank you. I never dreamed anything like this could happen."

"It has, and I hope it has taught you to let the Lord handle your problems instead of running away."

"Yes, sir, I'm not ever going to be in this situation again."

The three witnesses came to him. The last one shook his hand. "Young feller, if we'd a knowed your name, we coulda found you and told you what happened after you left. We learned that man had been cheatin' at cards in other towns around here, but we had no way of findin' you. I'm sorry for all the trouble you've had, but I'm glad you came back."

"Thank you, I am too. And I appreciate your willingness to step up with the truth." Jake swallowed hard. "I owe my life to you and your friends."

The man tipped his hat and strode away. Jake grasped

Daniels's hand again. "I don't know how I can ever repay you for what you did today."

Daniels clapped his free hand on Jake's shoulder. "Like I said, it's all been taken care of. And that reminds me, I have one more thing for you."

He reached into his jacket and removed an envelope. "This is from Derreck. He wanted you to be able to get home without any problem."

Jake stared at the envelope, then back up at Daniels. "I don't know what to say. I've never had so many people taking care of me." He didn't know how much the envelope contained, but by the weight of it, the money was sufficient to meet his needs.

Daniels grinned. "Son, God asks His children to take care of each other. The best way to repay us is to live your life for Him and to let others know what God did for you."

"I will, sir. I will." And that was a promise he intended to keep, and someday he'd pay back every penny.

"Are you heading up to Oklahoma this afternoon?"

"No, sir, the first thing I have to do is check on my uncle's ranch. I don't know what I'll find there, but I need to take care of that last bit of my old life." Going there first would add at least two weeks to his return, but it needed to be done.

"Godspeed, then. If you're ever in these parts, look me up and let me know how you're getting along." The lawyer set his hat on his head and walked through the doors.

For almost a year he'd thought of himself as a murderer, but now all the things he wanted and needed to do swept across his mind like the winds across the prairie. God had a plan for his life, but before he could seek that plan, he had to find a way to take care of Lucinda.

He couldn't go back and ask her to marry him, a penniless

cowboy. First he'd find out about the Lazy S and see what God had in store from that point.

⚬

The next week passed, and Lucinda's shoulder healed to the point she no longer needed the sling. Although the February weather had been warmer the past few days, Aunt Mellie told her the committee had moved the church social into the meeting hall recently completed in town.

Now the day had arrived. After preparing the food, she and Dove gathered supplies to decorate the containers for their dinners and settled at the table to work.

Dove said, "Your aunt Clara was sweet to find these trimmings and paper to use on our dinners."

Lucinda reached over for a piece of ribbon. "We'll have to do a better job than this if we hope to fool our escorts."

Dove giggled. "Well, actually, I don't want to fool Martin too much. If he doesn't have any idea which one is mine, he won't know when to bid."

"I hadn't thought of that. I guess we'll have to give them a hint."

Aunt Clara swept into the room carrying two patchwork pieces. "Here is just the thing to cover the dinners until you get to the church. I pieced these together in hopes of making a quilt later, but they can be put to good use now."

Lucinda held one of the large squares up to the light. "Aunt Clara, these are beautiful. Are you sure you don't mind letting us borrow them?"

"*Pshaw.* No, dear, I want you to have them." She peered at their decorating efforts. "*Hmm.* I believe we need a little more lace and ribbons. We want the young men to be tempted by their beauty as well as the good food inside. I'll be back in a minute."

Lucinda had chosen a basket instead of a box and finished securing blue ribbons on it. She picked up a length of yellow. "I think I'll make mine all yellow and blue. Those are my favorite colors." Who else might want to bid on her supper? Only a few young men lived on the ranches unless you counted the cowboys there too.

Lucinda furrowed her brow. "Oh dear, I do hope some stranger doesn't bid higher than Luke."

Dove laughed. "I don't think there's a chance of that. Luke has money he can spend, but most of the others don't." She held up her container. "See, I think the red bows make the brown paper look very festive."

Aunt Clara set a basket of trimmings on the floor. "Here are some other pretties. I used some of them on mine."

Lucinda giggled. "Aunt Clara! You fixed up one for yourself?"

"And why not? I'm as good a cook as any lady in these parts, and a mite better than most. It'll be fun to see who wants a taste of my homemade bread, jam cake, and fried chicken."

Lucinda pictured Aunt Clara with one of the few single men in town. Perhaps Joe at the livery stables or perhaps even Deputy Claymore. His wife died several years ago, and he was around Aunt Clara's age, and so was that man who worked at the hotel. Maybe Aunt Clara would have fun after all.

Aunt Mellie entered the kitchen, pulling on her gloves. "You girls about ready? Luke and Martin will be here any minute. You need to get those pretties covered and out of sight."

Lucinda set her basket in the middle of a patchwork piece and wrapped it securely. Then Dove did the same with her box. Aunt Mellie hugged Lucinda. "I'm so glad you're going with Luke. He's a fine young man. You'll have fun."

"I hope so, Aunt Mellie. I know I must not think about Jake today, but that's so hard. I miss him, and I'll continue to pray for him." Her heart still held hope for his return.

Noise of a wagon outside signaled Luke's arrival. She hurried out to meet it, making sure her basket was well covered.

When they arrived in town, Luke stopped the wagon, secured the horses, then came around to help Lucinda down. "Sure you won't give me a peek at your box before you add it to the others?" He smiled at her as she stepped down.

"No, you can't have a peek. You'll have to wait like everyone else. But if you're really nice, I might give you a hint."

"That's all I can ask, then, and I'll make sure I'm especially nice."

Inside the meeting hall a small bandstand had been set up for the four men who would provide entertainment. Garlands of red and white hearts decorated the stage. With a start, Lucinda realized that tomorrow was Valentine's Day. At a time and place like this, how could she keep Luke's mind on friendship only? She groaned silently.

After depositing their dinners, Lucinda and Dove rejoined Luke and Martin. Several other young men and women from their church as well as a few who didn't attend gathered in the building when the band struck up a tune.

She gasped in surprise. She hadn't known what to expect from the violins, a big bass, and an instrument Luke called a banjo, but it wasn't this. "What is he doing with that violin? That's the strangest sound I ever heard."

"That's fiddle music." Luke tapped his foot. "We all love it around here."

One of the men stepped forward. "Now, gents, it's time to choose your lady fair for a little do-si-do."

Luke grabbed her hand and led her to where men and women lined up across from each other. The music changed, and the man called out words that meant absolutely nothing to

Lucinda. She didn't know left from right in the frenzy of movement. Finally Luke noticed her distress and pulled her out of the circle of dancers.

She fanned her face and tried to catch her breath. "What in the world was that?"

"I'm sorry. I didn't even think about your not knowing how to dance."

"Well, I know how to dance, but that's not like any I've ever done." Indeed, the waltzes in Boston were what she thought of as dancing, or perhaps the ballet, not this crazy whirling and swinging by the hand from one place to another and from one partner to another.

Luke frowned. "We do it all the time around here. I'll have to teach you what to do."

Not today he wouldn't. So much activity in such a short time left her ready to collapse.

Dove and Martin joined them. Dove laughed. "Lucinda, we'll have to teach you how to do-si-do."

"That's what Luke just said, but I don't think so. My shoulder still hurts too much."

Luke looked concerned. "I'm so sorry. I should have known better than to take you dancing so soon after your accident. I'll sit out the dances with you."

Lucinda waved him away. "Please, just go have fun. I'll enjoy watching."

She gladly watched the whirl of the dancers, and even caught on to some of the patterns in the dance. Her foot tapped to the music. Although the sounds were unlike anything she'd ever heard before, she enjoyed its fast pace and infectious gaiety.

When the music ended, the three came to her, laughing and fanning themselves. She nodded toward the stage. "Look, they're stacking the dinners on the tables over there. I do believe the auction is about to begin."

Luke looked a bit alarmed. "What about that hint you promised me?"

Lucinda smiled. "My hint is that mine isn't a box."

The bidding began, and Lucinda began to have doubts about her box. What if someone else bid more than Luke did? Then, as more boxes were taken, she realized most of them knew which boxes they wanted and usually got the right one. She clapped with glee when Matt bid on Caroline's box and won it. A giggle escaped Lucinda's throat.

Dove nudged her. "I wonder what Mrs. Frankston will have to say about that?"

"Nothing good I'm sure." Her friend had read Lucinda's mind. She nudged Dove back. "Our boxes are up next." She grinned and glanced at Luke, and he grinned back. Well, so much for secrecy. Lucinda sat back and enjoyed the bidding. Four young men got involved in the bidding at first, but finally Luke had only one competitor. She scrunched her eyebrows and leaned forward.

Hank! He was the one bidding against Luke. Hank caught her eye and laughed, but he didn't go up after Luke's last bid. She breathed in relief as Luke claimed his prize and headed toward her.

When the auction finally ended, not only had Luke and Martin bid on the right dinners, but also Aunt Clara had a gentleman buy hers. She smiled and winked at the girls as she made her way to a table with Deputy Claymore. Leave it to Aunt Clara to find one of the most eligible older men in all of Barton Creek.

Lucinda followed Luke to a table where Dove and Martin sat, as did two other young couples.

Luke bit into a chicken leg. He licked his lips. "Best fried chicken I ever ate."

"It is?" She laughed. "You should have seen my first attempts. Even Matt wouldn't eat what I cooked."

"I must say you've learned since then. Can't wait to taste the pie." He winked as he took a bite of corn bread.

One of the girls tilted her head and peered at Lucinda. "You know what I think? You should let us call you Lucy. Lucy and Luke make cute names for a couple." Then she laughed as though she had made a great joke.

Heat rose in Lucinda's face. They weren't a couple! Then reality struck her; she hadn't thought of Jake all evening. Watching the dancing and the bidding had pushed him from her mind. Jake said he wanted her to get on with her life. If this is what the Lord wanted her to do, then perhaps the time had come to put Jake in the past and look to her future in Barton Creek.

Chapter 27

*A*fter four days of hard riding, Jake approached his uncle's ranch with fear and anxiety gripping his soul. Trees surrounded the house, and the corral held several horses, just as when he'd left. A brown and white collie ran out to investigate. Jake slowed his horse and dismounted as the dog jumped on him.

"Rusty, I can't believe you're still here." He grabbed the dog behind its ears and ran his thumbs through the silky coat. "You remember me, don't you, boy?" Rusty lapped at Jake's face.

"Jake, boy, is it really you?" A weathered-looking man strode toward Jake and the dog.

"Hello, Zeke. Yes, it's me all right." He reached out and grasped the man's outstretched hand. His uncle's ranch foreman hadn't changed a bit. "It's good to see you."

"And it's good to see you too. We've wondered all this time where you'd gone to and if you'd ever come back." Zeke guided Jake toward the house with Rusty nipping at their heels.

Jake grinned. "I can't believe old Rusty still remembers me. I missed him." His pa gave him Rusty as a puppy for Christmas. The dog had been his constant companion after that. He had regretted leaving Rusty behind when he rode away from the Lazy S.

Zeke opened the door. "Come on in. How long you reckon you'll be staying around these parts?"

"I don't know. I have some business to take care of in Oklahoma." When Jake entered the house, he stepped back in time. Everything looked the same as it did before his aunt and uncle died. He wasn't prepared for the feelings of grief that washed over him now.

Zeke motioned for him to follow him to the kitchen. "Della, look who's here. It's Jake himself."

A round-faced woman with graying hair turned around from the sink. Her eyes opened wide, and a smile lifted the corners of her mouth. "Oh, my, it is you." She opened her arms for a hug. "We didn't know where you'd gone or what happened to you. But I prayed for your safety every day."

"Your prayers helped save me." Jake wrapped his arms around her and breathed in the familiar scent of soap and cooking grease of the woman who'd been the ranch cook and housekeeper for many years. Her arms around him felt good and safe after all this time of uncertainty.

He stepped back. "Everything looks just like they left it."

Zeke hooked his hat on a peg by the door. "Della and I married not long after your aunt and uncle died. We figured we could run the ranch together until you came back." Then his brow furrowed. "You said you had business in Oklahoma?"

Jake grinned and sat at the table. Della set a cup of coffee before him and a plate of cookies. He grabbed two of them. It'd been a long time since he'd enjoyed any of Della's sugar cookies. The tender morsels melted in his mouth and reminded him of Lucinda's at Christmas.

He peered at Zeke. "I've been working up on a spread in the Oklahoma Territory. Met a pretty girl there, and I aim to go back and claim her as my bride—that is, if no one else has spoken for her by now."

Della beamed. "Well, I declare, that's more cause for celebration. When do we get to meet her?"

Jake rubbed the back of his neck. "That I can't say. I'm thinking about getting me a spread up there with the money my pa left me if it's still available." It hadn't been much, but it would be a start to his dream. He'd rather leave here and go back than to have Lucinda so far away from the only family she had left.

"The money's in the bank." Zeke rose, went to the desk in the corner, and pulled out a bank statement to hand to him. Jake glanced down at the amount listed. As he'd feared, it wasn't much.

Zeke continued, "When you didn't come back, I took over running the ranch. I'm willing to buy the Lazy S and pay a fair price for it. Put that with the money in the bank and you should have enough to get you started."

Zeke buy the ranch? Jake let the idea settle in his brain. That he hadn't counted on, but then he'd considered selling it before he left for Oklahoma. This made it easier for him to leave right away.

"I don't know what to say except thank you. I know Uncle Earl would want you to have it since you've been here so many years."

The older man sipped his coffee. "It's too good a place to let go."

"I can see that." He pushed back his chair. "This puts a new light on my visit. I'll be heading out soon as we can close the deal and I check in at the bank and make arrangements for the money to be transferred to the Barton Creek bank. I sure don't want to be riding alone with that amount of cash or even a bank draft on me."

Della ran her hands over her apron. "But you just got here, son. Do you have to leave so soon?"

Jake hugged her again. "Yep, that little gal up in Oklahoma won't wait for me forever. She has no idea I'm coming back for

242

her." He prayed no one else had claimed her heart.

"What do you mean she doesn't know you're coming for her?" Della pulled back and searched his face with her eyes.

"It's a long story, and I'll tell you all about it later. But first I'd like to get some of this trail dust off." He'd have to tell them everything, but now he didn't mind others hearing the story. God had saved him, and he wanted the whole world to know.

"Go on back to your old room. Some of your things are still there. Make yourself at home. Supper will be ready in a little bit." Della shoved him toward his room.

It looked as though he'd never left. The patchwork quilt on the bed had been his mother's. His first thought was whether or not Della would let him take it with him. Of course she would.

After cleaning up, he examined the contents of the drawers in the old maple chest. Several shirts lay folded as if waiting for his selection. A blue one caught his eye, and he pulled it out. He shoved his arms into it and discovered it still fit. In fact, it fit better than it had before. Aunt Josey had always made his clothes a little larger than needed so he'd grow into them, and now he had.

During supper, Jake enjoyed the home cooking he remembered from younger days. Della prepared more food than the three of them could eat with extra fried steak, mashed potatoes, gravy, homemade biscuits, and her home-canned green beans.

He explained to them what had happened in the time since he'd left the Lazy S. When he finished, Della sat with tear-filled eyes. "No wonder you want to get back to your girl. And I'm so thrilled about your finding Jesus. He's been taking care of you for sure." Then she jumped up from the table and hurried to the side board.

A minute or so later she returned to the table with a black velvet pouch. She set it on the table and pushed the tiny bag toward him. "This is your ma's wedding ring. I saved it for you, not knowing if you'd ever come back. But this would be perfect for your young lady."

Jake touched the soft nap then wrapped his fingers around it. Something of his mother's. "How did you come by this?"

"Your sister Carrie had it. She showed it to me one day and said she hoped to wear it at her own marriage."

Della's face blurred as Jake fought back the tears rising in his eyes. Both his ma and Carrie gone, but God had shown him another miracle in this ring being preserved.

He blinked and held the ring in his hand. The gold band had been engraved with flowers and his mother's name. Jake held it up to the light, and the glow from it brought back all the good memories of his childhood.

"Yes, God has been more than good to me." His fingers closed around the ring. "And I thank you for keeping my belongings all this time. I hope Lucinda will be free and will wear my mother's ring."

Zeke clapped him on the back. "She couldn't find a better man." Then he swept his hand through the air. "Look around. You'll find a few other family things. We kept as many as we could. You take whatever you want. I'll give you an extra horse to carry it on too."

Jake marveled at his good fortune. God had supplied for all his needs and then some. He'd be forever grateful to the man seated at the table with him. He rubbed his thumb over the engraved surface of the ring. As soon as possible, he'd begin the final part of his journey back to Lucinda.

⚜

Jake and Zeke rode back to the ranch after transferring the deed to the Lazy S over to Zeke. Because of the ranch's remote location and lack of a telegraph, settling his affairs had taken longer than he'd planned. Then days of heavy rain and flooding delayed him even more. It was March already, and he itched to get going.

"I can't believe my father left any money. I thought he'd drunk and gambled it all away. With that money and this from the sale today, I should be able to buy a nice spread for Lucinda and me." Ben would help him buy stock and get a house started. It'd been over two months since he'd left Oklahoma, but it wouldn't take that long to get back there.

"Your uncle planned on telling you about it when you came of age, but he died before he had a chance."

Jake shook his head soberly. If he'd known about the money, he'd have spent it or lost it all in card games. Even then the Lord was looking out for him.

"I'm going to head on back to Oklahoma now that our business is finished. I figure from the maps we looked at it's about five hundred or so miles to Barton Creek. If I can make twenty to twenty-five miles a day, I should be back in three weeks or so."

"Reckon that's about right. With all the things you need to take with you, and the extra horse, you'll be a little slower."

"Think I can take Rusty with me?" The collie would make a good traveling companion and be another part of childhood.

"Don't see why not. He's your dog anyways."

They rode in comfortable silence back to the ranch. If he made just the right time, he'd be in Barton Creek for Lucinda's eighteenth birthday, and that was one celebration he looked forward to with all his heart.

❧

A day of traveling behind him, Jake slowed his horse and searched for a place to camp for the night. Della had made sure he had food enough for several days. Now he looked forward to her biscuits and bacon. Zeke had been more than generous with the fine horse he provided to carry the load of things Jake decided to take back to Oklahoma.

Once he had a small fire going, he filled a black tin pot to make coffee. He'd have to remember to refill the canteens with water at the next stream or river so he wouldn't run low.

Rusty scampered around, exploring the terrain and taking care of his business. The collie made a fine companion for travel. Jake felt safer with his beloved pet by his side.

After his meal, Jake sat by the dancing flames and dreamed of a future with Lucinda. With the money from his father and the sale of his uncle's ranch, Jake now had enough to purchase a piece of land and to stock a few head of cattle. With Lucinda by his side, they would have a grand ranch. He didn't want to stop, but riding without any rest would be taking risks he didn't need. Besides, March could bring more rough weather, and he'd need all his strength to battle the elements.

Rusty nuzzled his hand. Jake reached up and scratched the dog behind its ears. "Well, Rusty, I've missed you. You'll be a fine dog for my ranch and a good pet for children." His and Lucinda's children would love the collie if God answered his prayers.

Jake leaned against a large rock and looked toward the black heavens. "Thank You, Lord, for Zeke and Della, Marshal Derreck, and Mr. Daniels. You sent wonderful people into my life to look after me." Then he remembered how Luke Anderson had admired Lucinda and added, "Lord, I know Lucinda has no reason to believe I'll come back to her, but please let her wait."

The judge in Rio Alto had written a letter to prove that Jake had killed Henry Girard in self-defense. Daniels had requested the letter just in case Jake ran into any trouble with the deputy back in Barton Creek or anywhere along the trail. The lawyer didn't think Jake would really need the document, but Jake appreciated the sense of security the letter gave.

He checked the horses one last time before settling down for the night under the star-filled heavens. God sat on His throne and took care of life on Earth. But what if he was too late? His heart wrenched with the idea, and his whole body ached. Lucinda's loving spirit was a good quality for a wife, and her beauty was a bonus.

Rusty barked beside him. Luke scratched the dog behind his ears. If Lucinda belonged to someone else, he would not buy land in Oklahoma. He'd go back to the Lazy S and work with Zeke.

Chapter 28

*B*en pulled up on the reins of his team. "I'm heading down to the smithy's for some supplies. I know you have a long list, so I'll be back to help you load it." The last time the family had been in town was for the box social. More snowstorms had kept the family cooped up for several weeks. Now with the early March thaw, this trip into town came as a welcome change.

He helped Mellie down from her seat and kissed her cheek. "I'll see you in a little while. You get your things, and I'll be down at the bank."

She fingered the collar of his shirt under his heavy jacket. "Think I'll buy material for a few shirts for you and Matt. Yours have seen better days, and Matt's are getting too little."

"Whatever you say, my love." He wrapped the reins around the hitching post. "I'll leave the team here so Luke and Mr. Anderson can load your things."

Mellie nodded and headed into the store. Ben had only gone a few yards down the street when Luke came running after him.

"Mr. Haynes, Mr. Haynes, wait up a minute."

Ben stopped and waited. "What's on your mind, young man?"

Luke inhaled deeply. His breath came out in a whoosh of air. "I have something to ask of you."

Ben smiled. "And what might that be?" From what he'd observed at the box social, the young man was interested in

Lucinda. Then he noticed Mellie had followed Luke outside. She stood a few feet away as though she too knew what Luke wanted.

The boy licked his lips. "Sir, I would count it a great pleasure to have your permission to call on Miss Lucinda." Pink tinged his cheeks.

Ben pondered the words. Not knowing for certain about Jake's fate, he had no reason to deny the request, although Lucinda may not agree. Still, the time had come for her to move toward her future here in Barton Creek. Mellie covered her mouth with her hand, waiting for his response. He reached out and grasped Luke's hand.

"I think that would be a fine idea. You have my blessings."

Luke's face now glowed redder than embers after a fire. He pumped Ben's hand. "Thank you. Thank you, sir. I promise to treat her with respect."

He stepped back, and a wide smile graced his lips. "Wowee! Can't wait to tell Pa." He turned and ran into Mellie. He reached out his hand to her arm. "Oh, I'm sorry, Mrs. Haynes. Did you hear? I'm going to come calling on Lucinda." He didn't wait for an answer but bounded back into the store.

Mellie bit her lip. "I hope that wasn't a mistake. No telling what Bea's going to have to say about it."

Ben hugged her. "Well, that's none of our concern. Luke will have to deal with his ma." He stepped back. "Now, let's get on with our business."

❧

Lucinda and Becky sat in the main room of the ranch house with their sewing. Uncle Ben and Aunt Mellie had gone into Barton Creek for ranch business and supplies, leaving the two girls behind. Lucinda pierced the cloth with her needle then let it drop to her lap. "I wish there had been room in the wagon for us. It's rather boring around here right now."

With two months gone by, Jake should have been in Texas by now and his fate decided. If only she could know what that fate was. The past eight weeks had been the longest of her life, especially with the bad weather keeping them inside.

Becky looked up from her stitching. "I would rather be out riding Daisy than doing this."

Aunt Clara walked in. "*Hmm*. Sounds to me like two girls I know need something exciting to do. How about a picnic down by the creek? It's a fine sunny day."

"Oh, good, now I can ride Daisy. Let's go change clothes." Becky stuffed her embroidery piece into the sewing basket.

Lucinda laughed. "Thank you, Aunt Clara. This will be fun."

When she and Becky returned in their riding attire, a red cloth covered a basket set on the table. Aunt Clara untied her apron. "I see you're all ready to go. Get your horses. I asked Matt to hitch the team to the wagon."

Lucinda hurried out to the stables with Becky behind her. Matt tightened the harness on the team. He crossed his arms over his chest, a frown forming on his face. "Have you forgotten what happened last time you went out? Pa would be mighty angry with me if I let you three ladies go out alone."

"Oh, Matt, it'll be all right. We're just going to the creek, and that's still on our land." She had forgotten her uncle's warning but felt perfectly safe here on the ranch.

"Don't make any difference. I'm going with you. And if I see Monk or Hank coming in, I'll get one of them to go too."

Lucinda laughed in relief. At least he didn't deny them the pleasure of the outing. "That's fine, but I think you want to go along for some of Aunt Clara's cooking instead of protecting me."

Becky headed into the stable. "C'mon. We're wasting time."

Half an hour later the four of them laid out their meal on the cloth that had covered the basket. Lucinda lifted her face toward the sun and basked in its warm spring rays. So different from Boston where the first days of March still brought snow and freezing weather. "I love springtime, but it comes so much later in Boston."

Becky joined her. "I like spring too, 'cause I know school will be out soon, and I'll have all summer to ride Daisy."

Aunt Clara set a plate of fried chicken on the cloth. "I much prefer fall myself. The trees are so vibrant with color, and it means the holidays are getting closer."

Lucinda agreed. Fall in New England provided some of the most beautiful scenery she'd ever seen. She had arrived in Barton Creek too late to witness such a display in Oklahoma, but surely the trees here turned from green to the brilliant gold and red of autumn just as they did in Massachusetts.

Matt finished securing the horses and joined them. After a short prayer, Lucinda filled her plate. What a pleasant way to spend an afternoon. The only thing that could make it nicer would be if Jake were with them. Images of her own house and a kitchen where she and Jake sat with their children as a family meandered through her mind. She could almost feel his arms about her.

A finger poked her arm, and the images disappeared. "I'm sorry. Did I miss something?"

Aunt Clara sat on a stool she had brought. "I was commenting on what a fine young man Mr. Luke is. You two made quite a couple at the social."

Lucinda felt the heat rising in her cheeks. "Well, I don't think we were the only ones. I saw you with Deputy Claymore, and he seemed to be quite happy."

Now Aunt Clara turned pink. She began gathering the

remains of the lunch. "Yes, I did have a good time, but everyone noticed you and Luke."

Lucinda bit her lip. Being with Luke had been pleasant, and he had expressed a desire to see her more often. His intentions seemed to be focused on a deeper relationship than friendship, and she didn't feel ready for that so soon. She'd much rather they be good friends, but she'd comply if her aunt and uncle wanted her to accept Luke's affection and Jake didn't return.

All her life, Lucinda had been taught not to question God's authority and His workings in her life. She had obeyed, but now she couldn't truly understand why He had let Jake ride away. Suddenly Matt jumped up. "I don't like the looks of that sky to the north. Either a cold front is coming or a bad storm or both. Let's get back to the house."

Aunt Clara finished packing away the remains of the meal. "You're right, Matt. Let's hurry."

The skies roiled with clouds covering the sun. Without its warmth, the air now carried a chill in the slight wind that blew across the creek.

Matt helped Aunt Clara up into the wagon then mounted his horse. She flicked the reins and headed for the ranch.

In the distance a jagged streak of lightning split the sky, and seconds later, thunder rumbled through the air. Lucinda kicked Misty into a fast trot. Those clouds held rain, and from the flashes across the sky, a great deal would fall.

They arrived at the ranch before the first drops splattered on the ground and were able to get into the house. Matt grabbed the horses' reins and led them into the barn. Lucinda stared out the window as the sky grew darker. Where were Aunt Mellie and Uncle Ben? She prayed they would be home before heavy rains came.

The trip into town had been quite interesting today. The best news Ben had heard concerned the telegraph lines. Mayor Frankston promised the lines would be installed by the end of the month, and Barton Creek would have connections with the rest of the world. He also said telephone lines wouldn't be far behind. He intended for Barton Creek to catch up with the more populated areas of Oklahoma.

That suited Ben just fine. Barton Creek had gone long enough without a telegraph office. More progress for the territory with the telegraph coming. He figured in another ten years Oklahoma would be a state, and that was something he would be glad to see.

"I'm glad the bank didn't have a problem with our borrowing the money to restock the cattle we lost. Sam and I will go next week to purchase what we need to get our herds back up to good numbers." Both men needed new stock in order to make any profit this year, and the bank's willingness to advance the money helped.

"Yes, and I'm glad we used the money Amanda left us to pay off most of our mortgage. I believe that helped Mr. Monroe make his decision."

Then her eyes twinkled. "Wasn't Luke cute the way he finally got up the courage to ask your permission to court Lucinda?"

Ben chuckled. "Cute isn't exactly the word I'd use. I hesitated to give it without asking Lucinda, but he seemed so anxious, and she seemed to enjoy being with him at the box social."

Mellie nodded. "It's for the best, and time for Lucinda to think about her future. As much as I loved Jake, sitting around, moping, and waiting for what will never be isn't healthy."

"I agree. We must do all we can to secure that future." No

one in town knew Lucinda would be a wealthy young woman when her birthday passed, and he intended to keep it that way. No need to attract those with less-than-honorable intentions.

Dark clouds rolled across the sky. He didn't like the looks of them, but if they were lucky, they might reach the ranch before the rain hit. This time of year meant unpredictable weather. This storm could cause the creek to overflow if the sky held as much water as he believed it did.

Mellie clutched his arm. "Look at that lightning! Oh, hurry, Ben. I don't want to be away from the house if a storm is coming."

Ben agreed and urged his horses to a faster gait. The temperature dropped several degrees, and a chill filled his heart. That could mean real trouble ahead. When cold air from the north mixed with the warm air they'd been having, tornadoes could result.

Large drops of rain spotted his coat as they approached the house. Matt ran from the stables to meet them. Ben hopped down from the wagon. "Help me get the supplies inside, then take care of the horses."

Monk and Hank rode in. Hank dismounted and hurried to help unload the wagon. "There's a lot of rain in those clouds. A lot of wind too. It's coming fast."

Mellie ran into the house to escape the rain that began falling harder. The men emptied the wagon, and Matt led the horses to the barn. Ben followed with Monk and Hank and their horses.

Ben heard the ping of hail on the roof. "Let the horses loose. I think this is going be a bad one. See how dark it is?" At three o'clock in the afternoon, the skies were greenish black. Ben's heart skipped a beat. The way those clouds swirled into one long tail meant only one thing. He had to get the women to safety.

He ran toward the house. "Tornado! Hurry! Get to the storm

cellar. Mellie, get the girls." Marble-sized hailstones bounced on the ground and scattered about his feet.

Mellie ran outside, Becky and Lucinda close behind, with Aunt Clara bringing up the rear. Mellie took one look to the north and urged the girls to run faster. Matt stood with Hank and Monk holding the shelter door open. Ben ran to help Aunt Clara. He held her arm and pulled her toward the storm cellar.

Monk helped the ladies first. Ben made sure they were in safe, then urged the men to go down. He took one last look at the twisting mass of clouds headed their way, then slammed the door shut and secured it behind him.

$$\sim\!\!\downarrow\!\!\sim$$

Lucinda sat huddled with Becky in the dim light of the shelter. The winds overhead roared and pounded on the door. From the grim look on Aunt Mellie's and Uncle Ben's faces, the storm was a bad one. Lucinda had never heard such noise from winds. She'd been in nor'easters and hurricanes, but never a tornado.

For what seemed like an eternity, but in reality lasted only a few minutes, the storm raged. Then silence came. No one said a word, but all sat still and listened.

Finally Monk stood. "Want me to go and take a look, boss?"

Uncle Ben shook his head. "No, we'll do it together." He turned to Aunt Mellie. "You stay here with the girls, and I'll let you know when it's safe to come out."

He climbed the stairs and opened the door. A lighter sky shone through, but rain still fell. The others followed and closed the door behind him.

The light from the lanterns cast strange shadows on the walls of the shelter. Shelves held canned foods and other supplies in case they had to remain there for any length of time. Her uncle's prayer after they settled in the shelter had been answered. They sat here in safety, but what had happened outside?

The door opened again and Uncle Ben came down the steps. "It looks bad, Mellie. I hate for you to see everything, but we can't put it off forever."

Lucinda's breath caught in her throat. Aunt Mellie headed for the steps. Lucinda grabbed Becky's hand. They would see the aftermath together.

When Lucinda stepped outside, the rain had stopped, but destruction lay everywhere. Her hand went to her mouth. "Oh, no!" The roof of the house had blown away, and two walls were gone. She could see some things still standing inside. Only half of the barn remained standing. Several stalls stood intact, but the rest lay in rubble.

Aunt Mellie's wail echoed in the air. Uncle Ben wrapped his arms around her.

"Oh, Ben, it's all gone. Everything we've worked so hard for." Her shoulders shook with sobs.

Uncle Ben held her against his chest. "I know it looks bad, but we're all safe. We can replace things and rebuild. God will provide for us. He's never let us down."

Total helplessness descended over Lucinda. She had never seen anything like this before. She hugged Becky, whose tears dampened the front of Lucinda's blouse.

Uncle Ben embraced Aunt Mellie tighter. "Go on and see what you can find in the house. I think some things can be saved. The men and I will round up the animals." He stepped back and released her.

Misty and Daisy? Where were they? Lucinda feared for the horses' lives. How could they live through such a storm?

Aunt Mellie squared her shoulders and marched toward the

house. She called out to Becky and Lucinda. "Come, girls. We must see what we can find to save."

Aunt Clara followed Aunt Mellie toward the house. "I declare, this is worse than the one I survived back in Kansas. I wonder what's left."

Inside, Lucinda discovered several amazing things. The china cabinet and hutch stood unscathed against one wall. Not a piece of china or glassware had broken in the turmoil. Only a part of the roof had blown away; the other part collapsed onto the back part of the house over the bedrooms.

Aunt Mellie stood in front of the cabinet for a moment with tears streaming down her face. "I can't believe what I'm seeing. Thank You, Lord."

Aunt Clara beckoned from what was left of the kitchen. "I've found some pots and pans."

Her two aunts picked up stray pots and other utensils. Lucinda and Becky lifted smaller pieces of debris from the floor, looking for anything salvageable. They found bits and pieces, some broken almost beyond recognition, and some intact. Lucinda picked up the vase she'd brought Aunt Mellie from Boston. It lay under a cushion from a chair without so much as a crack to mar the surface. She held it close to her chest, thankful for this remembrance of her mother. When they uncovered Uncle Ben's pipes and humidors, only one looked too broken to be fixed.

After she placed the pipes and vase on the wagon, she told her aunt, "I'm going to walk around a bit."

She stepped carefully over the debris in the yard, swallowing the tears that threatened to come. No need to cry over things that couldn't be undone. God had spared their lives, and they were more important than things. Like Uncle Ben said, things could be replaced and a house rebuilt, but life was priceless.

The landscape didn't escape the brunt of the storm either.

The tops of trees looked as though someone had twisted the branches right out of them, and still others had broken limbs hanging loose.

Something white in the trees near the barn caught her attention. She hurried over to investigate. Suddenly she realized those things draped over the naked tree branches were clothes. Upon closer inspection, she realized one of Aunt Mellie's petticoats adorned a limb. She then recognized others as pieces of her own private clothing. Even Aunt Clara's corset had found a home in the branches.

At first the sight mortified Lucinda. Their undergarments out where anyone could see them! She stood on tiptoe, but the elusive clothing fluttered just out of reach. The laces and hooks of the corset flapped in a slight breeze that sprang up. Then she giggled, and soon full-blown laughter filled her.

Becky ran up beside her. "What's so funny?"

Lucinda pointed to the tree. Then Becky burst into laughter too. "Is that what I think it is?" The two girls hugged each other then collapsed to the ground. Lucinda's eyes watered, and she could hardly breathe.

"We must get those down before Aunt Clara comes and sees them." Lucinda eyed the branches. "Come, climb on my back, and I think you can reach it." Becky hitched up her skirts and climbed aboard a crouching Lucinda. Gasping a bit at the weight, Lucinda stood, and Becky stretched out her arms. "Can you reach it?"

"Yes, and Ma's petticoat too." The items dropped to the ground beside Lucinda. Becky retrieved several other items and let them fall.

Uncle Ben came around the barn leading Misty and Daisy. Matt followed with two other horses. Matt yelled, "What in the world is that?"

"Daisy!" Becky screamed in relief. She jumped from Lucinda's back and ran over to wrap her arms around the horse's neck. Meanwhile, Lucinda grabbed up the garments they had salvaged.

"What were you doing on Lucinda's back, young lady?" The set of Uncle Ben's jaw reflected anger, but the twinkle in his eye betrayed him.

Lucinda defended her cousin. "Some of Aunt Mellie's and Aunt Clara's unmentionables landed in the tree. We wanted to get the things down before they saw them. Aunt Clara would be mortified."

Uncle Ben chuckled and glanced up at the tree. "I see a few more things, but we don't have time to worry about them now. I have the wagon, and we need to load it with what we can and head into town before nightfall."

Lucinda deposited her load on the wagon and hurried into the house to tell her aunts. The two ladies had managed to salvage many kitchen items now stacked in a corner. She found the ladies in a bedroom inspecting the damage there.

When Lucinda delivered her uncle's message, Aunt Mellie shook her head. "I don't know where to begin." She surveyed the debris. "We should look for things we really need. Tell Ben we'll be out in a few minutes."

They managed to fill the wagon with various items of clothing and pieces Aunt Mellie didn't want to leave behind. Uncle Ben covered others in the house as much as he could with quilts and moved a few items to a spot where they would be protected from further damage.

Lucinda found her quilt and a few pieces of clothing and loaded them onto the wagon. Hank and Monk rode up with two more horses. Monk shoved his hat back on his head. "Hank and I are going to stay here and guard what's left. We can sleep in the barn on our bedrolls. We'll do more cleaning up while there's still daylight."

Ben grasped the cowboy's hand. "Thank you. We appreciate that. Matt and I'll be back in the morning to help."

Five minutes later, Uncle Ben drove the wagon out to the road to town. Lucinda turned for one last look at the destruction left behind. Nothing would ever be the same.

Chapter 29

*L*ucinda awoke and glanced around at unfamiliar surroundings. Then the storm and its aftermath came plunging back. She shuddered to think what might have happened without the safety of the shelter.

Even though she had no chores this morning and no meal to help prepare, Lucinda could not sleep. She eased off the bed to keep from disturbing Aunt Clara, who still slept soundly. Becky had bedded down on the floor last night, and she stirred as Lucinda dressed.

Her cousin's sleep-filled voice rose from the covers. "Is it morning?" She yawned and sat up. "Oh, I forgot. We're in the hotel. No chores today. No school either. I'm going back to sleep." She pulled the blanket up over her shoulder and hugged her pillow.

Lucinda entertained no such thoughts. They rode into town last night just as night fell, but the damage to a few buildings was still visible. The hotel stood unharmed, as had the boarding house. God had spared the places needed for housing. Again, one of God's miracles to provide for His children.

She slipped out of the room into the hall. Her stomach rumbled at the aroma of coffee and frying meat wafting up the stairs. The clerk behind the desk greeted her. "Good morning, Miss Bishop. I trust you had a good night."

"Yes, I did. Thank you. Is the dining room serving breakfast yet?"

"Yes, ma'am. Go on in. I think Mr. and Mrs. Haynes are already there."

"Thank you." The management had tried to bring a little opulence to the hotel with a round burgundy velvet settee in the center of the lobby. She had noticed the cut-glass doors on her first day in Barton Creek, and thankfully, they had survived the storm.

Uncle Ben waved for her to join their table when she entered the dining room. She wove her way among the dark wood tables to where her aunt and uncle sat.

"You're up early this morning." Her uncle stood when she approached, then held the chair while she seated herself.

Lucinda picked up a napkin and laid it across her lap. "I didn't see any sense in staying in bed wide awake. I left Aunt Clara and Becky soundly sleeping."

A woman approached the table. Uncle Ben introduced her. "This is Nell, who takes care of the dining service here at the hotel. Nell, this is our niece, Lucinda Bishop."

"I'm pleased to meet you, Miss Bishop. What can I bring you for breakfast?"

"Some scrambled eggs and toast will be fine. And I'll have hot tea to drink."

Nell nodded and disappeared into what must be the kitchen area. Lucinda scanned the room. A number of people had come in for breakfast. Last night the hotel had been full, and Uncle Ben had been fortunate to secure two rooms. Matt had gone down to the livery and slept in the wagon.

She listened to the chatter of patrons around her. All the conversation revolved around the storm. Many farms and ranches had been hit, as well as buildings on the north side of town according to what she heard, but midtown only had a few broken windows from the hail.

Uncle Ben set his coffee cup on the table. "Mayor Frankston has called a special meeting on the church grounds later this morning. He plans to talk about rebuilding the school and some of the houses on that end of town. He also wants to see how many others suffered losses and what can be done."

Aunt Mellie laid down her fork. "I'm happy he's being so prompt in seeing to the needs of others. We'll need help getting the steeple repaired and patching the holes in the roof of the church."

Nell returned with Lucinda's meal. She placed the food on the table and stood with her hands on her hips. "This is the time we're going to find out just what these folks of Barton Creek are made of. Our first disaster will reveal whether we can be a town united in recovery or selfish in wanting personal needs tended to first."

Uncle Ben nodded and continued the conversation with Nell. Lucinda tuned out their voices. She prayed Dove's family had managed to find shelter and were safe because she hadn't seen them in town.

Just as they finished their meal, Aunt Clara made her appearance. She hurried to their table. "I can't believe I slept so late. Why didn't you wake me, Lucinda? There's so much to be done."

"You needed the sleep after our trip last night." Lucinda offered Aunt Clara her place. "I'm all finished eating and want to take a walk around."

"Thank you, my dear. I'm famished." The older woman sank into the chair.

Lucinda strolled to the entrance to the hotel and stepped out onto the porch in front. She leaned on the scrollwork railing to better observe the street. In the distance at the north end, the beautiful white steeple on the church lay toppled in the yard, and the school had lost its roof. The general store had a few broken windows, as did the depot.

The rains left the street a muddy mess of ruts and ridges. More people than she'd seen at any time she'd been in town strode up and down wooden walkways on either side of the street. Most were headed for the bank, the boarding house, or the general store.

When would life ever get back to normal? Her birthday was only weeks away, but all thoughts of a special celebration left her. The people here needed too many things for her aunt and uncle to spend money on a party.

A seed of an idea planted itself in her mind—an idea for which she would need professional advice—and she knew just who could give it. But first she had a more important errand to run.

⚶

Five minutes later, Lucinda walked out of the jail disappointed. No one had heard anything. The marshal had stopped by on his way back to Kansas and let Deputy Claymore know that he had sent Jake on to Rio Alto to face the judge there. Derreck had business to take care of elsewhere and didn't finish the journey. She again rued the fact no wire service came to Barton Creek. The mayor said soon, but not in time to help find out about Jake.

She strolled up the street and greeted those she knew from church. Men picked up broken glass and roofing material from the streets. Several stores covered broken windows with blankets or quilts. Other men on rooftops made repairs to stave off any more damage to the property below.

Lucinda returned to the hotel, where she found paper and pen to write a letter to Mr. Sutton. Would Mr. Sutton think her impractical in her desires? She had no idea how much money her trust fund actually held, but according to her lawyer, it was substantial. Her own needs were minimal, but the people of

Barton Creek as well as Aunt Mellie and Uncle Ben had great ones. Rebuilding would cost money, and lots of it.

With renewed determination, she sealed the letter and hurried to post it. If all went according to plan, she'd have a wonderful gift to give the people of Barton Creek on her eighteenth birthday.

With a day of no chores or meal preparation ahead, what could she do to pass the time? An idea occurred. Why not go back to the ranch and see what else could be salvaged and brought to town? Surely she could find more clothes and other things in all the rubble. She hastened her steps and met Uncle Ben exiting the hotel.

"Oh, I'm glad you're here. I want to go back out to the ranch and see what I can find that is still usable."

Her uncle furrowed his brow. "Your aunts are staying in town to help with things at the church. Maybe you should stay and do that."

Her heart fell. "Please let me go back. I can get Misty and ride out to see Dove and find out if they had much damage."

He pondered for a moment, then nodded. "All right. Get changed. Monk came in this morning to pick up supplies to do some repairs. He and Matt can ride back with you. Go on and let your aunt know where you'll be."

She threw her arms around his neck. "Thank you. I'll hurry."

"I have one condition."

"Oh, what is that?" Lucinda stepped back with trepidation.

"If you do go to see Dove, you'll let one of the men go with you. Understand?"

"Of course I will." With light feet, she raced up to her room, thankful she still wore the riding clothes from the picnic yesterday. Could it have been only yesterday? The picnic now seemed a distant memory in the light of present circumstances.

She didn't see Aunt Mellie or Aunt Clara, so she hastily wrote a note and left it where they would find it. Then she hurried to meet Monk at the livery stable. She climbed up into the wagon and waited for him.

He expressed surprise at seeing her but accepted her explanation. Once on the trail back to the ranch, she glanced up at the clear skies, so different from yesterday. The amount of damage in such a short time amazed her. All around the strength of the storm showed itself from the broken limbs of trees to strange debris caught in the branches.

Why hadn't she brought Becky with her? Her cousin would be sorely disappointed to learn Lucinda had returned to the ranch without her. The trip would have given Becky another opportunity to ride Daisy. Perhaps they could take the horse back to town for her.

❦

When the house and barns came into view, Lucinda sucked in her breath. It looked even worse today even though the men had worked to remove some of the trash. Tornadoes did crazy things as evidenced in how part of the house stood intact and the other part in ruins. The chimney rose like a beacon over the damaged front room. The beautiful furniture there could not be salvaged. Rain and wind had done their work.

Lucinda stood on the porch and took in all the rubble. "Monk, where does all the stuff that disappeared go? We found clothes in the trees, but what about the furniture and things? It's so weird."

"Don't know how to answer that, missy. It's a mighty powerful force. Those things could be down the road a piece, or they may have fallen miles away. After every big storm strange stories crop up about where something landed."

Would they ever be able to repair so much damage? "I guess there's nothing to do about it now but to see what is left that we can salvage. I'm going to search in my bedroom. Are you going to be in the barn?"

"Yes, but Matt and Hank are going out to check on the herd and round up what's left. Your uncle needs to know what his losses are and what Morris and Fowler lost too."

"That reminds me, I want to ride over and visit with Dove to see what happened there. Will you be able to go with me? I promised Uncle Ben I wouldn't ride off alone."

"I can do that." He stepped back. "You be careful in there now. We checked it out last night, and the remaining walls are sturdy, but there's probably broken glass and such under all that debris. We don't want you getting hurt or nothing."

She nodded and made her way across the ruins to her room. She picked up pieces of wood and tossed them aside and hunted for whatever could be rescued. Under several boards, one trunk sat with only deep scratches to mar the outside. Lucinda lifted the lid with trembling hands.

The contents lay virtually undisturbed. She lifted a few pieces of clothing saved for warmer weather. They felt damp from the water soaked up by the trunk, but otherwise wearable. The skirts and tops could be aired out and dried. She spread out a few things and left the lid open. Later it would go on the wagon to be taken back to town.

Her bed no longer had a mattress. Monk or Hank must have moved it because it had lain there yesterday. She picked her way to Becky's side of the room and lifted more debris from the floor. She bent over to retrieve a pair of shoes, and a footstep sounded behind her.

A gloved hand reached around and covered her mouth,

pressing hard. The other hand held a gun to her neck. An acrid taste of blood filled her mouth.

"Don't fight me, Lucinda. I have a job to do, and I aim to do it. Just be still, and don't scream."

The veins in her neck throbbed and pounded in her head. Who was this man? She squirmed in an effort to get free but stopped when he pressed the gun deeper against her neck, its cold steel like ice against her skin. Where was Monk? Why wasn't he protecting her?

"I'm going to remove my hand. Screaming won't do you any good. All your men left you here alone."

No, Monk had to be in the barn. He promised. With the gun still against her neck, he moved his other hand to grasp her arm and push her forward. Her scream pierced the air. He jerked her back and she fell, hitting her head. The room whirled around in a haze. She was going to die.

Lucinda staggered when the man pulled her up and shoved her against the wall, his gun still pointed at her.

Jake! She'd never know if he was dead or alive. *Dear God, please don't let this happen.*

"Uncle Rudolph can have the money," she begged.

"Just following orders. You've been a hard one to kill, but now—"

A shot rang out, and the man's gun fell to the floor. He yelled and reached for it. Another shot, and the gun skittered further away. Lucinda covered her ears and closed her eyes. Another shot split the air. Her attacker cursed and fell at her feet.

Monk ran over to her and pulled her up. "It's all right now."

His gun still pointed at the man, he snarled, "Don't move, or I'll shoot, and you won't be able to."

Then Matt stumbled over the debris to her side. "Lucinda, are you all right?"

She clung to him. "Oh, Matt, I…I was so…so scared. He was going to…kill me."

Matt smoothed her hair. "We're here now, and he's not going to do anything." He searched her eyes. "Think you can make it back to town?"

She nodded. Monk and Hank tied up the man. When her eyes met his, she flinched and grabbed for Matt. The man's eyes bore nothing but evil, something she had never seen before. She now understood what people meant when they said someone was full of the devil.

Lucinda straightened her shoulders. "My head hurts. I don't know what I hit, but I have a lump on my head."

Matt touched her forehead. "And you have a gash to go with it. It's bleeding a little." He picked up a piece of sheeting and pressed it against the cut. His other hand reached behind her and held up a large brick that had spots of blood on one corner.

Lucinda's mouth gaped open. "Aunt Clara's bed-warming brick? I don't believe it."

He grinned and dropped the brick then put his hand under her arm. He led her out of the mess. Hank dragged the attacker out to the corral to get the man's horse.

Lucinda peered up at Monk. "I was afraid you'd left me alone."

Monk shook his head. "I was out behind the stables checkin' some damage back there when I seen a strange horse near the corral. I sneaked around the back to make sure you were OK."

Matt nodded. "And that's about the time Hank and I came back to take you over to the Morrises. Monk was inching his way to the side of the house and motioned for us to be quiet and get off our horses. By the time we joined him, he'd just shot that guy."

Lucinda hugged Monk. "You said you'd take care of me, and you did."

"Glad I was in time, missy." His face reddened, and he coughed. "*Hmm*. Let's get you back to town. Hank and I'll tote this man to the jail."

Matt examined her cut. "This doesn't look too bad now. I'll drive the wagon and tie my horse behind it. You rest in the back."

Lucinda remembered the horses. "I want to take Misty and Daisy back with us. I'll ride in the wagon if you'll let them go with us."

Matt grinned. "I can take care of that. Becky sure will be happy to have Daisy in town with her."

She climbed into the back of the wagon where Matt had arranged a quilt and a pillow for her to lie down. He brought her trunk and a few other things she'd set aside and placed them beside her in the wagon.

"I think we're all set to go now." Matt finished securing the horses and climbed up on the seat.

Lucinda settled herself on the blanket. How was she going to explain the cut on her head and the blood on her shirtwaist?

⚓

Ben finished ordering the supplies he'd need to rebuild the house and strolled back to the hotel. When the wire service, electricity, and telephones came in a few months, Barton Creek would be on its way to becoming a thriving town. The new governor appointed by President McKinley promised many improvements for the territory. Someday Oklahoma would be a great state.

If Matt had good news about the bunkhouse, they might be able to move back to the ranch soon. Since it had two rooms with a kitchen, they could all live there if it wasn't damaged too much while they rebuilt the house. Many friends were in the same circumstances, but they would pull together and recover from their losses. One thing he'd learned, homesteaders and ranchers were hardy people, and one storm wouldn't keep them down.

Ben headed for the jail to speak with Claymore. If only they could find out what had happened with Jake, but news traveled slowly from other areas. He had his hand on the doorknob when a familiar wagon and driver turned onto Main.

Ben's eyes opened wide. It couldn't be. Matt drove the wagon with Misty and Daisy hitched to the back, and his hired men rode with a stranger between them. His throat tightened and bile rose in his throat. The wagon drew closer.

"Where's Lucinda, and who is that man?"

His niece sat up in the back of the wagon. "I'm right here, Uncle Ben."

He hurried to her, then frowned at the blood on her shirt and the cut on her head. His heart beat double time. The man on the horse between Monk and Hank greeted Ben with a smirk. At that moment he wanted to drag the man off his horse and beat him to a pulp. His fists clenched beside him. "What did that man do to you?"

"It's a long story. Help me down and I'll tell you."

He reached up, grasped her waist, then settled her on the ground. "I'm listening."

The more she talked, the tighter his fists became until his nails cut into his hands. Anger, revulsion, then rage raced through him. The heat of his anger flooded his body and face until he was ready to explode.

Deputy Claymore stepped out from the jail. Ben pointed at the stranger. "Arrest him, Claymore. He tried to kill Lucinda."

Monk and Hank pulled the man from his horse. Monk shoved him toward the deputy. "Ben's right. I stopped him before he could. He's not talkin', but maybe sittin' in the jail awhile will loosen his tongue."

Ben fought for control and clamped his teeth together. He didn't want Lucinda to hear the words threatening to spew forth. He started to follow the men into the jail but stopped and hugged Lucinda. "Go back to the hotel. Try to get to your room without Mellie or Clara seeing you. I'll tell Mellie about this later, but I don't want them coming down here, and knowing Aunt Clara, that's the first thing she'd do."

"I understand. I'll go around the back way. Maybe they're still at the church." She hurried toward the street behind the hotel. Ben waited until she disappeared around the corner, then tugged on the brim of his hat and strode into the jail.

Hank and Monk explained what had taken place at the ranch. Ben listened without changing expression. That man could have killed her, or done even worse, if his men hadn't been on the alert. "It's a good thing the three of you kept your word not to leave her alone. You saved her life."

Claymore held a paper in his hand. "Man's name is Barlow, Jesse Barlow. He's from back east far as I can tell from what Hank found in the saddlebags. Monk shot the gun right out of his hand, and the hand's still bleeding as well as his shoulder. I sent for Doc to come take a look at it."

At that moment, Ben didn't care if the man bled to death. "If he's from back east, that means Rudolph Bishop probably hired him to kill Lucinda."

Ben paced back and forth. This man could well be responsible for the accidents with Lucinda, but the sheriff needed proof. "See if Doc still has the bullet he took from Lucinda. I want to see if it matches the bullets in the rifle Hank brought in."

"All right, and I'll send someone to wire the Boston police

and ask them to question Mr. Bishop. Maybe he'll tell them something if he thinks his hired gun confessed."

Ben slapped his hand on the desk. "We caught this man red-handed, and he'll stand trial for that no matter what we learn from Bishop." He wanted Rudolph to pay for this, but making sure Barlow stayed in jail was more important.

"We'll do what we can. The circuit judge will be here next week. I'll make sure he stays put until then."

Ben stared at the cell where the man sat with his back toward them. "I want to kill him with my bare hands, but if I did that, then I'd be no better than he is." He strode from the room to keep from having to look at Barlow again. How would he explain this to Mellie?

※

Lucinda changed into the one extra shirtwaist she'd managed to bring last night and brushed her hair. She pulled it back to the nape of her neck and secured it in a bow. The bump on her head throbbed, but at least she could arrange her hair so that it and the cut didn't show.

Her reflection stared back from the mirror. Although no outward sign of the attack was visible, her insides still trembled. How could she pretend nothing had happened with her aunts and Becky? Lucinda squared her shoulders and took a deep breath, then let it out slowly before going to find her aunt.

Aunt Mellie had just unlocked the door to her room. Her face shone with excitement. "You missed a wonderful time at the church. Come in so we can tell you about it."

Lucinda smiled and hoped it masked the fear still gripping her nerves. She found a chair and sank into it. Becky bounced in with a big grin and a twinkle in her eye. "Matt brought Daisy here, and Bobby Frankston and I are going to ride this afternoon."

Aunt Clara's eyebrows arched. "Well, I declare. That boy has some sense in him after all. Must have a little spunk too, unless his mother has changed her way of thinking."

Aunt Mellie hugged her daughter. "I'm not sure that's happened, but I'm glad you're friends again." She patted the bed beside her. "Sit and listen to what we're going to do."

Lucinda squeezed Becky's hand, and pushed the incident from this morning out of her mind. Uncle Ben could tell them about the attack later. Her curiosity rose as to what the news about the church could be.

Aunt Mellie folded her hands. "We were talking about how so many of us need repairs on our houses, barns, and such, so we decided to organize a good old-fashioned barn raising."

Lucinda tilted her head and furrowed her brow. A barn raising? She remembered reading about something like that in a book. "Isn't that like a big party where everyone gets together and helps to build a barn in one day or something like that?"

"Exactly. And ours is scheduled for the day of your birthday." Aunt Mellie's face glowed with satisfaction.

"My birthday?" Lucinda's heart lurched. What did that have to do with building a barn?

"Yes, we can have your party the same day. Everybody will be there, so we can celebrate two things at one time. It will be a grand celebration."

"But, Aunt Mellie, I really—"

"Don't want a party." Aunt Clara finished the sentence. "I understand, but it's already been decided. Everyone brings food to the barn raising, so all we'll need to do is bake a cake for you. The ladies at church this morning were quite excited about the whole thing."

Lucinda swallowed hard. Aunt Mellie would go ahead in spite of any protest from Lucinda. They chattered about the plans, but she remembered the letter she'd sent this morning. Her spirits lifted. Perhaps the party would be the perfect time to give her gift to the city. One thing was for certain: if her money couldn't be used for good, she didn't want it. Of course Uncle Ben might argue, but she looked forward to everyone's surprise when she revealed her idea. The fact that no one but Aunt Mellie and Uncle Ben knew the amount of her inheritance made the surprise even more exciting.

Chapter 30

*A*fter two weeks of hard riding, Jake shouted in glee as he crossed over the Red River into Oklahoma Territory. He was almost home. The word filled him with the warmth of the love he knew waited for him there. The only blot on the future was his uncertainty of what had happened to Lucinda or what she now felt about him. Still, he had to believe in his heart that she was safe and had waited for him.

Rusty barked and ran alongside Jake. "Hey, boy, you're going to love the Haynes ranch, and they're going to love you."

When he stopped to rest the horses and eat, he pulled a notepad from his pocket and studied the dates written there. If he traveled at the pace of the past days, he would be in Barton Creek in time for Lucinda's eighteenth birthday. What better way to celebrate than to ask her to marry him. He pictured life with Lucinda in the future. The image so excited him that he packed up the remains of his noon meal and mounted Baron.

"We're almost there. Lucinda, I'm coming home."

⚜

Lucinda stepped out of the bunkhouse into the early-morning air. Dew kissed the sparse grass growing around the doorway. She loved this time of morning. Everything looked fresh and new on this day, March 21, that marked her eighteenth birthday as well as the first day of spring. The incident after the storm now remained as only a dim memory.

Her life in Boston rarely gave her the opportunity to witness the dawning of a day or the setting of the sun, two things she had grown to love in these open spaces. Never had she seen such spectacular colors. No creation of man could rival God's palette of pink and lavender in early morning, or the brilliant hues of orange and gold in the evening.

Although the air held a chill, the sweet smell of field clover and the spring bulbs in bloom warmed Lucinda's heart. She thanked the Lord for life and friends who loved her. The man who tried to kill her had been accused by her uncle Rudolph, and the prisoner turned on Rudolph. Now Rudolph awaited trial in Boston for the attempt on her life.

The satisfaction of knowing he'd pay for what he'd done didn't take away the pain of her loss. Greed had driven Rudolph Bishop and had led to his destruction. Lucinda renewed her vow to use her money for good and not evil. Mr. Sutton had yet to answer her letter, but even if he didn't approve her decision, it was hers to make when the money arrived.

The sun peeked over the horizon and flooded the sky with more golden light. Becky emerged from the bunkhouse. "You must be excited about today or you would still be in bed. This is the first time you've ever been up before me."

Lucinda laughed. "You forget the day after the tornado? I do believe you slept until ten that day."

A faint tinge of crimson crept up the girl's cheeks. "Oh, yes, I forgot." Then she grabbed Lucinda's hand. "Let's go get the eggs, and then after breakfast we can get started on the decorations."

Lucinda allowed Becky to pull her along to the henhouse. Although the place was damaged, most of the chickens were saved. She relished the task this morning in light of what could have been. This would be the most wonderful birthday she ever had. Nearly everyone from town would be here on the ranch today to raise the walls of the new barn and to begin a new roof for the main house.

With their chore completed, Lucinda followed Becky back to their temporary home. Lucinda stopped in front of the bunkhouse. Across the way the ranch house stood with new walls, ready for a roof to be added.

She had overheard her aunt and uncle talking about the big mortgage they had taken on the house to pay for the rebuilding and new additions. Wouldn't they be surprised when she made her announcement about the plans for her inheritance? Yes, all of Barton Creek would benefit if everything worked out as it should. She raised her face to the sun-filled sky. "Thank You, Lord, for Your bountiful blessings. I know You have wonderful plans for this day, and I can hardly wait to see them all."

Full of joy, she ran inside to help Aunt Mellie and Aunt Clara with breakfast.

⚕

After breakfast, Ben sought to have a few minutes alone with Mellie. He found her out in her garden checking on the plants emerging as new life in the rich soil.

"Looks like you'll have a good crop of vegetables after all."

Mellie jumped. "Benjamin Haynes, don't sneak up on me like that. You scared me half out of my wits." She stood and dusted her hands together.

"Sorry, my dear, didn't realize I was so quiet." He slipped an arm around her waist.

"And what is on your mind this morning, Mr. Haynes?"

He grinned. "You read me like a book. I've been having second thoughts about giving Luke permission to court Lucinda.

I believe Luke has his mind set on marriage, but Lucinda isn't near ready to be a bride."

Mellie frowned. "I keep thinking of how unkind Bea has been toward our family and the Morrises. Perhaps we were a little hasty in our wishes for Lucinda to have a proper suitor."

Ben rued their quick approval of Luke's request. Ben loved Lucinda like his own daughter and wanted only the best for her. His doubts now concerned him.

He hugged Mellie to his side. "I wish we hadn't been so busy with repairing damage from the storm. Do you think we ought to speak with her about it before Luke comes today? I have a feeling he'll be declaring his intentions soon."

"I don't know. I think I need to pray about this some more. We do want what's best for her, but we also must consider her feelings."

"I'll wait, then." He pulled out his pocket watch. "Time's getting on. People will be arriving soon. We can discuss this later."

Ben kissed Mellie on the forehead and ambled off in the direction of the corrals. The past few weeks had been busy indeed. Four other barns had been raised as well as the steeple on the church repaired. Several other homes awaited their turns for help from neighbors. The banks had been generous in extending credit, but Ben wondered how many had truly over-extended in an effort to replace what had been lost. His own indebtedness would take awhile to pay, but he had made sure the payments would not be beyond his resources.

Shortly before nine, the first workers arrived and unloaded wagons of lumber and supplies for the barn. Mellie and Aunt Clara greeted the women and showed them where to put their food offerings. Pride for his wife and his aunt filled him with contentment this morning.

Much would be accomplished today, but so much still needed

to be done. If the weather held up, their house could be ready for full occupancy in another month. Bea and Carl Anderson drove up with a wagon of supplies. For times like these, he was thankful neighbors could put aside differences and band together for the good of all.

⚬

The generosity of friends who brought food and tools to help with the barn still amazed Lucinda. Today would mark the fourth time she had seen the love and caring of Barton Creek citizens. Nothing like this had ever occurred in Boston, even after a hurricane.

She joined the ladies setting out food on the checkered cloth-covered tables. Tables groaned under the weight of pies, cakes, fried chicken, and tons of vegetables and fresh bread. No one would go hungry this day, and the weather had cooperated with temperatures in the sixties.

Young children ran through the yards and played on the makeshift swings Uncle Ben provided for them. Would she ever have the privilege of having a child to love and cherish as these women did?

Six months ago, before she came here, she would have scoffed at the idea of performing all the tasks she so enjoyed today. Her mother would be surprised but pleased with the changes that had come to her life. Aunt Mellie and Uncle Ben had worked hard to make her happy, and she loved them for it.

The way of life left back in Boston became a more distant memory with each passing day. Her dream now was to marry a young man and carry on the tradition of the West with either cattle or crops, whichever her husband wanted to do.

If only that husband could be Jake. Her promise not to think about him today slipped by the wayside as she imagined him standing with her to celebrate her special birthday.

⤜

Jake rode into Barton Creek, but the bank, Anderson's store, and even the saloon showed no signs of life. Boards covered broken windows, and other repairs were in evidence. He whistled below his breath. The only other time he'd seen anything like this had been after a tornado.

The jail appeared intact. Jake dismounted his horse and entered the building. Deputy Claymore's chair landed with a thud against the floor as he jumped to his feet.

"Jake Starnes! Of all the... I didn't think we'd ever see you again."

Jake laughed and retrieved the letter from his pocket. "I've been set free. Here, see."

The deputy read the letter with understanding dawning in his eyes. "Acquitted due to self-defense. Now that's what I call a miracle." He handed the letter back and offered his hand in greeting. "Welcome back to Barton Creek. I know one little lady who is going to be mighty happy to see you."

Jake shoved his hat back on his head. "I'm praying so. But where is everyone? The town looks deserted."

"Oh, everybody's out to the Haynes place. They're having a barn raising. Lots of damage from the storm and plenty of folk lost homes and barns."

Jake's voice caught in his throat. "A storm? Lucinda? Is she all right? Were any of the Hayneses hurt?"

"No, they're all fine. In fact, today's Lucinda's birthday, and they're combining the celebration with the barn raising. I'd be out there myself, but I have a prisoner to guard. My deputy will be coming to relieve me, so I can go out and enjoy the party."

281

"I thought I had the date right and would be here in time for her birthday." Jake's hand rose to pat the buttoned pocket guarding the velvet pouch with the ring. "I'll get on my way now. Thank you."

His boots echoed across the boards as he headed for Baron. He didn't have a minute to lose in getting to the ranch. His heels goaded Baron into a fast trot with his supply horse and Rusty following behind. In less than an hour he'd find out whether he had a future with Lucinda or not.

⤔

The men had constructed the walls to the barn and raised them with lightning speed. Lucinda glanced at the tiny watch pinned to her bodice. Almost two o'clock. Time for the meal to begin.

Aunt Clara rang the big brass handbell, calling the workers to the food-laden tables. They all gathered around, and Uncle Ben led them in a prayer, thanking God for His provisions. Lucinda's stomach fluttered with the big secret she held and would reveal later today. She stood back as hungry workers swarmed around the tables. Laughter rang out, and the women dishing up vegetables smiled broadly at the compliments coming their way.

"Lucinda, here you are. I've been looking for you."

She turned to find Luke standing behind her. "Oh, hello, Luke. I saw you arrive, but you've been too busy with the men for me to speak with you."

His smile revealed the dimple in his left cheek. "That's why I'm here now. Would you do me the honor of dining with me?"

Lucinda had not intentionally avoided Luke but hoped he'd be too busy helping others to be concerned with her. However, as hostess, she must remember her manners. "That will be delightful."

He grinned then pulled a folded envelope from his pants

pocket. "I almost forgot; the postmaster asked me to give you this. It came in on the stage this morning."

The return address jumped out at her. The letter from Mr. Sutton had arrived. Excitement tingled through her. As much as she wanted to read it at the moment, she didn't want to do it with Luke standing so near.

"Thank you. I'll read it while you get our food." She waited until he joined the line at the tables then turned away to slip her finger under the flap. Her hands trembled as she removed the sheet. Her eyes skimmed the letter, and then she wanted to shout and jump for joy. Mr. Sutton agreed with her! The funds would be transferred to the Barton Creek bank as soon as possible. Enclosed he included a bank draft to help her get started on her mission. At the sight of the amount, she sucked in her breath. So much. How could it be? Surely he'd made a mistake and sent it all.

With this amount, her aunt and uncle could rebuild their house in fine fashion, pay off the mortgage, and still have plenty to help the church and others in town. Excitement coursed through Lucinda's veins. She couldn't wait to make her announcement and would do it soon.

Luke rejoined her. "From the sparkle in your eyes, the letter must have been good news."

Lucinda accepted the plate he handed her. "Yes, it was. This will be a good day."

"It's already a great day with the weather cooperating and being your birthday."

"Oh, but it's going to get even better." She glanced up as Dove and Martin joined them. "I'm happy you two decided to come over. This food looks delicious."

Dove settled beside her, and the two men kneeled nearby.

Luke placed his plate on a napkin spread on the ground and moved to sit next to Lucinda.

Her friends talked about the weather and how many people had come to help, but Lucinda tuned them out. Her joy waned. What if the people here didn't want her help? She hadn't even thought of that. Not everyone welcomed help from an outsider. They might consider it charity.

Luke tapped her arm. "Lucinda, are you all right? You look distressed about something."

She swallowed hard. "I'm fine." She smiled and fingered a piece of homemade bread. "I guess I'm just anxious to get all the repairs done and move back into the house."

Dove nodded. "I understand that. We were so fortunate that the storm passed several miles west of us. We only had the rain and the creek flooded, but no damage."

Talk returned to the rebuilding efforts in town. An idea formed in Lucinda's mind. She wouldn't give specific amounts to anyone. Instead, she would talk with the banker and set up a fund to be given to people as they had need. Common sense told her she must put back some for her own funds, as she couldn't live off her aunt and uncle the rest of her life.

Dove grabbed her hand. "You men take our plates to the cleanup, then meet us at the tables over there. It's time for Lucinda to open her gifts while dessert is served."

She and Dove scrambled to the area set aside. Aunt Mellie had told everyone that gifts were not necessary, but a stack of them were piled on a table.

Friends and neighbors gathered around. Lucinda picked up a box wrapped in yellow paper. It came from Dove and contained one of the samplers she had created. "Friends are the sunshine in our lives" stated the carefully embroidered letters. Lucinda hugged her friend.

Each package contained something handmade by the giver. The caring efforts behind the gifts warmed Lucinda's heart. They had truly accepted her as a part of the Barton Creek community.

Luke leaned over her shoulder. "I would like to have a word with you after this is over, if I may."

Lucinda nodded and bit her lip as he walked away. She reached out and squeezed Dove's hand. In her heart she knew what he wanted. The signs had been there all along. No matter how she tried to show only friendship, Luke pressed for more, and more she couldn't give him now, and perhaps never.

The workers milled about, preparing to continue their building. The time had come for her revelation. Lucinda stepped up onto a stool and clapped her hands. "May I have your attention, please?"

The crowd quieted and gathered around her once again. She licked her lips then began.

⚓

Jake rode up to find Lucinda calling for people to gather around her. He dismounted and stood on the fringes and kept out of sight. Her lilting voice carried to his ears, and no sound had ever been sweeter. She had grown even more beautiful in the months he'd been gone. A yellow bow that matched her dress caught her dark hair up in back, letting it cascade over her shoulders like a waterfall.

"First, I want to thank all of you for coming to help Uncle Ben and for bringing all this wonderful food. The gifts you brought for me are accepted with gratitude for welcoming me, a stranger, to your town. Each gift will be treasured for many years to come."

Heads nodded, and people smiled at each other. That's when he noticed Luke standing near her. The look on the young man's

285

face mirrored the feelings Jake held. Despair clutched his soul with iron talons. He was too late. She belonged to Luke.

Still, he couldn't take his leave without seeing her. Then she spoke again. "Now I have a surprise for each of you. Birthdays are a time for giving, and I'm giving a gift to Barton Creek. Most of you don't know that I am to receive an inheritance since I turned eighteen today."

Jake's head tilted, and he frowned. He should have known from the things Ben had said. He had no right to seek her favor. But why not? He had money enough to take care of their needs.

The murmur of voices through the crowds grew silent once again. They waited for her to continue.

"I have a check here which I will deposit into a special account for the people of Barton Creek. The money is to be used to help you make repairs, replace lost furniture and equipment, and to rebuild what was destroyed."

Stunned silence greeted her words, before a cheer arose as they shouted their words of thanksgiving. Jake's eyes opened wide. She came from wealth, but he'd had no idea to what extent. Then her words dawned on him. Let her give all her money away if that's what she wanted. He had more than enough for them both. Never had his love been so strong as at this moment.

He pushed his way through the crowd that became quieter as people recognized him and murmured among themselves. His gaze never left Lucinda as she accepted thanks from the people. Then she turned, and her eyes locked with his. All color drained from her face, and she reached to steady herself. He continued to stride toward her, mesmerized by her gaze. She jumped down from the stool and ran to his outstretched hands.

Lucinda stopped in front of him with tears rolling down her cheeks. "It truly is you, not a vision." She grasped his hands.

He pulled her closer. "I'm not a vision, and I'm a free man."

"But how? No, I don't care. You're here; that's all that matters."

Jake released her hands and wrapped his arms around her, oblivious to the crowd now gathered around. Her head rested just below his chin. He leaned down slightly and kissed her hair. "I've come home a free man, Lucinda. The judge and some witnesses said I shot that man in self-defense. He declared me innocent and let me go."

⁂

Lucinda's heart leapt in her chest. His arms tightened about her. She lifted her head toward his. He hesitated a moment then leaned closer and whispered, "I'll kiss you proper when we don't have such an audience." Then his lips brushed across her forehead.

Lucinda's skin tingled with the brief kiss, and she held tightly to his hand. At the moment she wished everyone would disappear, but men and women crowded around them. Aunt Mellie and Uncle Ben pushed their way through. Aunt Mellie grabbed Jake around the waist.

"I can't believe it's really you. We've prayed for this day, and here you are." She brushed tears from her cheeks.

Aunt Clara pushed herself forward. "Is this the young man I've heard so much about?" She eyed him up and down then declared, "You are just as handsome as they said." Her chubby arms embraced Lucinda. "My dear, this is the best birthday gift you could ever have."

Charlotte Frankston stepped forward to confront Jake. "How did you get here? Did you kill that marshal and escape? Where's our deputy?" She turned and searched the crowd.

Lucinda cringed at the animosity in the words and squeezed Jake's hand. "He's a free man. He only killed in self-defense."

Aunt Clara slapped her hands on her hips. "Charlotte

Frankston, this is a family matter, and you aren't a member of this family, so keep your hateful opinions to yourself."

Lucinda gasped as did Aunt Mellie, who grabbed the elderly woman. "Aunt Clara, please. Let's not have a scene."

Charlotte Frankston narrowed her eyes and marched away.

Jake still held her hand as he talked with Uncle Ben. Across the way Luke stood with Dove and Martin on either side. The misery in his eyes aroused her sympathy, but he'd recover, and maybe then he'd see what a wonderful girl Dove was and turn his affections her way.

The crowd dispersed as men returned to their tasks and women began the job of cleaning up from the dinner. Jake said, "Let's take a walk."

Lucinda strolled beside him away from the gathering. So many words she wanted to say, but none could pass the lump that blocked her throat and threatened to fill her eyes with tears, happy tears. All the days of waiting seemed now no more than a brief interlude, yet in those days God had worked in both of their lives to bring them to this point. He promised to answer prayers when she prayed believing He would. She wanted to sing, shout, and praise God for this miracle. She would wait until Jake had his say, but if he didn't do it soon, she might burst.

When they reached the trees, he stopped and took both her hands in his. "I've looked forward to this moment since the first day I learned I was a free man. I was afraid you'd find someone else, but deep in my soul I believed you'd be here waiting for me."

"And I believed you would return because of God's promise that something good can come from something bad if we love Him."

"I love you with all my heart, and I'm ready to get a ranch of my own. I want you to work beside me. If your aunt and uncle give their blessing, will you marry me, Lucinda?"

"Oh, yes, yes, and I love you too, Jacob Starnes." Her whole being filled with the love she'd harbored for so many months. "But please call me Lucy, a name more suitable for my new life as the wife of a rancher."

Jake laughed and lifted her from the ground with his hug. "Lucy it will be." He set her back down, and his fingers lifted her chin. His lips touched hers lightly then pressed harder as her hands went up around his neck. The kiss fulfilled every dream she'd had and sealed a love no longer blighted by the past but anointed with hope for the future.

Look for
BOOK TWO OF THE
Winds Across the Prairie Series

—— *Morning for Dove* ——
BY MARTHA ROGERS

W HEN LUKE ANDERSON FALLS IN LOVE WITH Dove Morris, he is aware of her Native American heritage. What he is not prepared for is the prejudice suddenly exhibited by his family. Can he convince his parents that love knows no boundaries of race or culture when it comes from God?

Morning for Dove

Chapter 1

Oklahoma Territory 1897

*T*oday was not a good day for a wedding. It was Lucinda Bishop's wedding day, and he wasn't the groom. The sun may be shining outside, but Luke Anderson's gut rolled and tumbled like the dark clouds before a storm. His feelings should have been under control by now, and they had been up until this moment. Now her image rolled through his mind like pictures on a stereo-optic machine.

He shook his head and snatched off his tie. Anger filled his heart. His eyes closed tight and prayed for God to take away his feelings. All thoughts of Lucinda must be put away as part of his past and not his future.

Calm swept through him as he let the Lord's peace take over. Still he'd rather do anything else, like stay behind and keep the store open. Pa didn't worry about the business he'd be losing by closing down for the day because most of the townsfolk would be at the church. He shrugged his arms into the sleeves of his jacket. He hated having to wear a suit in this heat. With his tie now securely back in place, Luke headed downstairs to meet his parents.

His mother tilted her head and looked him over from head to foot. "I must say you do look especially handsome today." She nodded her approval and turned for the door.

Luke tugged at his collar and forced himself to smile. She must have thought he'd come down in his work clothes.

His sister beamed at him. "You are handsome, even if you are my brother."

Luke shook his head and followed her outside. "You look very pretty yourself, Alice."

She looked up at him and furrowed her brow. "Thank you, I think."

Luke relaxed at his sister's comments. He usually ridiculed or teased her, but she did look pretty today with her blonde curls dancing on her shoulders. At sixteen, she had the notice of a few boys in her class at school, but Pa kept a close watch on his only daughter. The tightness in his chest loosened. He'd get through this day.

Since the church was only a few blocks down the street, they would walk, but his younger brother Will ran ahead. When they reached the churchyard, wagons, surreys, and horses filled the area. Pa had been right. People from all over were here. He looked forward more to the celebration afterward than the actual ceremony.

He followed the rest of his family into the church and down to a pew. The sanctuary filled quickly, and the music began. Instead of paying attention, Luke tugged once again at the demon collar and tie and wished for relief from the heat. The organ swelled with a melody, and everyone stood. Dove, Lucy's best friend, walked down the aisle followed by the bride.

Never had Lucy looked more beautiful. He had to admit deep in his heart that she'd never been his. Even when he courted her, her heart had belonged to Jake. Luke should have known he'd never make her forget that cowboy.

Then his gaze fell on Dove, and his throat tightened. Although he'd known her for years, he'd never seen her as any more than the part Cherokee daughter of Sam Morris. Now her bronzed complexion and dark eyes glowed with a beauty that stunned him. He had looked right through her when they had been at the box social last spring and on other social occasions. At those events, she'd been with someone else, and he'd seen only Lucinda. Dove was quiet and didn't say much when around others their age, and he had spoken directly to her only a few times at church. Today he saw her with new eyes.

Lucy Bishop then appeared. He still thought of her as Lucinda, but she preferred Lucy now. When she reached the altar on the arm of her uncle Ben, Luke sat down as did the congregation. He ignored the words of the minister and concentrated on Dove. He regretted not doing so before now and intended to get to know her better at the festivities later in the day.

With that resolve, Luke glanced to his left and right. Jake and the Haynes family had many friends judging by the number of people in attendance. Even Chester Fowler had come. He'd been less than friendly with Ben Haynes and Sam Morris the few times Luke had seen them together. Something about the man bothered Luke, but he couldn't quite put a finger on it.

From the corner of his eye he noticed Bobby Frankston staring to the side of the altar. Luke followed the boy's gaze to find Becky Haynes at the other end. She stood with Dove beside Lucy as an attendant. Her attention had been drawn to Bobby's, and a faint bloom reddened her cheeks. That blush didn't come from the heat. Luke chuckled to himself. It looked to him like another boy had fallen in love.

When the ceremony ended, the couple left the church and headed to the hotel where the Haynes planned a lavish celebration for their niece.

When Luke joined the other guests there, tables laden with thin slices of beef, chicken, and ham along with a variety of breads, vegetables, and fruit filled one end of the room and beckoned to him. After filling his plate, he moved to the side of the room and bit into a piece of chicken. At least the food tasted good.

He gaze swept around the room. The hotel dining hall had been cleared of almost all of its tables, and people milled about talking with one another and balancing plates of food. Mr. and Mrs. Haynes had spared no expense for their niece.

Courting Lucy last spring had been a more than pleasant experience, but now the time had come for him to move on with his life. He planned to partner with his father in their general store and had already changed the name to Anderson's Mercantile. Pa had great plans to expand the business and add new merchandise to attract more customers.

In his perusal of the room, his gaze came to rest on Dove Morris. The pale yellow dress she wore emphasized her dark hair and almost black eyes. He'd never seen such flawless complexion on anyone besides Lucy. But where Lucy's was fair, Dove's reflected the heritage of her Indian blood. She smiled now at something the guest beside her said, and it lit up Dove's face.

At that moment she turned in Luke's direction. Her eyes locked with his and widened as though surprised to see him. A sharp tingle skittered through his heart. Before he could catch his breath, she turned back to the woman beside her. The tightness in his chest lessened, but he still stared at her even though she no longer looked at him.

Twice now something had coursed through his veins as he observed her. An explanation for those feelings eluded him. Strange, nothing like that had happened with Lucy when he was with her. Whatever this feeling happened to be, one thing was certain; he had to speak to Dove. Still, after what happened with Lucy, he would take his time and not rush into a relationship so quickly this time.

He made his way in her direction, not allowing his eyes to lose contact with her face. When he stood by her side, her head barely reached his shoulder. He had never truly paid any attention to how tiny and petite she was, even when he'd seen her in the store and at church. A sudden urge to stand taller and make a good impression overcame him. "Miss Morris, what a pleasure to see you this afternoon."

Her lips quivered then broke into a smile. "Luke Anderson. It's a pleasure to see you too. Wasn't the wedding lovely?"

"Yes, it was." But not as lovely as the girl standing before him. "Would you like some refreshment?"

"I would like that. Thank you." Her soft voice melted his resolve. He had to know more about this beautiful young woman. How her beauty had escaped his notice was something he didn't understand. He straightened his shoulders and grasped her hand to tuck it over his arm. She'd certainly grown up while he had been so smitten with Lucy Bishop.